COPPER COUNTRY

Other Books by Kristin Neva

SNOW COUNTRY
A Copper Island Novel
Book One

HEAVY
Finding Meaning after a Terminal Diagnosis
A Young Family's First Year with ALS

Tervetuloa!

Welcome to Copper Island. If you're here for the first time, I can't wait to introduce you to this beautiful setting and the quirky characters who live on these pages.

Although I set the story near two fictional towns, Douglass and Quincy, I attempted to accurately reflect the culture and spirit of Michigan's Keweenaw Peninsula. Since Finns once made up 20% of the population, they had a noticeable impact on the local culture. Many people continue to use a few Finnish words, and residents from diverse ethnic backgrounds embrace the traditional sauna and participate in Finnish festivals.

Like all names in the book, my character Russ's surname is used fictitiously. I chose Saarinen because it is a beautiful Finnish name meaning "of the island."

If you've read *Snow Country*, the first novel in the series, you'll soon realize that Aimee and Russ's story doesn't pick up where we left off at the end of book one. Each story stands alone, but the two books overlap for about seven months. *Copper Country* begins in June, five months after Beth arrived on the island in *Snow Country*.

One of the conflicts in *Copper Country* comes when Russ and Aimee learn how different their churches are. Although Pinehurst Community Church and the Lord's People Church are fictional, many couples who come from different church backgrounds deal with similar issues.

It is my hope that exploring these themes will spur us all on toward love and grace.

Thank you for visiting.

Kiitos,

Kristin

KRISTIN NEVA

COPPER COUNTRY

A Copper Island Novel
❧ *Two* ❧

THE
CHRISTMAS TREE
HOUSE

Explore Copper Island @ KristinNeva.com

Glossary
of Finnish and Yooper Words

bush— woods; forest

camp— hunting or recreational cabin

downstate— the Lower Peninsula of Michigan, below the Mackinac Bridge

hey— also *eh*, a word used at the end of sentences to elicit an affirmative response or to add emphasis to a statement

hyvää päivää— Finnish for good day

kiitos— Finnish for thank you

Kuparisaari— Finnish for Copper Island

Lapp— a descendent of the *Sami* (Laplander) people of Finland

näkemiin— Finnish for goodbye

nisu— Finnish for sweet cardamom bread

päivää päivää— Finnish greeting, literally day day

pannukakku— Finnish for oven pancake; a bready, custard-like dish baked in a pan, similar to Mexican flan but with flour

pasty—	a regional dish of cubed potatoes, carrots, rutabaga, beef, and pork stuffed in a flour shell and baked—ingredients vary, but always includes potatoes and usually some type of meat
riisipuuro—	Finnish for creamy rice porridge; rice simmered in milk and sweetened with sugar—it is often sprinkled with a cinnamon/sugar mixture and sometimes served with raisins, similar to Mexican *arroz con leche*
Sami—	also Laplander, the indigenous Finno-Ugric people of Northern Europe
sisu—	the Finnish spirit of resilience and determination in the face of adversity; a word with deep cultural significance to Finns and Finnish Americans
tervetuloa—	Finnish for welcome
UP—	the Upper Peninsula of Michigan, spoken as each letter *U - P*
Yooper—	a resident of the Upper Peninsula of Michigan
Yooper Scooper—	a wide, sheet metal snow shovel that slides on the ground
yous—	plural of *you*, found in some Northern US dialects, also spelled *youse*, rhymes with *news*

For my mom,
who gives so much of herself.

And in memory of my dad,
who was always present and gentle.

Chapter 1

Russ Saarinen lifted a plastic bottle above his head and poured water into his mouth. The sun evaporated sweat off his back, and wind blew from Lake Superior onto the island, rustling new, green leaves at the tops of gnarled trees. It didn't matter to him what Aimee thought. He liked his private oasis hidden in a glade of a sugar maple forest.

"I hit something," Danny called out.

"Yeah. You saw the size of those rocks I sent out on the sled." Russ stared down the nine-foot trench he and his best friend had dug under the old hunting cabin. "Aimee should be back soon with lunch."

"Your two favorite things, hey." Danny laughed.

Russ grinned. Hot pasties and his beautiful girlfriend. He found it hard to believe she liked *him*.

"It's metal!" Excitement filled Danny's voice.

Russ grabbed a flashlight and crawled into the hole. "Let me see."

After the frost lifted and the ground dried, June offered the first opportunity for Russ to make a crawl space. He didn't want to endure another winter without insulation under the floorboards.

Beneath the cabin, Danny sat with his legs crossed as he used the tip of a spade to knock dirt from the trench wall. He jabbed at the boulder, exposing orangeish yellow glints. "It's float copper."

Russ clawed at the rock behind Danny to expose the split-pea-soup green of oxidized copper. "This has got to be at least six feet long." They had trenched along the specimen, which was only revealed after Danny tried to give himself more elbow room to dig.

A faint drone turned to the distinct sputtering of a four-stroke engine as his four-wheeler neared the cabin. "Aimee's back." Russ grabbed a shovel from the sled they had pushed into the hole. He piled dirt alongside the copper in an attempt to bury it. "Don't tell her. Help me cover this up."

"Don't tell her?" Danny laughed. He threw his shovel in the sled and leaned back against the dirt wall. "You can't keep secrets from her."

Russ knew by that he meant *can't*, rather than *mustn't* or *shouldn't*. Russ could never lie, at least not well. As a kid, he'd walk into the house and his father would ask, "What have you been up to?" If he was into mischief, his mouth would become dry. His dad would repeat the question, "*What* have you been up to?" in a tone that expected truth, and Russ would break.

"Just help me cover it up." Russ scowled at Danny in a way that would be offensive to anybody but a best friend.

"Come on, man. You're the engineer. You know dirt ain't going to stick to the side of that rock." Danny pulled off his leather gloves and threw them in the sled. "Why don't you want her to know?"

Russ stopped his futile attempt. He sat back and combed his blond beard with his fingers. The four-wheeler got louder, slowed to an idle, and went quiet altogether. "She'd want me to sell it."

"What's wrong with that?" Danny asked.

Russ sighed and shook his head. "I just want to insulate down here."

"Hey, guys," Aimee yelled into the trench, "the pasties are

here."

In the cabin, Russ pulled the table down from the wall, and a single leg dropped to the floor to support the free end. Hinges attached the other end to the wall so the table could be folded up like an old ironing board to give room to walk about the sixteen-by-twenty-foot cabin. Aimee set a paper sack of pasties on the table, and Russ and Danny pulled up stools.

"How's the digging?" Aimee asked while the guys tore open the foil wrappers. "Did you make good progress while I was gone?"

Russ buried his face into his pasty.

"Well?" Aimee pressed.

Russ shrugged. "We won't be able to dig it out. It's hopeless."

Chewing through his words, Danny said, "It's a bit premature to call it hopeless."

Russ narrowed his eyes. "I'll have to jack up the cabin to insulate underneath."

Aimee set her untouched pasty on the table. "What's going on, Russ?" A look of consternation spread across her face.

He could have quickly changed her look to glee by telling her about the copper, but he didn't want to. He wished he hadn't found it. He took another bite of his pasty and swallowed hard.

"*What's* going on?" Aimee repeated the question.

Russ threw his hands up. "All right, all right. I'll tell you."

Danny laughed. "Told you."

It was only going to be a matter of time. Keeping a secret from Aimee—especially Aimee—was never an option. She had trust issues to begin with. "We found copper under the cabin."

"Where's the copper?" Aimee scanned the room. It wasn't unusual to find float copper in the Keweenaw. Usually small nuggets. Less typically, people find boulders or flat sheets of copper that were sheared off a larger deposit and then pushed to the surface by ancient glaciers.

"It's too big to pull out." Russ casually took another bite of his pasty and methodically chewed.

"How big?" Aimee turned to Danny.

Danny spread his arms out wide. "Big."

"I've got to see this." Aimee picked at her pasty until the guys finished eating, and then led the way outside.

By the time Russ crawled into the trench, Aimee had already dug a hole under the edge of the copper.

She shrieked. "It's at least a foot thick, maybe thicker."

He cringed. "It's not coming out, and besides, I can still insulate with it here."

"We can get it out. We'll move the whole cabin if we have to. This has to be worth a fortune." Aimee talked that way, using the plural pronoun, as if everything they did was a team effort, as if they were married, even though they had only been dating a few months.

"I'm not moving *my* cabin." Russ crossed his arms and leaned back against the trench wall.

"You guys all right down there?" Danny called. "Your first fight, hey."

"No, man. We're good." Russ lowered his voice. "You've seen enough. Let's go."

"I want to see how long this is." Aimee glanced up at Russ. Her white smile reflected the sunlight at the other end of the trench.

Russ laughed at her infectious enthusiasm. She was gorgeous even with dirt smeared on her forehead and cheeks. With caramel-brown hair and olive skin, she looked Italian. She didn't know what her roots were. Aimee Mallon. Her surname sounded Italian. She thought it was Irish. In any case, she wasn't Finnish, which would be another strike against her in his parents' eyes.

He didn't care, but his parents wanted him to marry a girl from the Lord's People Church. Every summer LPs from across the country converged somewhere for preaching and meals and, for the young adults, an opportunity to meet a mate. At one church convention, Russ approached a woman, but she rebuffed him, so he never tried again. Now he found it hard to believe Aimee was his girlfriend.

Aimee lay on her side and searched for the end of the specimen. "We could use this to purchase Koski's property next door. That one guy got a couple hundred thousand dollars for a big piece of copper."

"He got a headache. He couldn't get it off his property for several years."

"If it's going to take several years, we best start now," she retorted.

"Aimee." Russ sighed. "I don't want to take it out."

Aimee stopped her work and sat up. "I grew up poor, and I don't want to be poor again. This shack of yours isn't in my dream."

"This cabin's got everything *I* need."

"It doesn't even have a toilet that flushes." She crossed her arms and scowled.

"Hey, that's a composting toilet. That cost more than any other toilet you'll ever sit on."

"I need to head out," Danny called down. "Aimee, do you want a ride home or are you staying?"

Aimee looked at Russ and raised her eyebrows.

"Stay." He smiled at her and then crawled out of the hole while Aimee continued her search for the end of the copper boulder. Russ called back, "Don't waste your time working down there."

"Ha ha." Exaggerated laughter came from below the cabin.

Danny slapped Russ's back as they headed toward the four-wheeler. "You guys are fighting. It's getting serious."

"After Beth left, you still think arguing's a sign of passion, hey." Russ shook his head.

Danny ignored the jab.

Russ felt bad for the guy. His best friend was head over heels in love with Beth and even told her so, but she just thanked him. Beth had returned to California, and Russ could tell Danny wasn't getting over her. "Sorry, man."

The guys climbed onto Russ's ATV, and Danny leaned back and put his hands on the rack behind the seat. Russ zigzagged through woods under a canopy of sugar maple leaves. He took different routes to minimize the impact on his neighbor's property and to obscure his location. The cabin sat in the middle of a forty-acre parcel on what the old Finns called *Kuparisaari*, Copper Island, the top half of the Keweenaw Peninsula that juts into the south side of Lake Superior. He bought the land-locked property cheap because there was no easement, which was fine with Russ. The cabin was off the electrical grid with no access by road. Russ rode in on a four-wheeler or snowmobile. Old man Koski who sold the land to him wanted to sell the adjoining property for four times the price, even though he'd be unlikely to find another buyer in his lifetime. At least he was nice enough to let Russ park his truck and trailers on his property near the road.

"Have you heard from her?" Russ yelled over the noise of the engine.

"No." That single word carried significant pain. Danny wasn't typically a man of few words.

Danny was good for Russ, drawing him out of his shell. He got to know Danny through the Copper Island youth hockey league years ago. His parents were okay with him playing with Danny when they were kids, but in middle school, they encouraged him to stick with the LP Church kids. The two reconnected when Russ started taking college classes in his junior year of high school and had more freedom. They'd snowmobile, hunt, or just hang out. Danny was polite and didn't talk about his religion, so Russ's parents overlooked the fact he wasn't from their church.

Russ dropped Danny off at his Jeep Cherokee. "Not a word about the copper, right?"

"Of course not." Danny craned his neck up as a helicopter passed low overhead. "I think that's the sheriff."

The helicopter flew west toward Russ's property.

"Anyway, I was saying, if word got out, Koski would double his already ridiculous price."

Back at the cabin, Russ kicked off his boots by the door. Aimee was sweeping out the dirt they had tracked in during lunch. She had stowed the kitchen table and pushed the stools against the wall. A trash bag sat by the door, ready for Russ to haul it out to the burn barrel. Normally, he'd walk right into the cabin with his boots as he did over lunch, but he knew he'd hear *mister* if he tried that. Aimee called him *mister* whenever she wanted to correct his ways, like keeping food out of his beard. Aimee collected the dirt in a dustpan and threw it out the door. She hung the broom on a nail. "Okay, mister."

"What'd I do?" Russ took a few steps past Aimee and grabbed a water bottle out of his propane refrigerator. He sat on the love seat that also unfolded into his bed.

"Why don't you want to get that copper out?"

"I don't want the hassle." He avoided eye contact.

"It's huge. I can't find the end of it." Excitement rang in her voice.

"All the more reason to leave it there."

Aimee joined Russ on the love seat, the only soft seat in the cabin. "I don't understand you."

"What's there to understand?" He sighed inwardly. She was optimistic for her future, only one semester away from graduation, but he knew better. He had tried the corporate thing, but they betrayed him, so he created a simple life in his off-the-grid cabin. He was independent and that's the way he liked it. "I don't need money. Most people who win the lottery end up broke and unhappy."

"You're dirt poor, so we don't want to pass up an opportunity to cash in on a literal buried treasure."

"I'm not poor," he countered.

"Look at this place." She waved an arm. "This is worse than the house I grew up in, and we were poor."

He looked around the cabin, trying to see it through her eyes. Maybe it was a little drab, but it met his needs—and his desires. "Aimee, there's more to life than a nice house. I have independence."

"Man can't be an island unto himself."

"Listen to you. You're quoting John Donne."

"I don't know who that is. I'm quoting Louisa Herrala."

"You've been talking to Lou about me?" After Aimee's friend and mentor, Louisa, was diagnosed with ALS a few months prior, she moved to California to live with her daugh-ter.

"Of course I talk to her about you." Aimee elbowed Russ and smiled. "Lou said you'll eventually figure out you need somebody in your life."

"Look, lady," Russ tried to use the same tone as Aimee's *mister*, but it sounded contrived.

She laughed.

"Look, I'm having fun dating you, but I don't know if this is going any further."

"Why not?" She narrowed her eyes.

"We want different things. I want my forty and a mule. You want a McMansion and a Mustang."

Aimee's face broke into a grin, and her eyes twinkled. "That's about the stupidest thing I've heard."

"Poetry's not my forte, but my point is I like my little life, and you *don't*. You want a nice house. I want my small cabin. You want to be a paralegal. I hate lawyers."

"You want kids someday, don't you? You're already twenty-nine. You have twelve brothers and sisters. How can you not want at least one or two?" She looked at him with puppy dog eyes.

He felt his resolve crumbling. "I haven't thought that far ahead. But then there's the issue of my family, now that you bring it up."

"Yeah, when do I get to meet them?" She stuck out her lower lip.

"It's complicated." Russ put his arm around her and pulled her close.

Chapter 2

"Why do I like guys who aren't head over heels for me?" Aimee asked Tammy, another waitress at the Heikki Lunta, when they met at the order window.

"What are you talking about? Russ likes you." Tammy attached a ticket to the carousel, balanced a plate of eggs, bacon, and hash browns and a plate of pancakes on one arm, grabbed another plate with an omelet, turned on her heels, and walked out to the dining room floor.

The red, wood-clad diner sat on a steep side street in Douglass and overlooked the canal that cut through the middle of the Keweenaw Peninsula. Tranquil water reflected the hill that rose up on the other side of the canal. The rising sun shone on the lift bridge, which connected Copper Island to the rest of the peninsula. Locals filled half the tables on the mid-June day, as the college students had left town and the tourists hadn't yet arrived.

Aimee was back to work at the diner now that the spring semester was over. Between this job and waitressing evenings at the Cornucopia, she hoped to pick up enough hours to pay down her Visa bill and have enough credit to pay for classes and books in the fall. Just one more semester and she'd be done with her paralegal coursework. She'd graduate from college and then find a stable, professional job. She wouldn't need to worry about making ends meet ever again.

Aimee served chocolate milk to the lone customer at the counter, Mikey, a young man with an intellectual disability and the heart of a child. "What can I get you, hon?" She didn't bother giving him a menu, because he couldn't read.

"I got three dollars and fifty-seven cents." Mikey strewed crumpled bills and loose change on the counter.

"That'll buy you whatever you want." It didn't matter how much he had, because Aimee always covered the rest from her tips.

"Pancakes and bacon. Lots of syrup."

"The syrup's right there, hon. You can drink it if you want." Aimee winked.

Mikey laughed.

Aimee returned to the order window, snapped the order on the carousel, and continued her conversation. "Russ *likes* me, but he's not head over heels for me, not like Danny was with Beth. And if you remember, I hung out with Danny for the longest time, and he didn't even think we were dating."

Tammy laughed. "At least you're attracted to nice guys." Tammy was not. She liked fun guys—bad boys. A few were overbearing, borderline abusive. She was trying to break up with one now, but he wasn't taking no for an answer.

Aimee had been propositioned by fun-loving guys who came into the Cornucopia. She waited on a table of four college-aged boys the other night. She was the bouncy, bubbly version of herself—the Aimee who made good tips. When the customers left, she found a note with a telephone number and message—*Beautiful, let's hook up sometime. Text me for some discreet fun.* She was flattered but thought the guy, whichever one he was, was disgusting, not even considerate enough to remember or use her name.

Russ was different. He might not be thinking of marriage, yet, but he respected her and was sweet. He picked wildflowers for her birthday. "Buttercups for my buttercup," he wrote on a homemade card. He gave them to her and apologized that they were the only flowers in bloom in early June, when she turned twenty-five. Visiting a florist or even the floral department of Shop-Mart would not have occurred to her adorable geek. Beth talked about picking a man like her father. Aimee wanted the exact opposite of her father. She wanted somebody kind and present.

Aimee wiped the counter, where she liked working when things were slow because it was where people sat when they were eating alone. They tended to be chatty, which made time pass quickly.

"Uncle Mak," Aimee said as the big man entered the Heikki Lunta.

"*Hyvää päivää*," Mak barked. "Good morning." His yellowed, coffee-stained teeth matched his bushy blond beard and full head of hair. His light-blue eyes looked young, except when he smiled—the wrinkles showed his sixty-three years. Mak took a stool at the counter, where Aimee had already set a cup and was pouring coffee into it. "Yous got *pannukakku*?"

"We sure do. I'll put your order in."

"With extra berry sauce." Mak set down a fancy journal with the word *Inspire* embossed on the cover and placed a metal pen on top of it. He sipped his coffee.

Aimee put the order in, dropped off Mikey's pancakes and bacon, and made the rounds with a coffee pot.

"Aimee, you hear from Beth?" Mak asked when she passed by.

"Yeah. I called her a few weeks ago to see how Louisa was doing," Aimee said when she returned. "She asked about you and how everyone was doing, except Danny, although I knew she wanted to know especially about him."

Mak opened his journal and readied his pen. "What you think went wrong between them two?" Mak frowned.

"Uncle Mak, are you putting them in your book?"

"I need inspiration. What went wrong?" Her uncle mined the lives of his family and friends for plotlines. He was working on a western romance under the pen name Iris MacDowell. "I got to find out. I'm in da middle of da dark moment and have to find out how it ends."

Aimee shrugged and smiled. Mak set his pen down and sipped his coffee.

"Aimee, more chocolate milk, please," Mikey asked from a few stools down.

"Sure, hon." She refilled his glass.

"What about Russ? How's yous twos doing?" Mak asked.

Aimee laughed. "I can't figure that man out."

"Mysterious men are intriguing, makes good fiction."

"It's not that he's mysterious. All I have to do is give him a look, like this," Aimee raised one eyebrow, "and he caves under pressure, tells me everything I want to know."

Mak let out a belly laugh.

"But it's weird he hasn't said much about his family and I haven't met them. Is it a problem I'm not a Finn?"

"Nah, they don't care about that. We Finns like to tease non-Finns and half-Finns for not having *sisu*, but on da other hand, we've got hundreds of dumb-Finn jokes. Have you heard da one about Eino's new chainsaw?" Mak didn't wait for an answer. "He brought it back to da store and told 'em it don't cut faster than his hand saws. The guy says, 'Let's take a look,' and…" Mak snorted a laugh and slapped the counter. "…he started it up. Eino yelled, 'What's that noise?'"

Mikey snorted and laughed like Mak. Aimee suspected he didn't get the joke, rather he thought Mak's laugh was hysterical. Aimee laughed, too, but more at Mak for how he told the joke than the joke itself. She could've predicted the ending as soon as he asked if she heard about Eino's new chainsaw. A bell dinged, and Aimee headed toward the kitchen, as other bells over the front door rang with customers either coming or going.

"Here's your *pannukakku*." Aimee set a large piece of the Finnish oven pancake in front of Mak.

"*Kiitos*. Thank you." He took a bite and licked his lips. "Da Saarinens are LPs, eh?" Mak returned to the mystery of Russ's parents.

"Well, yeah, but Russ doesn't go any more. He's kind of shunned organized religion."

Mak scribbled something in his journal.

"Uncle Mak, Russ would not want you to use that."

"Hello, Aimee." Russ took a seat on the stool next to Mak. "Hey, Mak."

"Speak of da devil." Mak chuckled.

Mikey laughed in turn.

"You've been talking about me?" Russ asked as Aimee poured his coffee.

"Mak asked about us." Aimee shot Russ a smile that made his high, bony cheeks turn pink.

"Yep, you're a man of mystery," Mak said.

Russ looked pained.

Aimee put in his order, which was the same every time— pancakes, hash browns, and bacon, extra crispy.

When she returned, Russ leaned forward and whispered, "Does he know?"

Aimee knew he meant the copper. "No," she said.

"What was that?" Mak grabbed his journal and pen. He raised an eyebrow.

Russ rolled his eyes and groaned. "Okay, fine, but you have to promise not to tell anybody."

"Promise," Mak said.

Russ looked down at the journal and then up at Mak, who snapped the book shut.

Russ leaned over and lowered his voice. "I found float copper."

"And?" Mak sounded unimpressed.

Float copper was all over the Keweenaw. Long before Europeans first discovered its treasures, Native Americans plucked float copper off the surface and forged tools.

Russ glanced over each shoulder, making sure nobody was within earshot. "And it's big."

Mak opened up his journal.

"You can't use this," Russ pleaded.

"Did you dig it out?" Aimee asked.

"Just enough from the top and bottom to determine how thick it is, about a foot thick, and then I used my metal detector to ascertain the edges. I calculated two to three cubic meters." Russ looked back and forth between Aimee and Mak. "It'd have a mass of about 24,000 kilograms." Russ smiled broadly, looking at them expectantly. "That's about five-and-a-half tons," he said.

"Wow," Aimee and Mak said in unison.

"How much is that worth?" Aimee asked.

"At today's spot rate, scrap value of the copper's about $30,000. But I bet a mineral museum would pay more."

"So you're going to take it out?" Aimee asked.

Russ shook his head. "No. I was just curious if I could figure out how big it was without having to take it out."

After her morning shift, Aimee grabbed a to-go box of leftover *pannukakku* and walked a few blocks out of Douglass and onto the lift bridge to Quincy. As bells rang, a gate blocked the sidewalk and the lanes of traffic. The bridge lifted, and a sailboat motored underneath. As soon as the mast was clear, the bridge began to lower. Aimee tilted her face toward the warm noon sun.

Her phone chirped with a text message. Aimee brightened. Maybe Russ wanted to stop by before her evening shift. He sometimes did that if he didn't have contracting work, which was often. She could continue the conversation they had started about their future, *if* they had a future.

The text was from a number she didn't recognize. Area code 602. Kids from all over the country came to Douglass State University, so she was familiar with a few other area codes, but not this one. She used to get random text messages when she first got her number, but she hadn't received any for the last few years. She opened the message. *Sweetheart I want to see you.*

Oh, brother. Another fun guy. She didn't remember giving her number to anybody. Besides, who would call her sweetheart? Her dad had used that term of endearment. He also called her kiddo, and beloved, which is what he said Aimee meant. He rarely used her actual name. She loved it when she was a kid, but now she shuddered when she heard those nicknames, ever since she abandoned hope he would return.

She slipped the phone back into her purse. With the deck down and gates up, she continued over the lift bridge and into Quincy, Douglass's twin town. She looked over her shoulder at the sunlight sparkling off the water. Two speedboats motored toward each other and pulled long V-wakes behind them. The boats passed, and their wakes crossed, forming a woven pattern of water. As she walked, she thought of her dad.

Francis Mallon was sick with a disease that could have excused much of his behavior if it hadn't hurt so much. When he was sober, he played cards, cribbage, and any other board game. He laughed, he joked, and he worked. He had several different jobs. At a sawmill, as a butcher, as a logger. When he didn't have steady work, he'd get depressed and drink. She wasn't sure in which order that happened. Maybe he drank, got depressed, and then got laid off. In any case, her dad was a mean drunk. Aimee would see it coming and hide in her room. Rob stood between him and their mother. How could she love someone who'd hurt her mother and brother? He never hit Aimee. She wasn't sure how she would've felt about him if he had, but for her, the worst betrayal came when he left. He disappeared, and she hadn't heard from him since.

Two blocks down Main Street in Quincy, Aimee opened a door to a narrow staircase. She ascended the flight of stairs to her one-bedroom, street-side apartment above Dresses by Susan. She slipped off her shoes and aligned them neatly next to the door. She put the *pannukakku* in the refrigerator. On the kitchen table, bills stood on end in a napkin holder. She had jotted the due date in light pencil on the bottom left corner of each and ordered them from first to last due. She tried not to think about bills until she had to pay them, and then she prayed she'd have enough money. Her apartment was small but tidy with furniture assembled from Craigslist and Goodwill.

Aimee retrieved a feather duster from under the kitchen sink. She ran it across her coffee table. She dusted the framed prints that hung on her wall. She paused to study a photo of her family, taken months before her dad had taken off for good. She had hoped her dad's recovery would stick when he started bringing the family to church. Rob, who was three-and-a-half years older, graduated from high school that year and joined the military. They didn't talk often. Her mom lived in Quincy, but Aimee didn't see much of her. She was messed up in her own right—not a drinker, but she had other ways to numb the pain of life.

She ran the feather duster around the frame in a flourish. She would be the one to break the cycle. She was glad Russ came from a more stable family. She wondered when he was going to have her meet them.

Chapter 3

"Oh, good, you made it, Russ." His mother, Maari, glanced up from a half-peeled potato and greeted him with a smile. Russ breathed in the blended aroma of beef and turkey baking, each in a separate oven. "Did you join the Quincy congregation today?" Maari asked.

His parents attended a Lord's People assembly in the village near their home, but Russ rarely joined them. He had only attended the Quincy assembly once, but it was enough for his mom to assume that's where he went regularly.

"Didn't make it this morning." Russ carried a twelve-volt car battery through the kitchen where his adult sisters and two of his sisters-in-law worked at a long island peeling and cutting potatoes from a fifteen-pound bag that sat in the center. Water boiled in a large stockpot on one of the two kitchen ranges.

Every Sunday afternoon, most of the thirty-eight Saarinen family members converged on the banks of the Trap Rock River. There was nothing fancy about the house, except an oversized living room, dining room, and kitchen. The four bedrooms—a master suite, a nursery, a boys' dorm, and a girls' dorm—offered little privacy for an introvert like Russ, but such was the life in a family of thirteen kids.

When Russ was born, the family lived in a part of the house that had since been converted to a three-stall garage. His parents expanded the house when he was six and again when he was thirteen. Russ and his brothers, along with friends and family from their church, helped with the construction. Russ's dad, an electrician, exchanged professional services with other congregants, many of whom were contractors.

"You need a haircut, son. And shave off that beard," Maari scolded.

Russ grunted. He set the battery on the floor in the corner of the dining area and attached clamps from a charger he kept at the house.

Russ sat with his youngest brother, twelve-year-old Henri, at the card table where a 2,000-piece puzzle was in progress. Henri was born when Russ was in his second year at Douglass State but still living at home because he wasn't yet eighteen. Russ snapped pieces in place. His teenage sisters watched after his younger nieces and nephews, who ran around the living room. The older nieces and nephews were outside, probably catching spring peepers or playing soccer. Henri was more serious, like Russ at that age. Russ liked being around him, even when nothing was said—well, especially because nothing had to be said.

"Don't forsake the assembly of believers, son," his mother chided him.

Russ nodded. He had in fact been to church—at Pinehurst Community, where Aimee attended, however she hadn't seen him. Russ slipped in the back after the first service began and left early before Aimee arrived at the second service. He had to see what it was about, why it was so special to Aimee. She loved Pinehurst and liked talking about the sermon every week, so he wanted to see for himself.

Russ wanted to know all the facts before making a decision. Aimee talked about their future, but he wasn't sure he'd fit into her church, and he didn't think she'd like his. He wasn't keen on organized religion these days, anyhow, but church was important to Aimee and he definitely wanted to raise kids in a church. As for the last matter, he wondered where all the kids were at Pinehurst. When they released the kids to something called children's church, a dozen kids ran out of the sanctuary. There were a hundred little kids at every one of the Lord's People assemblies, but they stayed with their parents during the service.

"The convention's coming up," Maari called out from the kitchen. "Will you come with us, Russ? It's in Minneapolis this year."

Russ grunted, non-committal.

"Your Aunt Virginia's coming up from North Carolina. All her girls are coming, too, with their families. Maybe your cousins could introduce you to their single friends."

"I don't need help finding a wife," he muttered.

"Yeah, right," one of his sisters needled. "When's the last time you combed your hair?"

Russ rolled his eyes. The women never let up.

Henri handed Russ a puzzle piece. "I think this goes over by you." Indeed, it fit.

Part of his hesitation having Aimee meet the family was that they were always teasing him about finding a wife, and they'd fawn over her. Of course, they'd also want her to join their church. He hadn't explained that dynamic to her, yet.

"Melissa Halone's single, and she's old, like you," another sister said.

"Isn't she our cousin?" Russ asked. "Anyway, there's a reason she's single."

"You shouldn't talk," a sister teased. The women laughed.

"She's your third cousin. It doesn't even count," Maari said.

"I'm having a hard time concentrating on the puzzle." Russ snapped a couple of pieces together and pushed them across the table toward Henri.

"You could go Finland." His eldest sister-in-law, Anna, spoke with a thick, Finnish accent, dropping the preposition *to*.

"I can't take this anymore." Russ stood and left Henri with the puzzle as the women cackled from the kitchen. He walked out to the garage.

"Hello." Russ's dad, Karl, took a drink from a Styrofoam cup. "Coffee's hot. Help yourself."

Russ's adult brothers and brothers-in-law sat in lawn chairs.

Russ grabbed a chair from a hook on the wall and placed it in the circle of men. He helped himself to a cup of coffee from the coffee maker that sat on his dad's workbench.

"What have you been up to?" his dad asked.

Russ avoided eye contact and combed his beard with his fingers. He didn't care to mention his girlfriend or the copper.

"*What* have you been up to?" Karl asked again.

"Oh, fine. But you guys have to promise not to say anything to anybody."

"Promise," murmured most.

"I found float copper." Russ smiled broadly.

"Yippee. I have a piece in my pocket right now." His brother Paul set his coffee cup on the floor and dug into the pocket of his khaki pants. He pulled out a flat, lumpy green rock. "I found this in my driveway this morning." He held it up.

"That's not float copper," Russ said. "That's a little chunk that got left behind with crushed mine rock." Piles of black rock lie all over the Keweenaw, left over from the underground mining days a century ago. "Anyway, what I found is big."

"How big?" one of his brothers-in-law asked.

"Big. It has a mass of..." Russ paused, sensing he might lose them. "It weighs about five-and-a-half tons."

"How did you manage to weigh it?" Karl asked. "And where did you find it?"

"I didn't weigh it. I estimated its volume and calculated its mass based on the density of copper."

"So you're using your degree again, hey," Paul said.

The men laughed.

Russ attempted a smile. "It's under my cabin."

"How are you going to take it out?" a younger brother asked.

"I'm not, but I want to figure out how I would. What do

you think, Dad? How would you do it?"

"Is Koski going to give you an easement?"

"No. Well, I didn't ask, but I doubt it. He wants me to buy his property."

Paul laughed. "I think his property just got more expensive."

"Nobody can say anything about this. This is a small town. If word gets out…"

"Are we the only ones you told?" a brother-in-law asked.

"You and a couple other people—a few other people."

"And you're the genius," Paul said. They all laughed, including Russ, albeit uncomfortably.

Russ's parents called him gifted, but he didn't think so. He liked to read and simply remembered what he read. He thought if he were smarter, he could figure out how to be less awkward around people.

"What would you do, Dad?" Russ asked.

"First, I'd buy that property before Koski finds out."

Later that evening, Russ sat with Aimee in a corner booth at the Black Fly, a bar in Douglass. His clan and others from the LP Church stayed out of bars, for the most part, and, if any were there by chance, they'd never admit to seeing him.

"Aren't you going to ask me about the sermon?" Aimee asked. "You always ask me about the sermon."

"What was the sermon about?" Russ sat patiently as she told him everything he had already heard, but he listened with interest because she also talked about her dad. Pastor Chip had preached from Colossians 3, about setting hearts on things above and getting rid of such things as anger and rage. Aimee was bitter her dad left the family and wasn't sure she could let go of her anger. "Why do you like Pinehurst so much?" He had never known someone so enthusiastic about church.

"It's family to me. Like a family I never had."

Aimee didn't talk much about her family, and though she pushed to meet Russ's family, she hadn't introduced him to her mom. "Isn't your mom around, and how about Rob?" Danny and Rob had been friends in high school, and Russ hung out with the two of them on occasion.

Her shoulders stiffened. "My mom's checked out. Rob's busy with his life. I love them, but they're not there for me."

Russ frowned. "At least you've got Mak and Lorna."

The aroma of garlic caught Russ's attention. A waitress set their large pizza loaded with sausage and veggies on the table—arguably the best thin crust pizza in the Copper Country. Russ pulled a slice off the pan and put the end in his mouth.

Aimee set a piece of pizza on her plate. "I'm glad I have my Uncle Mak and Aunt Lorna, but it's not the same as having parents who are involved. My mom's other sister, my Aunt Senja, goes to Pinehurst. She was the one who invited my family there. And Pinehurst welcomed us in. I feel at home there."

"Humph." He hadn't been impressed with her church. Russ set a second pizza slice on his plate.

Aimee smiled and reached out with a napkin. "Are you saving that for later?" She dabbed his beard to remove dangling cheese. "You should come with me Sunday, check it out."

Russ sat back in the booth and stroked his beard.

"Okay, mister, 'fess up."

"Oh, fine, I attended Pinehurst this morning."

"You did. How exciting!" Aimee shrieked.

Russ cringed.

"What'd you think?" Her eyes were filled with anticipation.

He searched for something positive to say. "The sermon was all right—although not exactly the one you remembered."

"Russ, you sat there and let me tell you all about it without saying a word." Aimee crumpled her napkin and threw it at him, bouncing it off his face. "You must have been at the first service. You should come with me next week. I usually sit with Danny and other people our age."

"I don't think I can go to Pinehurst, even if I wanted to." He left unsaid that he really didn't want to. It was too irreverent for his tastes. Rock music. Conversational prayers. Sermons that touched on Scripture then went off on tangents and personal stories. Why try to improve upon the Word of God?

"You're a grown adult. You can go wherever you want."

"I don't want to make waves. Have you ever thought of joining the Lord's People?"

"I didn't know you could join. I thought you had to be born into it."

"All kinds of people join, usually boyfriends or girlfriends of members, right before they get engaged."

Aimee squealed.

"No! I'm not saying anything by that." Russ looked around the room to see if anybody was looking at them.

"I could join. Where do I sign up?"

Russ felt flushed. He took another bite of pizza and methodically chewed and swallowed. "Hypothetically—not that this is going anywhere, not that I see a future —just hypothetically, could you see yourself joining the Church?"

"Well, I could try it. But you don't go to your church much anyhow, so why wouldn't we go to Pinehurst where I already go?"

"I can't leave the Church. All my work comes from people in the Church." The LPs supported the members' businesses. They wouldn't use anybody outside the Church unless the service wasn't available within. "Besides, everyone in my family attends the Church. It's expected I will, too."

"Speaking of your family, when do I get to meet them?"

"Look, Aimee, my family will love you, and that's what I'm afraid of. I get enough grief from them already about finding a…"

"A what?" Aimee prodded him.

"…wife." Russ reluctantly finished.

A smile spread across her face.

Man, she was beautiful. Russ looked away before continuing. "We need to figure out first if there's a future here. I'm not sure if we have the same desires."

Aimee raised an eyebrow. "Do you plan on being a hermit for the rest of your life?"

"I'm not a hermit." Russ put his head down to work on another piece of pizza.

"You live in a cabin with no electricity. You drive an ATV across someone else's property, never taking the same route twice. You charge batteries at your parents' house, You have a $3,000 toilet to separate your urine from your solids—that's weird."

Russ looked up.

Aimee laughed. "You have cheese dangling from your beard. Again."

"Then why do you even like me?"

"It'll come off." Aimee dabbed his beard with a napkin.

"No, I mean why do you like me if you think I'm weird?"

"Because you're kind and patient. You spend time with me and listen to me. You even love me."

"I never said that."

"You show it. That's why I fell for you. After Danny told me I had the wrong impression of my relationship with him, you were so gentle with me. You didn't say much, but you saw I was sad and you comforted me."

Russ had taken over Danny's role driving Aimee around after Danny started dating Beth. When they broke up and Beth went back to California, Russ kept chauffeuring Aimee, which turned into a friendship.

"I have a lot of sisters," he finally said.

"That's good. They made you who you are. You have a tender heart. I love that about you. Even though you're a geek, you're my adorable geek."

For a moment, Russ was ready to throw caution to the wind. He steeled his resolve. "But you're not interested in my lifestyle." The property came with the old hunting cabin, which was at the time so dilapidated it wasn't even on the tax rolls. That suited Russ fine, because the property taxes for the land were only $200 per year. He bristled at the thought that in a free nation a man can't truly own property—he can merely rent it from the government. Other than that, it was paid in full. "You want money and a comfortable life, but you're up to your eyes in debt. Wealth's an attitude. I'm not poor because I'm content with what I have and I don't buy things I can't afford. I'm a minimalist."

"Why are you so anti-stuff?"

Russ laughed. "You mean not materialistic?"

"No, that's not what I mean. I don't think it's materialistic to want a toilet that flushes. It's not materialistic to want a water heater so I can have a hot shower, or to be able to blow-dry my hair without starting up a generator. It'd be nice to have two or three bedrooms so our kids don't have to sleep in the same room as us when they turn fourteen."

"Why would it matter if they slept in the same room?"

Aimee raised an eyebrow.

Russ felt heat rise to his face. *Oh!* He studied her. She was cute when she was mad. Streaks of hazel variegated her huge brown eyes. Her silky caramel hair hung over one shoulder. Her V-neck T-shirt accentuated the curve of her neck, the curve of her... Whoa, cowboy! He tried to rein in his mind. "I'm independent." Russ looked down at his plate.

"That's not what relationships are about."

Russ sighed. "I don't mean independent from people like you or my family. I mean I'm independent from financial obligations. I don't work for anybody, and nobody can ruin my life."

"Russ, you worked for a horrible company. They hurt you, but you need to let it go."

Aimee's phone pinged. She flipped it over and read a text message. She slipped it in her purse and picked up a slice of pizza.

"Who's that?"

"It's nobody."

"If it's nobody then why won't you tell me?" Russ set his pizza on his plate and leaned forward.

"It's just a guy who wants to see me. I don't even know who he is or how he got my number."

Russ chuckled nervously.

Chapter 4

Aimee surveyed the cabin from the love seat where she cuddled next to Russ, after he had picked her up after her morning shift at the Heikki Lunta. Soft pine floors with grout-filled cracks. Plywood countertop. Paneled walls. Curtain-less windows. "It needs a woman's touch."

"What are you talking about?"

Aimee laughed. "For starters, we could get rid of the outhouses tacked to the wall." Russ had so many quirks and odd interests she didn't even ask about the half-dozen pictures of outhouses next to the table.

Russ bobbed his head left and right as if he was considering it. "I painted the ceiling to brighten it up. I disinfected the well, put in a pump. I put in the shower stall and the composting toilet." Russ nodded to the four-foot by six-foot closet in the opposite corner of the cabin. "This has come a long way in the last year."

Aimee grimaced. She always tried to remember to use the toilet before she visited Russ's cabin. There was no septic system on the property, only an outhouse, so Russ had purchased a waterless toilet before winter set in last year. She didn't care for either option. To shower, he turned on a generator to pump water into a cistern near the ceiling and then waited hours for it to get to room temperature before taking a quick shower. Aimee hated cold showers. She'd had enough of them growing up. She wasn't about to subject herself to them willingly.

The kitchen was rustic. Russ didn't need or want any appliance other than his propane cooking burners and a propane-powered fridge the size of a cooler, both of which sat atop a plywood counter. He brought in a replacement propane tank every few weeks. He heated the cabin with a wood stove, which he fueled with trees he cut down on his property and split himself. The cabin had one propane light, and for instant-on lighting, Russ had rigged up LEDs run off 12-volt batteries, which he charged when he visited Danny or his parents.

Aimee knew how to be poor. Her family had lived most summers without electricity as her dad never paid bills in full or on time. They relied on the humanity of the power company to feed their meter in the winter.

Russ's phone dinged. Aimee reached over to grab it for him off the end table where it lay on a Bible.

"Don't look at it. It could be some gal who wants to see me," Russ said. "I don't look at your phone to see who texts you."

She laughed. It seemed the text she had gotten while they were at the Black Fly had rocked him a bit. Good. "Yeah, right." She tossed her hair and, as she handed the phone to Russ, read aloud the short text message from Danny, "I've got a job for you."

"Why are you reading my messages when you won't even tell me who texted you?" He frowned.

Aimee shrugged and smiled. He *was* jealous. That might be a good sign. "At least you have work." Russ was a building contractor in the Keweenaw, as was everyone, it seemed. There wasn't enough work to go around in the summer and no work at all in the winter. Aimee peered over Russ's shoulder at the text message exchange.

Are you available now? And after Russ affirmed he was, Danny replied, *Maribel Myers. Bring plywood.*

"This won't be paid work, will it?" Aimee asked.

"Doesn't look like it. Let's go."

Aimee rode behind Russ on his four-wheeler through the maple trees across Koski's property to his truck and construction trailer. Russ backed his truck up to the trailer and hitched it up. They drove up the county road about a mile, past Koski's house, and into Maribel's driveway. Rusted farm equipment littered the yard between a dilapidated house and an old barn.

"She's your neighbor." Aimee was surprised they had arrived so soon.

"Never met her. I've seen her clear her driveway in that old plow truck. She's an old widow, no kids. Danny looks after her."

Russ knocked on the front door, and Danny yelled from inside to come in.

"Danny, give me my gun back," a woman yelled.

"It's okay, guys, you can come in," Danny called out.

Danny, dressed in a Michigan State Police uniform, was in the kitchen with the agitated woman.

"I don't know them, Danny. I don't know them." The woman paced.

"It's okay, Maribel. They're friends." Danny repeated 'it's okay' until Maribel stood still and glared at Aimee and Russ.

"Russ is a builder. I asked him to come to patch that up." Danny gestured to a window. Shards of glass stuck out from the edges of the kitchen window sash. Behind the broken pane, a few squares of duct tape stuck to a screen, which was torn and flapping in the breeze.

"What happened?" Russ asked.

Maribel turned toward the window. "I shot a squirrel. Danny, would you go get it?"

"Yeah, I'll grab it later, after we put a board over this window."

"You shot a gun from inside the house?" Aimee moved closer to Russ, and he grabbed her hand.

"She forgot her window was down," Danny said as if it were the only unusual thing about it.

"Danny, I need my gun." Maribel frowned.

"Now Maribel, you're not exactly thinking clearly these days. It might be best if you give me a call when you need a squirrel shot."

"Danny, you're the one who's not thinking clear. A squirrel will never wait around that long. Squirrels don't even wait for me to go outside to shoot them. And I don't need my gun just for squirrels. I need protection from Vance."

Danny smiled at her in a way that seemed to put Maribel at ease, as if he were taking her seriously. He turned to Russ. "Do you have a piece of plywood you can put over this window?"

Russ nodded. "Sure, and I'll take measurements for a new pane. I can come back another day to put it in."

Danny and Russ pulled the kitchen table away from the window. Russ pulled a tape measure off his belt and measured the outside and inside dimensions of the sash. Aimee never saw him write down numbers when he worked on building projects. He just remembered them.

"Aimee, could you keep Maribel company?" Danny called over his shoulder as he and Russ headed for the door.

Maribel watched with sad eyes as Danny carried her .22 rifle out with him, and then she shook her head, as though ridding herself of the memory. She smiled pleasantly at Aimee. "Have a seat. Have a seat. Would you like coffee?"

"That'd be delightful," Aimee said in the voice she used for unhappy customers.

Maribel retrieved a mug from the cupboard and filled it from a percolator pot that sat on the kitchen stove. "Here's yours."

Aimee took the mug and sat at the kitchen table. Maribel topped off her coffee and joined her, leaning back in her chair and crossing her legs. Her oily, salt-and-pepper hair conformed to the shape of her skull. Age had softened her once-strong features of high cheekbones and square jaw. She gazed intensely at Aimee, as if trying to remember who she was.

Aimee smiled and sipped her coffee. "Wow. That's strong."

Maribel laughed. "That's how Henry likes it."

"Who's Henry?"

"Henry's my husband."

Aimee looked around, confused. She thought Russ had said she was a widow.

"He's not here." Maribel furrowed her brow. "He died."

Russ and Danny returned to the kitchen with plywood and a drill. Russ moved around the table and placed the plywood over the lower sash. He retrieved a few screws from his pocket and put them in his mouth. With one screw, he tacked the top right corner of the plywood to the window.

"Your husband's a hard worker." Maribel nodded approvingly at Russ.

"He's not my husband." Aimee smiled as Russ glanced her way.

"He will be," Maribel said decisively.

Danny scoffed. "Don't make wedding plans. She said I'd marry Beth." Pain was evident on his face.

"You will." Maribel cradled her mug in her hands and looked at Aimee sternly. "I've been getting things mixed up lately, but as my reality dims, I can see beyond it clearly." She leaned forward. "He loves you," she whispered. "He loves you. I can see it in his eyes."

Russ looked back to Aimee with a serious expression on his face. He pulled the last screw out of his mouth and fastened the plywood.

"I have something for you." Maribel stood. "I can't give you the dresser, because that's for Danny and Beth, but I have a quilt for you. Come, I'll show you. I'll show you." Maribel led the way down the hallway to a bedroom with a twin bed in disarray and clothes strewn about the floor. Maribel opened the closet and rummaged around a bit, eventually pulling down sheets and blankets. "It's not here. It's not here. I'll look in the other room."

She led the way into another room with another twin bed, where Danny and Russ joined them. A number of boxes sat on the floor next to an antique dresser.

"Is that Beth's and your dresser?" Aimee asked Danny.

Danny's face looked pained, and Aimee regretted teasing him. The poor guy was heartbroken.

"I'm looking for a quilt. It's a beautiful quilt but it's too big for my bed. It's made for two. It's made for two." Maribel opened the closet and stood looking up at boxes. "Henry's mother made it for us. She's an excellent quilter." Maribel searched under the bed. She became as agitated as when Russ and Aimee had first arrived.

"It's okay," Danny said.

"It's Vance," Maribel said. "He's done took my quilt. Arrest him, Danny."

On the way back to the cabin, Aimee rested her forehead against the side window, catching glimpses of white here and there in the most shaded parts of the bush where winter stretches into June. How sad for Maribel to live alone. Her husband dead. No kids.

"Do you want to meet my mom?" Aimee asked Russ, after he unhitched the construction trailer.

"Now?"

"Yeah. Seeing Maribel makes me think I should see her." She felt guilty for not doing more for her mom, but conflicted because she needed to get herself through school before she could be of much help anyway.

Russ looked apprehensive. "Isn't it a little too soon for me to meet her?"

"She's not going to fawn all over you, if that's what you're worried about. We'll see if she even notices you."

They climbed back into his truck and headed up the gravel road, past Koski's, past Maribel's. As they neared the top of the hill, Aimee looked out the back window at Lake Superior off in the distance. She loved the view. Russ paused at a stop sign and rolled across the intersection onto a paved road in worse condition than the gravel. They passed the Johnsons' timber-framed house, Danny's little blue house, and Louisa Herrala's empty farmhouse. They came to another stop sign at US Highway 41. As Russ waited for traffic to pass to turn right toward Quincy, Aimee decided they should take a detour. "Go straight," she told him.

Russ glanced at her, shrugged, and drove across the highway and down a road that ran nearly parallel to the highway. A few miles in the distance, the Quincy Shaft House stood tall.

They approached a cluster of houses behind an old mine hoist, a steel-framed right triangle with a large wheel on top. The perpendicular part of the frame was on the southeast side, and the angled part of the frame sloped down at fifty-four degrees to match the copper vein under it. At the turn of the twentieth century, miners descended into the shaft that pierced the basalt rock and copper. They blasted, picked, and loaded copper into carts pulled to the surface by a large cable that ran over the pulley. The workers lived in houses built by the mining companies in little villages called locations—Mesnard Location, Boston Location, Phoenix Location.

"I grew up in that house." Aimee nodded to a square structure with vinyl siding, new windows, and a cement driveway complete with a basketball hoop and a Honda Odyssey.

"That's nice." Russ stopped the truck across the street from the house.

"Not when I lived there. My dad bought it for $20,000. It looked like Maribel's house with paint peeling off the clapboard. It was rougher on the inside." Aimee smiled. "But our toilet flushed." She grimaced. "Even when we had to flush it using a bucket we filled with the old hand pump."

The hand pump was gone, and the grass was greener. She had remembered enough. "Let's go. You know where the subsidized housing in Quincy is, hey?"

Russ nodded and drove back to the highway. They rode in silence as they headed down the hill.

At the apartment complex, Aimee led Russ down the hallway and knocked on her mom's door. She could hear muffled voices and dramatic music inside. She knocked again. No answer. She knocked loudly.

"Come in," her mom yelled from within.

Aimee led Russ to the living room where a TV played

a soap opera and her mom sat on a couch holding a can of Mountain Dew. Aimee motioned to Russ to have a seat in a chair, and she sat on the couch with her mother. "Hi, Mom, I brought somebody for you to meet."

"Who's that?" Her mother glanced at Russ and then turned back to her show.

Aimee sighed. Why did she even try? "His name's Russ. We're dating."

Her mother remained fixated on the television screen as suspenseful music built to a crescendo and the camera framed a mustached man in a suit deep in thought. When the show went to a commercial, she offered Russ a snaggletoothed smile. If the state of her health weren't evident in the lack of a neck and her swollen ankles, her decayed teeth were a dead giveaway. Her mom was never the same after Dad left. With few job skills, she could only find part-time, minimum wage work, and they lost the house to foreclosure. She always had issues controlling her diet, but when she got depressed, she pretty much gave up and her weight ballooned.

"Russ, this is my mom, Sophia."

Russ smiled awkwardly.

Sophia frowned. "Have you heard from Rob?" she asked Aimee.

"A few months ago. He's doing all right, working in Las Vegas—computer work."

"You still in school, hey?" Her mom sipped her Mountain Dew.

"Yeah. One semester left."

"What are you studying?"

"Paralegal." Aimee had told her that dozens of times over the last few years. She tried to give her mother the benefit of the doubt, telling herself it was hard for her mom to remember such an unfamiliar profession, like trying to remember foreign names. At least she cared enough to ask.

Sophia watched with interest a commercial she had likely seen a hundred times. She took another drink.

"Mom, Russ was asking about my heritage. Do I have any

Italian in me?"

"Not on my side." Sophia had pale white skin and dark hair with streaks of gray.

"How about on Dad's side?"

"Frank's dad was a Lapp."

"I'm part Finnish?" Aimee directed her question to her mother, but looked at Russ and tossed her hair. "Mom?"

Sophia didn't respond, her eyes glued to the TV watching the soap opera.

"The Lapps *are* Finns, right, Russ?"

"Yep. The Sami are the indigenous Finno-Ugric people of Northern Finland. That explains your dark hair and eyes."

Sophia dropped her chin, furrowing her eyebrows as she examined Russ.

He grimaced and looked toward Aimee.

She nodded. "I think we'll go."

"Okay," her mother mumbled, "make sure the door closes on your way out. The latch sticks."

When they were back in the truck, Aimee sighed. "So that's it. If you get me, it's only me."

"And if you marry me, you marry my whole family."

Aimee smiled at the thought.

As they drove through Quincy on the way to Aimee's apartment, her mobile phone chirped. The text message was the same 602 number. *Kiddo, got your number from Rob. I want to see you.*

"Your other boyfriend?" Russ's attempt at sarcasm would have amused her, had she not been so upset.

Aimee's lips felt numb. "My dad."

Chapter 5

*R*uss glanced at Aimee in the passenger seat of his truck as she held her phone in her lap and stared at the screen. He pulled up to her apartment, hoping she wouldn't get out. He didn't want her to leave when she was so upset.

"I can't believe it." Aimee's voice cracked. "My dad wants to see me."

He didn't know what to say. "Should we drive someplace?" he finally asked.

Her eyes remain fixed on the small screen. "Yeah."

"Let's head out to the lake. We have plenty of daylight left." Russ drove out of Quincy and headed east along the canal. When he didn't know what to say, he found it was best to say nothing.

A mile down the road, Aimee broke the silence, spitting out the words. "After ten years, my dad sends me a text message. He doesn't even have the decency to call me."

Russ had never heard so much anger in her voice. "Maybe he knew you'd be shocked, wanted to put the ball in your court." He said the words tentatively.

Aimee sighed. "What should I do?"

An hour earlier, Russ wouldn't have hesitated—of course she should get back in touch with her dad. Family is important. But after meeting her mom, Russ wasn't so sure. Every family has issues. He had issues growing up LP, feeling like a misfit on the hockey team and in college, but his parents were always engaged in his life—at least as much as they could be with thirteen kids.

"What's your dad like?" Russ asked.

Aimee put her phone in the cup holder. "He was funny. A joker." She let out a short, uncomfortable laugh and then frowned. "Except when he drank, then he was mean." She reached over and rubbed Russ's neck.

Her touch sent electricity through his body, and he tried to focus on the conversation. "Ten years, hey."

"He left when I was fifteen. He had run off before, but he always came back weeks later sober and broke. But then he disappeared for good." Aimee's chin drooped. "It took a year before I gave up looking for him every morning when I came out of my room. My mom lost the house when I was seventeen, so I went to live with one of my friends, and my mom moved into subsidized housing." Her voice trembled.

Russ pulled off the road next to a scrapyard. When he reached for her hand, the dam broke. He caressed her hand as she cried.

Aimee scooted over to the center seat and leaned her head against his shoulder. "Sorry," she said.

He reached behind the seat and grabbed a roll of toilet paper and handed it to her.

"How romantic." Aimee smiled.

"It's for emergencies. This constitutes an emergency."

Aimee laughed as she wadded toilet paper in her hand. "You're adorable. You have a lot to learn about women if you think this constitutes an emergency." She turned the rearview mirror toward herself, blotted her smeared mascara, and then blew her nose. "Louisa Herrala says there's a reason God made tears." She smiled up at him.

"You have a little black…" He touched her nose.

She leaned forward to look into the rearview mirror, and with a bit more toilet paper rubbed mascara off her nose. "I wonder what my dad wants."

"I guess there's only one way to find out."

"I need to think about it. Where's the 602 area code from?"

Russ searched on his phone. "Phoenix, Arizona."

Aimee lowered her eyebrows.

"Do you want to go home or should we go somewhere else?" Russ asked.

"Let's go somewhere." Aimee's brown eyes brightened, her enthusiasm back in a surprisingly sudden shift in mood.

Russ drove along the canal past an old smelting plant, a historic site that once processed copper ore into ingots. Piles of man-made lava rock—chunks of black glass, the tailings from the furnace—lay next to the facility. The hillside rose up on the left, and every few hundred yards, streams of water carried run-off from the snowmelt down the hill to culverts under the road. They passed newer houses built along the canal and clusters of old houses built by mining companies over a century ago. The road curved northeast toward Torch Lake past relics from an industry long since dead. Old stamp mills had disintegrated to odd, rusted metal components sitting on top of crumbling cement structures. An old dredge boat, which was once the key instrument in a reclamation plant, sat beached on the stamp sand.

Russ stopped in the village to pick up food for the outing. "Would you want to wait in the truck while I run in?" He was taking enough of a risk driving through the village with her. Whoever was inside the convenience store was bound to know his family.

"Nah, I'll go in."

Russ swallowed hard. He walked to the entrance as she got out of the truck. She took a few quick steps to catch up with him, and he held the door open for her.

"Such a gentleman." Aimee smiled.

Russ frowned. It was something he would have done for anyone. He hoped she wouldn't make it obvious that they were a couple.

"Hey, Russ," the clerk said when he entered.

Russ nodded to the chatty woman who had tended the store since he was a kid.

"Where's the bathroom?" Aimee asked.

The clerk pointed to the back of the store.

"I just need to freshen up."

Russ hurriedly selected crackers, deli ham, cheese, and water and brought them up front. Maybe he could be back in the truck before she came back.

The clerk rang up his order. "So irritating when people come in to use the bathroom without making a purchase."

Russ studied the lottery tickets, which interested him in no way other than distracting him from the clerk's statement. As much as he wanted to defend Aimee, he willed himself to keep his mouth shut. Honesty is a virtuous curse in a world with flawed standards. His big mouth got him into trouble at his last company, where he had been living his dream until they ripped it from him.

The clerk stated the price, and Russ put cash on the counter. "You're quiet today, hey," she said.

Russ stroked his beard. With copper under his cabin and his girlfriend in the john, his mouth became dry. He simply nodded.

The woman handed Russ his change and bagged the merchandise.

"Hey, what'd you get?" Aimee sidled up to Russ, touching his arm, and he almost jumped out of his skin.

"Oh, she's with you?" The cashier said the words with interest.

Russ ignored the question, grabbed his bag, and made a beeline for the exit. Aimee followed a foot behind.

"Okay then, you stay out of trouble," the cashier called out as they left.

"What was that about?" Aimee asked when they were on the road again.

Russ shrugged and quickly changed the subject. "My family lives down there." Russ pointed to an intersecting road.

His family home was in Trap Rock, a valley that runs

between the copper spine of the Keweenaw Peninsula to the northwest and smaller hills to the southeast. His adult brothers purchased land from his parents, and two sisters married men from the Church who had property in the area. Russ wanted several miles of separation, so he bought his place on Quincy Hill.

They passed farms, horse ranches, and country homes—up and down hills and around a few bends until Lake Superior came into view. In a beachside park on Big Traverse Bay, Russ set their supper on a picnic table, kicked off his shoes, and buried his feet in the sand. Aimee sat next to him and rested her bare foot on his. Low bushes with tiny white flowers, the genesis of blueberries, covered sand dunes. The only shade came from a few Saskatoon trees, which would produce wild sugarplums in August. Russ often ate them right off the branches, and his sisters teased he looked like a giraffe. Lake Superior lapped up on the beach below them. The sun, having worked all day, had warmed the cool June day to seventy degrees.

"How're you doing?" Russ wondered if she was thinking about the text message from her dad.

"Great." Aimee smiled broadly. After she finished her crackers and cheese, she stood and rubbed his shoulders. "Let's go down by the water." Aimee took off her windbreaker and tied it around her waist.

He tossed the empty packaging into a trash can, and then they walked down the dune to the water's edge. Waves gently rolled in. Across the bay, the Huron Mountains rose above the horizon.

"It's beautiful," Aimee said.

Farther down the shoreline, several people were piling logs and driftwood into a tepee structure, undoubtedly for that night's Juhannus Day celebration. They were probably LP teens, who frequently gathered around fires on the beach, but for the Finnish summer solstice festival, the fires were particularly large.

"Let's go over there." Russ pointed in the opposite direction.

They walked the beach until they rounded a point and no one else was in sight. They sat, leaning against a driftwood log.

He grabbed her hand. Her skin was soft and smooth under his. "It doesn't get much better than this, hey," he said.

"It's nice being alone with you so you can act like you like me, and even hold my hand." Aimee squeezed his hand and gave him a flirtatious smile.

Russ scooted closer and put his arm around her shoulder. He felt a deep longing rise within him—desire, but not lust, something stronger. His mind worked. He liked her, maybe even loved her, but was a future with Aimee possible? Could she fit in with the Lord's People? Would she want to be LP? If he left the Church, what would happen to his business? Construction jobs were scarce as it was. If he started going to Pinehurst, business would dry up completely. Was this another time when he was supposed to do the right thing, no matter the consequence? What was the right thing?

"What's wrong?" Aimee asked.

"Just thinking." Russ smiled. "About us."

"Let's walk some more." Aimee stood, and a small butterfly tattoo on the back of her shoulder peeked out from under her tank top.

Russ hadn't noticed it before, but until then he hadn't seen her wear a sleeveless shirt. He stood and touched her shoulder, gently tracing the wings. "Did it hurt?"

Aimee shrugged. "Not as much as other things."

"Let's go that way." Russ nodded in the direction opposite from where they had come, away from the bonfire builders. He thought the butterfly was pretty, but the Lord's People don't accept tattoos. He and Aimee were from different worlds.

Chapter 6

"*H*ey, lady. What does a guy have to do to get coffee around here?" Russ teased Aimee when he walked into the Heikki Lunta.

Aimee faced the counter and smiled. "What's this? A block party?"

After taking a stool next to Danny, Russ leaned forward to see who was sitting on Danny's other side. "Hey, Koski." Now all he needed to do was keep his mouth shut about the copper.

"Hey, neighbor. Call me Bobby." Otto Robert Koski Jr. insisted on being called by his youthful name, even though he was in his seventies.

Aimee poured coffee for Russ and topped off Danny's and Koski's cups.

Russ blew over the top of his coffee and then took a sip. "Speaking of neighbors, how's Maribel doing, Danny?"

"She wants her gun back, that's for sure." Dressed in his trooper uniform, Danny often got breakfast at the restaurant after his night shifts.

"What happened to her gun?" Koski asked.

"I had to confiscate it, write a report for careless discharge. She shot out the glass in her kitchen window killing a squirrel. There's a court date. She'll probably have a competency hearing. We'll see if she shows up," Danny said.

"Doesn't she have other guns?" Koski asked.

"I suppose you should honk your horn if you decide to drop in for a visit." Danny laughed.

"Russ, I don't want you going back to replace the window." Aimee put on a stern face.

Russ met her gaze. "I don't want to die either."

She smiled at him.

Koski laughed. "Isn't that sweet. The man has somebody to live for."

"You can follow me in, Russ," Danny said. "I'll provide cover."

The door dinged. Mak took a few steps into the restaurant and bellowed, "*Hyvää päivää.*"

"*Päivää päivää,*" Koski replied.

Mak stopped in his tracks, looking at the men at the counter. "Oh, this is too good to be true. I'll be right back." He scurried out of the restaurant.

"Say, Russ," Koski leaned forward and peered around Danny, "I heard you might be wanting to buy that adjacent forty and make a road into your place."

Russ stroked his beard.

Aimee shrugged. "I better go put in your order."

Russ glanced over at Danny and then over to Aimee who stood at the pass-through window. She stuck his ticket on an order wheel. Russ's throat dried and his palms moistened. "No, no. No need to build a road."

The door clanged again. Mak scampered back into the restaurant with his journal and took a seat on the other side of Koski. "What'd I miss?" He opened the book and readied his pen.

"I was telling Russ he ought to buy that land and build a road." Koski sipped his coffee.

"Then what'd you say?" Mak leaned forward, directing his question to Russ.

"I said I didn't need a road." He combed his beard with his fingers.

"That's not what I heard." Koski winked at Aimee. "It's one

thing to be hauling yourself and propane tanks back and forth on the four-wheeler, but now you have a precious load."

Russ shook his head at Aimee.

She threw up her hands. "I didn't say anything."

Mak wrote feverishly.

Danny sat back on his stool with a look of amusement.

Russ sighed. "Okay, who'd you hear it from?" It was inevitable in a small town. Why couldn't he have kept his mouth shut? He wondered how high the price of the land was now.

Koski chuckled. "My wife is friends with your young lady's Aunt Senja." He nodded toward Aimee. "They was talking about yous and figured it might make sense to put a road in—make it easier for a lady to visit the place."

Russ exhaled. "That's something to think about."

Koski stood. "I gotta go."

"*Näkemiin,*" Mak said, and the others said goodbye in English.

The bell above the door rang upon Koski's exit.

"Have any of you said anything, to anybody?" Russ looked at Danny, Mak, and Aimee in turn.

"Russ, I think you're the only one telling people." Aimee grabbed his coffee cup and dumped it into the sink behind the counter. She placed the cup back on the counter and refilled it with hot coffee.

Danny laughed. "You can't keep a secret, brother. You best move on that land before word gets out."

Russ shook his head. "I'm not planning to take the copper off the property."

"You got to do somethin' with it," Mak said. "With somethin' that valuable on your property, when word gets out, you'll have people comin' to take a look."

Russ stiffened. Aimee set his pancakes, hash browns, and bacon—extra crispy—in front of him.

Russ pushed the plate back. "I can't eat."

Danny laughed. "I've never heard you say that. Relax, man."

Mak scribbled in his journal.

"You can't use this!" Russ said.

Chapter 7

"*O*kay, mister." Aimee pointed to a makeshift plywood door with a padlock that covered the opening to the trenched passage underneath the cabin. "How inconspicuous. No one will ever guess something valuable's under there." Sarcasm was Aimee's most potent weapon. "What are you going to do with that copper?"

"It's fine where it is." Russ flapped his hand, walking away from Aimee to the cabin entrance. "Why are you so obsessed with it?"

"I'm not the one who put up a no trespassing sign and boarded up a hole underneath my cabin."

Russ shrugged.

"Come to think of it," Aimee continued as she caught up to him, "you never take the same route in, so I doubt I just happened to see the one sign you posted. How many did you put up?" She surveyed the woods around the cabin.

"I put signs along the west boundary of my property."

"All along one side of your forty acres? How far is that?"

"A quarter of a mile." Russ sat on a step to the front door.

"Unbelievable. How many signs?"

Russ stroked his beard.

"*How* many signs, Russell?" Aimee raised an eyebrow.

"Fifty."

"Fifty no trespassing signs plus the signs nailed to the side of your cabin, hey." Aimee read the signs out loud, "Private Property, Trespassers Will Be Prosecuted, Keep Out."

Russ lowered his head. Apparently, the conversation with Koski had rattled him.

"You're paranoid. You need to sell the copper," she pressed.

"I couldn't get it off the property if I wanted to, which to be clear, I don't want to." Russ folded his arms. "I don't need the money and I don't have the money to buy Koski's property."

"So get a loan." Aimee shooed black flies away from her face.

"Aimee, I own this cabin, free and clear. I'm not going to go into debt over this."

"You have to spend money to make money."

Russ sighed. "That's where we're different. I'm not comfortable with the way you live on credit."

"It's the only chance I have to get ahead." She bit her lip.

"That's not true. You could figure out a way to get ahead without going into debt. You're going to be a slave to your debt."

"Look, Russ, I'm not smart enough to get a free ride through college."

Russ rolled his eyes.

"I couldn't even get a single scholarship, except for a few hundred dollars from Pinehurst to buy books one semester. And I had to petition for independent student status to get federal loans because my dad's nowhere to be found and my mom wouldn't get off the couch to fill out the form." Aimee stepped past Russ to the front door of the cabin. She needed to clean, sweep—anything to work out aggression. The door was locked and had a shiny new knob. "You changed the locks? Who would lock the door of a shack in the middle of the bush in the UP? Argh!"

As she stood facing the door, Russ reached around her and unlocked it. "Let's go inside and sit down."

"Fine," she snapped.

Russ clomped across the floor, depositing a trail of dirt.

"Are you forgetting something?" Aimee kicked off her shoes and put them neatly next to the door.

"Sorry." Russ put his boots next to the door. He reached for Aimee's hand, but she pulled it away.

She followed him to the couch and sat close to the armrest opposite him, leaving as much space between them as possible. "You said I'm going to be a slave to my debt. That's not true. I'm using debt as a tool, as an investment in my future. There's no way I can come close to paying for classes by waitressing—my income barely covers my rent and food. I need to break the cycle of poverty. And here you are, intentionally impoverished. You have so much talent, so much potential—so much invested in you by other people paying for your undergraduate and even giving you a free ride through a PhD program. You can contribute so much, but you throw it all away for your camp." Aimee motioned with her arms palms up to the room.

"I'm independent."

"No, you're not. You're one of the most dependent people I've ever met. You rely on your friends and family to charge your batteries. You keep your venison in your parents' freezer. You're dependent on people from a church you don't like to get enough work so you can pay for your propane tanks and meals. You skip meals and binge when you have food."

Russ was silent.

"I grew up with nothing." Aimee pulled her knees up to her chest. "I have nothing, and if I don't work my tail off now, I'll never have anything. You have the luxury of playing poor. All you have to do is hitch a ride back to Trap Rock Valley and you'll have a warm bed and food. I have nothing to fall back on."

Russ scooted closer to Aimee and rubbed her back. "What are you going to do about your dad?"

"What would you do?" She studied his face.

"I don't know."

"I wish Louisa Herrala were here. I talked to Beth. She said the ALS is not progressing as fast as they thought." Aimee felt her heart soften. She wasn't really upset with Russ, although she did wish she could see more of a future with him. His shack did not cut it. The text message from her dad had rekindled embers of anger that remained inside her. After all those years, her dad chose about the least personal, most noncommittal way to communicate.

Aimee leaned her head against Russ's shoulder. She felt thankful he seemed to take her venting in stride.

"I'll build Louisa a ramp if she decides to come back."

"Yay!" Aimee smiled. "See, Russ, that's why I love you. One more question—if you don't want to take the copper out, why did you build the door to the trench? Why not bury it?"

"I like to look at it."

"Russell, *you're* the one who's obsessed."

Chapter 8

*A*imee tossed a credit card statement on the kitchen table. She'd open it later. Right now she couldn't bring herself to look at it. She stepped into the living room and paused to study the picture of her family. The last photo she had where her mom smiled with her eyes. The last time they were a happy family.

She took the picture off the wall and sat on the couch with it. It was the last picture with the whole family, taken at Rob's graduation and just before he left for the Air Force. She didn't talk to him often. He had called a few weeks ago to wish her a happy birthday—he was doing okay, and she was glad.

She retrieved her cell phone and dialed his number.

"Hi, sis," he answered.

"Is this a good time to talk?"

"Sure. I'm at work but can take a short break." Rob worked in IT in Las Vegas, where he had been stationed with the Air Force. He stayed in for eight years, during which time the Air Force sent him to computer technician training, and he worked on base as a network administrator. "How's the geek?"

"I can call him that, but you can't. Russ is great. Well, mostly great, but that's not why I called. Did you give Dad my number?"

"I didn't think you'd mind. You missed him so much."

"So he called you? How did he get your number?" Aimee asked.

"I suppose he kept it all these years. It's the same 906 number I had when I left home. Remember when he got that janitorial job at the school and celebrated by getting us all cell phones—all with numbers one digit apart?" Rob laughed. "I think he lost that job a month later, but I managed to keep my phone."

"Yeah, I didn't." In the string of disappointments in Aimee's childhood, losing the phone barely ranked. "He texted he wants to see me."

"He texted me, too. I sent him your number, and I tried calling the old man, but he didn't answer—just sent me a text saying he can't talk. So forget him."

Aimee laughed. Rob's reaction didn't surprise her. His disdain for his dad started years earlier with the physical abuse. Rob had already joined the Air Force by the time Frank abandoned Aimee and his wife.

"I googled the number. It's a Phoenix area code. Are you going to see him?" Aimee asked.

"I doubt it. If he wants to make his way up to Vegas, I'll have dinner with him. Are you?"

"I haven't decided." Aimee felt like crying thinking about it. "I wish he had never texted. I get sad all over again. I don't have money to go to Phoenix anyway."

"I've got to get back to work. Say hi to the geek."

"Rob, stop."

"I would've never imagined you dating him. Isn't he an LP?"

"Yes. And goodbye."

After freshening up for the evening, Aimee walked out of Quincy, across the lift bridge, and into Douglass. Two blocks past the Heikki Lunta she entered The Sheldon House, where her Aunt Senja lived in an apartment on the fourth floor of the historic brick building. Aimee checked the time on her phone. She was early to the monthly prayer meeting and still working through her thoughts, so she took the staircase.

Aimee didn't consider herself hyper-spiritual. Hers was a practical Christianity—an alternative to the brokenness she lived through her first fourteen years. After her dad completed the first few steps of AA, he decided the whole family needed God.

Frank had chosen Pinehurst for their church because that was where his sister-in-law Senja, the only Christian he knew, went. Aimee had Christian friends, so she went willingly with the hope her life might become more like theirs. Her mom went submissively—not a mutual submissiveness that comes from respect and a nurturing environment, but a submissiveness born of fear. Rob refused to go, and Frank couldn't do much about it because Rob had two inches and twenty pounds on him. Besides, he was just weeks from graduation and had already enlisted in the Air Force.

Flowered wallpaper and dark-paneled wainscot decorated a hallway dimly lit with wall sconces. Her feet tread quietly on rich, burgundy carpet over a thick pad. She thought back to her first days at Pinehurst Church in the March before she turned fifteen. They had sat in the third pew next to Senja. Once her aunt picked her jaw off the floor, after seeing Frank and the family, she hugged each of them and beamed throughout the service. Sunday mornings were Aimee's refuge, her foundation that summer when everything changed. Rob left for the Air Force that June. Aimee got her learner's permit that summer, and Frank was going to teach her to drive, but then he left—for good. That was when her mom gave up on life.

Senja was a good aunt, but it was awkward to talk to her about family issues. Aimee eventually found a confidant in Louisa, but then Louisa was diagnosed with ALS and moved to California with her daughter. Rob was in Vegas, busy with his own life. Aimee only had Russ, but he acted as if they were undercover spies when they went out on dates. He didn't want to introduce her to his family. And to top it off, he lived like a hermit. Maybe he was right. They had different desires.

When she arrived at the door marked with an *ichthys*,

Aimee entered immediately. Nobody ever knocked on Senja's door on prayer night.

"Hello. You're early." Senja greeted her with a hug.

"Maybe we can talk before the others arrive." Even though she wasn't particularly close to Senja, Aimee was glad to have her in town. She worshiped with her every Sunday and prayed with her once a month.

Senja led her into the kitchen where she was preparing for her company. "What's on your mind?"

"My dad texted me."

"Really?" Senja raised her eyebrows.

"He wants to see me." Aimee leaned against the counter. "I'm not sure how I feel about that."

"That's understandable." Senja sliced cheese on a plate.

Aimee felt anger bubble below the surface, yet part of her dreamed. Maybe he had changed. Had gotten sober. Wanted to be her dad again. "Part of me wants to ignore him, but I feel guilty."

"You did nothing wrong, dear." Senja patted her shoulder and then went back to her preparations, pulling a box of crackers from a cupboard.

"I know. He ruined our lives. Mom was never the same. I barely remember what she was like back when life was normal." Aimee fell silent.

"Here, arrange these crackers and cheese on this tray." Senja stepped to the side and let Aimee take her spot at the counter.

Aimee placed the crackers and cheese on the tray in concentric circles. "Mom had no real job skills, so she had nothing to fall back on when Dad left. That's why I'm so determined to get my degree."

"Makes sense to me. I'm glad I got my degree." Senja was an accountant at Douglass State. She pulled a can of coffee down from the cupboard, filled a basket, and poured water into the coffee maker.

"But I don't know how I'm going to pay for my last semester. Russ thinks I'm already way over my head in debt. I can't get ahead while I'm paying for school, but if I quit, I'll never get out of this cycle of poverty."

Senja filled a kettle with water and placed it on the stove. "Frank and your mom had much bigger issues than the lack of a college education."

"I know, but if I quit, I'll be buried in debt with nothing to show for it. As it stands, I'll need to get a job making a lot of money just to keep my head above water."

"Most kids have student loans when they get out. You'll get a good job and pay it off. It'll be okay."

"I hope so. I'm not sure if Russ and I have a future. He wants to be Mr. Independent. I think he's being silly acting like Grizzly Adams."

"I came close to marriage once, but I don't feel qualified to help you sort through this one. So we'll have to bathe it in prayer."

Aimee nodded. Senja was a loving aunt, but she needed someone to guide her, not just pray. She missed Louisa.

The door opened. Bella Atkinson, the pastor's wife, entered, followed by Robin Clinton, the owner of a local gift shop called Robin's Nest. The prayer meeting began and Aimee shared with the group her financial situation and her relationship with Russ. They all listened empathetically and offered their prayers.

After prayer group, Bella gave Aimee a ride home.

"Do you think I should break up with Russ?" Aimee asked her point blank. "Are there too many red flags?"

"Money's a big issue. Chip and I have seen conflict over money many times in premarital counseling, but it's not a deal breaker. In fact, it's good when it comes up before the marriage, because it'll come up one way or the other. If both parties are willing to develop a common culture…" Bella chuckled. "Douglass and Quincy considered merging into one city years ago." She pulled onto the bridge that separated the two cities. "It went to a ballot, but the people of both cities voted it down. Neither city wanted to give up control. Each city wanted to keep its high school sports team."

Aimee smiled. "I can see why. Douglass was our biggest rival. Even if Quincy lost all our other games, if we beat Douglass it was a good season."

"When you have a marriage, both sides need to give. Think of how hard it would be for two cities to become one. Marriage requires the same sort of painful process."

Aimee nodded. She wasn't sure that either she or Russ was ready for that.

Chapter 9

Yapping echoed off concrete floors and brick walls as Russ stopped in front of a kennel that housed a large lab mix. Lucky, as the tag said on the chain-link gate, wagged its tail.

"You can pet him if you want." The shelter worker opened the gate.

Russ stepped in, and Lucky licked his hand before he could pat the dog's head. "Does he bark?"

"Sure, he's a dog." She laughed.

Lucky nuzzled against him. "Well, Lucky, today's not your lucky day. You're a little too friendly." Russ gave him a pat and exited the kennel.

The woman frowned. "You want an unfriendly dog?"

"I want a dog who'll deter trespassers. Do you have any rottweilers?"

The woman shook her head.

"Pit bulls?" The woman shook her head again, aghast.

"German shepherds?"

"We have a German shepherd. Come this way." The woman led Russ past smaller breeds—a pug, a howling beagle, and a terrier mix. "Here she is."

Heidi lay curled up with her chin on her front paws. She

pulled her eyes open enough to look at them, but moved no other muscle.

"She looks old," Russ said.

"We get a lot of dogs from the families of elderly folks who've passed away."

"I don't think you have a dog for me today. It's just as well," he said. "My girlfriend's a bit of a clean freak anyhow, probably wouldn't want the mess."

Besides, Aimee already thought he was off his rocker for boarding up the trench and changing the locks—and putting up over fifty signs. He imagined Aimee's reaction if he had adopted a guard dog. Maybe he was crazy, but if so, how would he know it? Russ frowned, and then relaxed. He remembered reading once that if you're wondering if you're crazy, you're not.

Russ left the animal shelter and drove north back into town. Earlier that day, he had a small job south of town replacing a faucet for a lady from his church. He had hoped to be building houses, but it seemed most of his work consisted of handyman-type jobs. Changing bathroom fixtures. Repairing broken windows. His real passion was new construction, creating something out of nothing. That's what he had loved about his engineering work.

When he had worked in research and development in the automotive industry, his company hired him to find innovative ways to solve problems. The focus was making something functional yet inexpensive. He tried to separate himself from any previous solution, which was almost impossible since people have come to take for granted the most complex tools ever known to mankind.

He had been successful and even had a patent to his name. He collected a small royalty on one of his inventions, as part of an incentive program, but he considered it blood money. There was nothing wrong with his invention, but he didn't like that the source of the money was a company that turned a blind eye to other products that hurt people. Of course, he wouldn't refuse the money, as that would just put more cash in their greedy pockets. But he didn't feel like he could spend it on himself, either, so he spent it on mission work.

Every November, Russ drove down to McAllen, Texas, and crossed the border into Reynosa, Mexico, where a missionary couple led work groups building houses for the families in a poor *colonia* located on an old garbage dump. Those small shacks made Russ's cabin look like a mansion. Aimee had no idea how good they all had it. He helped build a house the first year, but he was just one of many hands. He wanted his own project where he was thinking as much as doing, where he could create and innovate.

Driven by the smell of open sewer, he recruited local kids to help him dig a hole and build his first outhouse. The hard part about digging in the Copper Country was hitting rocks. The hard part about digging in the *colonia* was hitting trash—cans, tires, bottles—as the settlement sat on an old landfill.

Russ built beautiful, simple structures using materials he purchased at The Home Depot in Texas, and he drew instructions so the kids could build privies for others when they could scrounge up materials left over from house builds. Those pictures on the wall of his cabin reminded Russ of what was most important in life.

Driving west along the canal, Russ passed the Douglass State University campus, a mix of brick and glass buildings, one reaching up ten stories. It was as modern as any campus, but located in the heart of the Keweenaw. The contrast was stark. A technologically advanced, internationally recognized university with high-paid staff sitting in the middle of a rural, snowbound region with below-average incomes and run-down housing. It was a blessing for folks like Aimee. With otherwise stringent enrollment requirements, Douglass State opened its doors to local residents. The university, along with excellent primary and high schools, made the Copper Country one of the best places in the world to grow up poor. But, as Aimee pointed out, it still takes money to lift oneself out of poverty.

Russ stopped downtown at the hardware store, where he

picked up a few supplies. Hinges, a flush-mount handle, and truss hangers. Aimee was right. A padlocked door underneath his cabin was conspicuous. He'd cover up the trench and go in from the top. He needed to get a better look at that copper. Maybe he could get the copper out in pieces. He didn't need the money, but he could use it to help Aimee get through her last semester of college.

While he was there, he purchased a roll of window screen and glaze, and he had the hardware store cut a windowpane for Maribel Myers.

Crossing the bridge, Russ called Danny. "Are you available?"

"You bet. I'm at my folks'. I lit the sauna. Do you want to come over?"

"Later, but first I need cover. I'm on my way to Maribel's."

Russ picked up Danny, and they drove down the county road, past the stop sign where the pavement ended and the gravel road began, and down the hill with Lake Superior in view. Russ pulled into Maribel's driveway.

"Honk your horn." Danny used his cop voice.

Russ looked over at him as he followed the order.

"I usually come in my Trooper truck and chirp the siren."

Russ pulled to a stop in the driveway. "Maybe this isn't the best idea."

"We'll be okay." Danny opened the truck door. "Come on."

"Did you bring a gun?" Russ got out of the truck.

Danny laughed. "No. I wouldn't shoot an old lady."

As they walked toward the stoop, Maribel stepped out the front door with a double-barreled shotgun.

"Maribel, it's me, Danny. Russ and I came to fix that windowpane."

"All right, Danny." Maribel lowered her shotgun.

The men ascended the steps, and Maribel broke open the barrel of the rusted gun. No shotgun cartridges.

"Ha. It's not even loaded. Did Vance steal your shotgun shells?" Danny asked.

"Don't be an idiot. This is Henry's old gun. I have no idea

where the ammo is." Maribel led the way through the house and into the kitchen.

Russ removed the plywood and screen and then stepped out the back door onto a porch where he prepped the window sash for the new pane. He double-checked the measurements—he had remembered correctly. The pane would fit perfectly. Through the open window, he listened in on Maribel's conversation with Danny.

"Where's your fiancée, the one who looks like Rebecca Herrala?" Maribel asked bluntly, as she poured coffee into Danny's cup.

"Beth's not my fiancée. She moved back to California."

Russ heard the pattering of a helicopter. It passed overhead as it flew north. The sky was typically quiet in the UP. A regional commuter jet landed and departed twice a day, but he seldom heard it from his location. Occasionally, he noticed a contrail from a commercial airplane heading north at 35,000 feet.

"I want you to take that dresser so you have it when you get married. It's built for two. It's built for two," Maribel told Danny.

"Maribel, I'm not getting married. She left me." Danny's voice cracked.

In high school, the lanky, bookish Russ was an unlikely best friend for the athletic, ever-popular Danny Johnson. Ever the charmer, girls surrounded him, and Russ lived vicariously through him. But now for the first time, Russ had a girlfriend and Danny didn't.

Russ walked off the back porch and around the house to get the windowpane. The old house had mostly bare, clapboard siding and looked as if it hadn't been painted since it was built. Trees encroached on the house, filling what was probably once a strawberry farm. Too bad so many of the old farms were just fallow fields. Years before grocery stores stocked large, uniform, almost tasteless strawberries, the Keweenaw had supplied the Midwest with berries half the size but twice the flavor. Russ looked forward to the early weeks of

July when kids would set up roadside stands to sell the berries they picked from the few Copper Country strawberry farms that remained. So good.

Russ set the windowpane in the sash, jammed in new metal glazing points, and glazed around the edge of the window. The helicopter pattered to the north, occasionally coming into view as it made loops. It was the sheriff chopper, probably looking for marijuana growers.

Russ stepped back into the kitchen.

"Vance returned that quilt," Maribel said, looking at Russ. "It's for you and your fiancée. Your fiancée. That pretty girl. It's made for two."

"She's not my fiancée."

"Good grief." Maribel slammed her coffee cup on the table. "What's this world coming to? A bunch of grown men acting like boys."

Danny shrugged.

"When I was a girl, I was expected to grow up. I married Henry when I was eighteen years old. He was twenty-four. That was old to get married in those days. You kids these days act like you have all the time in the world. You don't. You don't."

"What happened to Henry?" Russ asked.

"He died. I watched him waste away. I watched him waste away."

"Sorry about that."

"You didn't do anything," Maribel snapped.

"If you need anything done around here, you let me know," Russ said. "Now if you don't mind, I'll take that frame with me and replace the screen for you."

The men excused themselves and drove back to the Johnsons'.

"You think it's true I'm acting like a boy?" Russ asked Danny after they settled on the cedar bench in the sauna, where the thermometer read 175 degrees.

Danny chuckled. He ladled water from a bucket at his feet and threw it on the stove. The rocks sizzled. Steam rose to the ceiling and rolled to the back wall and down onto the naked men. "You certainly aren't positioning yourself for a family, but I guess there's no harm in remaining single your whole life."

"It never occurred to me I'd ever have a girlfriend." Russ smiled.

"Do you love her?"

"I haven't decided, yet."

"Ha. You sound like Beth."

From Danny's tone, Russ knew that wasn't a compliment. "You hear anything from her?"

Danny shook his head and threw more water on the stove. "So what's the deal with you and Aimee?"

"I don't know." Russ shrugged. "I like her. But I like my lifestyle. My cabin. Being my own boss." He didn't know if he wanted to give up his independent life. Maybe he was more dependent than he thought, as Aimee had pointed out, but it wasn't absolute independence he craved, rather emancipation from the corporate world. "You wouldn't leave Michigan to follow Beth to California, and I don't want to leave either. She wants to live in a big city."

"You lived downstate before. It's not so bad. There's always weekends. Or maybe you could get a job lecturing and have your summers off. There's no better place to summer than in the Keweenaw." Danny threw another ladle of water on the stove.

"I'd never work for a corporation, much less a university. Corporate politics are bad enough." Russ grimaced. "Thanks for dredging up old memories. And could you stop with the steam already? It's already 175 in here." Russ looked around Danny's head at the thermometer. "Correction, 185."

"Dude, I'm not even Finnish, and I have more *sisu* than you." Danny threw another scoop on the stove.

Russ dipped a washcloth into a bucket and wrung the water out over his head. He covered his face with the cloth as he thought about Project Cousteau.

He had loved his job in spite of it being in the city. He had worked mostly on research and design, except for an occasional special project. Project Cousteau was a deep dive into customer complaints. It didn't take long to figure out the problem—an unmitigated pinch point. Most of the complaints were of fingers being pinched, but with no real damage. However, eleven people required stitches, and three children lost fingers. It could've been avoided, and he was curious as to why it was designed the way it was. He reviewed the engineering documentation and determined that the lead engineer, who had since been terminated from the company, did in fact propose an alternative design, but management overruled him. Russ made the same suggestion, but they shot him down, too.

Danny squirted him with the hose. "Earth to Russ."

"What was that for?"

"I asked you if you'd consider an engineering job with a city. Government jobs have their perks."

"You've got to be kidding. After they fired me, I reported the design flaw to the DOT and asked for whistleblower protection. They said I should've come before I got fired, as if I should have seen it coming. That's our government." Russ felt his face heat up, and it wasn't just from the sauna. He knew how it worked. DOT bureaucrats retired after twenty or thirty years and became private sector directors and vice presidents. There were too many ties for real accountability. Russ wiped his face with the washcloth. "Man, it's hot in here. Ready for a breather?"

In the late June evening, the men wrapped towels around their waists and stepped into the bright sun.

Russ said, "I'm thinking maybe I should ask Aimee to move in with me."

"Are you crazy?" Danny asked.

Russ was beginning to wonder.

"Your family would disown you," Danny said.

"Yeah, that doesn't go over too well with the Lord's People."

"Marriage is an important institution, not only because it's sacred, but because it provides legal protection."

"I hate the government."

Danny chuckled. "Remember, my friend, I *am* the government."

"I'm not talking about you. You're a good cop. I mean it's not any of the government's business what I do with my own life. Maybe we can have a church wedding but not file any papers."

"You're thinking about marriage, hey?" Danny asked.

"No, not really. I just like to think through all of the options."

"You might want to think how a wife will carry a baby and bags of groceries on a four-wheeler to the cabin over someone else's land."

"You have a point."

"So what are you doing with the copper?" Danny asked.

Russ combed his beard with his fingers and turned his back to Danny.

"Russ?"

"Oh, fine. I'll tell you."

Chapter 10

"*A* rug," Aimee said when she walked into Russ's cabin. "That's nice."

Russ stroked his beard.

"You took my advice to heart." Aimee looked around the cabin. It felt homier. "I told you this place needed a woman's touch. You covered up the trench outside and got rid of the outhouse pictures. There's hope for you yet."

"I moved the pictures to the wall next to the toilet." Russ walked through the cabin and sat on the love seat.

"Are you forgetting something?" Aimee pointed at her shoes by the door.

"Oh, that's right." Russ unlaced his boots and brought them to the door.

"You buy a new rug then walk into the house with your boots on." Aimee walked on the forest green carpet to check it out. The floor clicked. As she shifted her weight back and forth, she heard and felt clicking, like a loose board. "Mister, what's going on here?"

Russ sat back down on the love seat and stroked his beard.

"Russell?" Aimee put her hands on her hips and raised an eyebrow. Russ turned his face away. Aimee kneeled down and began to pull up the rug.

"Stop," Russ yelled.

Aimee rolled the carpet up. "A trap door? You've got to be kidding me."

"It can be useful when you sweep. Open it and push all the dirt inside."

"That's gross. And that's not why you put it there. Who do you think you are? Bilbo Baggins? You want to go down your hole and look at your Precious, hey."

"It's not like that. I'm thinking about taking it out, maybe piece by piece. If I can figure out how to cut it."

Aimee opened the trap door by pulling a ring handle out of its recessed holder. Cold, damp air rushed into the cabin. She knelt next to the hole. "It looks like an archaeological dig down there."

"Let me show you." Russ slipped into his boots.

He stood next to Aimee. She scooted over, and he sat on the floor with his feet dangling into the hole and lowered himself down. He sat cross-legged and turned on a flashlight. "Get your shoes and come down here."

Aimee joined Russ in the hole, where Russ had cleared a foot of dirt from the specimen and opened a two-foot gap between the copper and the bottom of the cabin. A short-handled spade shovel rested in a five-gallon bucket. It looked as if he had been hauling the dirt out one bucket at a time. A gallon of vinegar, a container of Morton salt, and a half-filled plastic container of liquid sat on a piece of plywood, along with a scrub brush.

"Take a look at this." Russ dipped the brush in the liquid and scrubbed a section of copper. "See?" He turned to Aimee with a wide smile.

"See what?" she asked.

"Here, get the light on it."

"It looks like copper."

"Not just copper. There's something else in it. I don't know what it is, or what that means for the value, but see those streaks of silver-colored material?"

"How do you find out what it is?" Aimee asked.

"I was a mechanical engineer, not a chemist or geologist. I tried to cut off a section over there." Russ pointed behind Aimee. "It's hard to cut. The copper gums up the disc on my grinder. I can't cut it with my Sawzall, either."

"You're taking it out?"

"That's my plan. I won't have peace living here with it under the cabin."

"Good. Have you checked into mineral rights?"

"What?" Russ's face soured.

"Mineral rights. When you purchased the property, were the mineral rights separated from the surface rights?"

"I have no idea what you're talking about."

"I had a class on property rights. You need to determine if you have the right to remove the minerals."

"We can look at the deed."

"We could do that," Aimee said, "but it would be best to have a lawyer look at it."

"I hate lawyers."

Aimee pursed her lips. "Russ, remember I'm going to be a paralegal. I'll be doing research for a law firm someday."

"I don't mean *you*. You'll be a good paralegal," Russ said. "I didn't have a good experience the last time I dealt with lawyers. I was so naïve I told them everything I knew. Yes, the engineers knew about the problem before they even produced it. Yes, they manufactured it with the design flaw. Yes, they shipped it anyhow. Yes, they continued to produce the item after receiving complaints. And when they asked what I'd say if called to testify, I told them I'd tell the truth. They fired me for *poor performance* a week later. Poor performance after getting an excellent review a month before." Russ pounded his fist on the table. "And no attorney would take my case."

He had never shared those details with her before and although she wanted to defend her chosen profession, she felt empathy for him. She had never seen him so worked up. "Now, mister, have you ever worked for somebody who didn't like contractors?" She said the words gently using her unhappy-customer-waitressing voice.

"Sure, I've had customers who've used me to fix shoddy work."

"There you go, Russ. There are good lawyers and bad lawyers." For such a smart guy, he lacked common sense when it came to some things. He needed to let it go.

Russ sighed and bowed his head.

"The lawyer can also tell you if the state has reserved mineral rights for this section of land," Aimee said.

"Seriously? The state? I hate the government." Russ huffed.

Aimee shook her head. "Fire up your laptop. I'll see what I can find."

After they crawled out, Russ pulled his laptop from a backpack and set it on the table. "You were right. We could do a lot with the copper. We could purchase that land, make a road, pay your tuition, pay down—"

"Whoa, mister." Aimee held up the back of her left hand. "Do you see a ring on this finger?"

Russ shook his head.

"I didn't think so. And I'm not taking a dime from you until I see a ring…" Aimee paused and cocked her head to study him. He looked so disappointed. "Except on a date. Then you can buy me dinner." Aimee smiled. "Now give me a hotspot."

Russ found his phone and fiddled with the settings. Aimee started the laptop and connected to the Internet through his phone. She searched the web for Michigan Mineral Rights. And it didn't take long to find what she was looking for.

"I thought you *wanted* me to take the copper out," Russ said. "Maybe we can pay down your debt."

Aimee liked the sound of the plural pronoun *we*, but she questioned if they had a future. "Take it out if you want, but I'll pay my own tuition and debt. It'd be a good idea if you bought the property and built a road to get to your house."

Her dad's text and the visit to her mom reminded her how important it was for her to finish her degree, to develop job skills and the ability to support herself. For whatever reason, she had chosen the paralegal path, and she had since found out that paralegals typically work in large cities for big law firms. Russ was on an entirely different path.

Aimee reviewed the search results, clicking in and out of screens that took mere seconds to load with an LTE connection. She laughed.

"What so funny?" Russ asked.

"I'm thinking how ridiculous it is that we're using the Internet in your rustic, landlocked cabin in the middle of a maple forest."

"You know it, hey. No electricity, but I have access to over a million terabytes of data."

"I'd prefer a toilet that flushed." Aimee turned the laptop part around. "Look at this map."

Russ came around the fold-down table.

"This is a Michigan DNR Land and Mineral Ownership map." Aimee pointed to the screen. She clicked on Houghton County, where square patches of pink and green decorated the map like an incomplete needlepoint design. She zoomed in to the area above Quincy. Colors designated each forty-acre parcel where the state reserved for itself surface rights and/or mineral rights. A blank square indicated the landowner had rights to the minerals. "Where's your property?"

Russ pointed to the screen. "Right there."

Aimee zoomed in further. "Which square? This red one or the white one?"

"I'm not sure."

"The disclaimer on this map says not to rely on the boundaries, as they're estimates. Yeah, you'll definitely need a lawyer."

"I hate lawyers."

"Russ, stop."

Aimee's phone chirped. A text message from the 602 number. *Aimee this is dad. Making my way home.*

Tears welled up in her eyes.

Russ read the text message over her shoulder and wrapped her in his arms. "It's going to be okay."

She took deep breaths, trying to calm her racing heart. Finally she turned to face him. "You better take me home. I work at the Cornucopia tonight, and then I have a morning shift at the Heikki Lunta tomorrow."

"Do you have time for a five-minute stop at Maribel's?" Russ asked.

Aimee shrugged. "I guess so."

As Russ pulled to a stop next to Maribel's old plow truck, Aimee asked, "Are you sure this is safe?"

Russ honked the horn. "Yeah. She can't find her shotgun shells."

He grabbed the screen from behind the seat, and as they approached the house, Maribel stepped out on the stoop and pointed a gun at them.

Russ grabbed Aimee's hand, pulling her behind him. "I guess she also has a rifle."

"Who goes there?" Maribel's voice was shrill.

"It's me, Russ—and Aimee. I have your new screen."

"All right." Maribel lowered the gun.

"What happened to the shotgun?" Russ asked.

"I was looking for ammo and found shells for Henry's old 30-30. Come in. Come in." Once in the kitchen, Maribel offered coffee.

"No thanks, ma'am," Aimee said with a smile. "Russ said this would just take a minute."

Russ pulled the table out and opened the window.

"I found that quilt for you." Maribel clapped her hands. "But you can't have it, yet. That boy needs to grow up first."

Russ turned his head quickly to look at Maribel.

Aimee laughed.

Maribel furrowed her brow and studied Aimee's face with an intense, almost frightening, gaze. "You have cold feet, too, eh. Maybe I was wrong. Maybe I was wrong. But I'm seldom wrong about such things." Maribel shook her head. "I was wrong about Rebecca and Chip, but other than that, I've called them all. Well, was wrong 'bout my brother, too. I set him up with Henry's sister—he made a fool out of himself, embarrassed me. Embarrassed me. My brother never did marry. Saddest thing I ever saw. Men are no good single."

Russ closed the window. "We need to go, Maribel."

"Okay. Okay. Now, what's your name again?"

"Aimee."

"Aimee, you let me know if that boy grows up. And tell Danny to stop by. I need to file a report. Vance has been at it again. This time he got Henry's pocket watch. It should've been in the box with the 30-30 shells. It's one thing for him to take a can of coffee, but to stoop to taking sentimental items, that's low. That's low. Never thought I'd see so much crime in the UP."

"Could you warm me up, Aimee?" Russ pushed his cup to the edge of the counter.

"I'd love to." She winked.

Heat rose to his face.

She grabbed the pot. "More coffee, guys?"

Mak and Danny nodded as she filled Russ's cup. The three men sat at the counter of the Heikki Lunta.

"You're gonna blow it up?" Mak asked.

"Are you talking about the copper?" Aimee topped off the other cups.

Russ frowned. "I thought you didn't care about the copper."

Aimee set the pot back on the burner. "Not really." She leaned against the back counter. "But I'm always interested in blowing stuff up. Did you look into mineral rights?"

"I wasn't planning on it. Don't you have tables to wait?"

"Nope." Aimee crossed her arms. "Tammy has those two, so you have me all to yourselves." Business was slow in June, the cool weeks after classes let out at Douglass State and before tourists flooded into the Copper Country from July through the fall colors in October.

"Well, anyway, it's hard to cut." Russ shoveled a forkful of hash browns into his mouth. He swallowed. "But I think I can blast it into pieces if I freeze it with liquid nitrogen. If I wait until January, when it's already ten-below, I can freeze it down even further and make it brittle."

"You thought of collateral damage to your cabin?" Danny asked.

Russ stiffened when Tammy came behind the counter to fill a coffee decanter. The others knew not to speak.

"What?" Tammy looked over her shoulder. "Why'd yous stop talking?"

"Guy talk," Aimee said, and Tammy shook her head.

After she left, Russ continued, "I'll lay blasting mats over the copper."

"What was that?" Mak leaned forward and peered around Danny, who was sitting between the two.

"He said blasting mats," Danny relayed.

Russ leaned around Danny. "Are you writing this down? You can't use this."

Mak looked up. "I'm not creative enough to think of my own plotlines. I won't say nothin' to nobody until you get it out."

"I don't even know what that means. That was a triple negative sentence." Russ shook his head.

"Russ, I've seen controlled explosions," Danny said. "Trust me, you don't want to blow it up, not even with blasting mats."

"Then how am I going to cut it up?"

"Have you tried water?" Mak asked.

"Huh?"

"High-pressure water. Cuts through anything." Mak scribbled notes.

"Thanks for the tip. But you still can't use this."

"Uncle Mak," Aimee interjected, "how's the other book coming along?"

"Figured out da ending. She'll be redeemed. She won't give in to her fatal flaw. I's tellin' Lorna 'bout da book. She says a book's like any other product—like herbs, pasties, gluten-free cupcakes—it's got to make da customers happy. If women want to be depressed, they can read the news. So I'll write a Happily-Ever-After ending."

"Romances don't always end happily," Danny said sharply.

"He's right, Uncle Mak. Life doesn't have happy endings. Look at my life." Aimee sighed.

"You got a lot of life to live, yet."

"Did you hear my dad's coming home?"

"No," Mak said, reaching for his journal again.

"You want something for your next book? Use this—dad leaves family high and dry, only to return ten years later as if nothing happened." Aimee buried her face in her hands and bent over the counter.

"Oh, dear, don't cry." Mak stood and clumsily patted her on the shoulder.

Aimee lifted her head.

"We're here for you." Russ hated to see Aimee so sad. It was the hardest part of loving.

"Yeah, it'll be okay," Danny said.

"Thanks, guys." Aimee wiped tears from the corners of her eyes. "I'm in a pretty sorry state when my best confidants are three men—an old Finn who writes chick lit, a cop depressed over unrequited love, and a Hobbit who wants to blow up copper under his cabin." She laughed through her tears.

The men looked at each other.

Aimee sighed. "I wish Louisa would come back, and I miss Beth."

Chapter 11

As the July sun warmed the peninsula, sea breezes from Lake Superior swept over the land and carried away the last of the black flies. Kids set up roadside strawberry stands, and the Heikki Lunta served fresh berry sauce on *pannukakku*. Tourists came first for Independence Day weekend, and then for the Strawberry Festival, and then for the great weather. Russ hadn't seen much of Aimee. He thought she might be coming around to his way of thinking on debt. She was always working, picking up extra shifts at both the Heikki Lunta during the day and at the Cornucopia in the evenings.

It was just as well because he was busy, too, having landed two decent-sized construction projects—a sauna and a two-stall garage with an attached space for a pet grooming business, both for Lord's People. While he had the work, he took advantage of long summer days. And then he'd drive his tired body home, take a quick, cold shower, and open his laptop to research Mak's idea for cutting copper.

A portable water-jet cutting system uses high-pressured water—60,000 pounds per square inch—and is capable of cutting through hardened steel. It would easily cut the copper. The idea seemed feasible until he contacted equipment manufacturers. Unfortunately, the machines cost over twenty grand. He figured he could piece together the components for half the cost, but it would take months to assemble and wouldn't produce more than 20,000 psi. So Russ put his church connections to work and found a contracting company in Minnesota that had a portable unit it used for cutting concrete. The owner, who was his dad's third cousin once removed, agreed to rent it to Russ. He'd bring it to the Keweenaw at the end of July when his family came for the summer church services. Even the rental was pricey, but Russ could take the money out of his Mexico mission outhouse fund and pay it back after he sold the specimens he planned to extract.

With a plan in place and the delivery date set, Russ needed time to prep the site. For once he wasn't thankful to have contracting work. He had to clear overburden from the float copper and build a makeshift floor in the hole so he wouldn't have to stand in mud created by the machine. He thought of jacking the cabin up a bit, but decided against it as it would expose his treasure.

One morning Russ woke to a thunderstorm. He had finished his client's garage roof the day before. Today's project was supposed to be the siding, but that would have to wait. There wasn't much he could do inside until the electrician—his dad—came the following week. A perfect day to work under his cabin.

Russ skipped breakfast and headed down into his hole. He used a hoe to pull dirt from the top of the copper. He scooped the dirt with a spade shovel into the five-gallon bucket. His phone rang. Maybe a client, but he didn't want more work. He shoveled more dirt into the bucket. The phone rang again. He popped his head up through the trap door. His phone was on the end table next to the love seat. He pulled himself out of the hole, but not in time to catch the call. Two missed calls from Aimee. He called her back.

"Screening your calls, hey?"

"No. I didn't get to the phone in time."

"We haven't seen each other for weeks. We've barely talked. Are we still a couple?"

"Of course," Russ said.

"Good. I don't have to work until tonight, and it's raining today, so it's a perfect day to hang out."

"Well." Russ hesitated. "I'm busy with a project."

"Oh, you have inside work?"

"Yeah," Russ stroked his beard, glad she couldn't see his face.

"Mister, what are you up to? I can hear it in your voice."

"Oh, okay. I'm renting a portable water-jet cutting machine at the end of the month. I need to prep the site."

"Never mind." She hung up.

Russ sighed and headed back down through the trap door.

The next morning it was still raining, but Russ decided to surprise Aimee at the Heikki Lunta. He didn't want to lose her. When the rain seemed to let up, he made a break for it through Koski's woods out to his truck. It wasn't too bad driving under a canopy of maples, but he got soaked when he parked the ATV and got into the truck. Danny was right—the arrangement wouldn't be practical with a wife and baby.

"You look like a river rat," Aimee said as she plunked a cup of coffee on the counter.

"You're beautiful." Russ sipped his hot drink.

Aimee smiled. "That was smooth. Has Danny been coaching you?"

"Did you walk over here today?" Russ asked.

She shook her head. "Took a taxi. I can walk in the cold and the snow, but not this. I'll put your order in after I ring up that table over there." Aimee made her way across the restaurant.

A man set a briefcase on the floor next to Russ and sat at the counter.

"Wet out there, hey." The man took off his jacket.

Russ nodded.

"Was gonna knock on doors this morning, but I'll have to wait this out."

Russ sipped his coffee and avoided eye contact.

The man stuck out his hand. "Vance Hoteham."

"Vance?"

"You, too? What a coincidence." Vance laughed.

"No, I'm Russ." Russ extended his hand and studied the man.

Vance sported a neat goatee and wore a dress shirt. A Country Satellite TV ID badge hung by a lanyard from his neck. "You live around here, hey?"

"Yep."

Vance smiled broadly. "Live in town or do you have land?"

"Land." Russ grunted the word and then sipped his coffee.

"Today's your lucky day. I've got a quota I need to make. I've got a wife and kid at home, so I've got to bring home the bacon, if you know what I mean."

Russ could feel Vance looking at him.

Vance leaned over and whispered, "I've got a promotion code I'm not even supposed to tell anybody. If somebody tells me 2-Months-Free, I've got to honor it, if you know what I mean." Vance sat up, and his voice boomed. "And we're running a special this month, buying people out of their overpriced contracts when they sign up with us. Who you got for a TV provider?"

"I don't have TV."

"Even better." Vance smiled broadly. "Don't need to worry about the old contract, so I can give you an even better price." He set his briefcase on the counter and rifled through it. He pulled out a stack of papers and set it on the counter. As he pulled out a calculator, an old-fashioned pocket watch fell on the counter. "Here's what we offer." Vance set a glossy brochure in front of Russ.

Russ studied the watch. "I'm not interested. It's against my religion." He reverted to his stand-by excuse when asked to do something he didn't want to do anyhow, like dance at a wedding.

"Are you an LP?"

"Yep."

"We have Internet service, too," Vance said, but without

the same enthusiasm.

"What can I get you to drink?" Aimee appeared with a coffee pot and topped off Russ's cup.

"I'll have coffee." Vance smiled. "Vance Hoteham."

"Vance?"

"What? Is everyone named Vance?" He laughed.

"Yeah, and I wear a name tag that says Aimee." She grabbed a cup from the counter behind her and poured his coffee. "Cream or sugar?"

"No, thanks. Say, where do you live?"

"In Quincy."

Vance looked disappointed.

"What do you think of his pocket watch, Aimee?" Russ motioned to the counter where it sat.

Aimee's mouth gaped open.

"Yeah, isn't that something." Vance picked up the watch. "An old lady gave it to me. Said I reminded her of her late husband."

"Do you remember her name?" Russ asked.

"Can't say that I do. I'm usually very good with names, Gus, but I don't recall hers. She's an old lady who lives up on the hill. She serves strong coffee. It grew hair on my chest."

Aimee made a disgusted face.

"I haven't been up on the hill since last fall. I suppose I should knock on a few doors up there again," Vance said.

Russ and Aimee looked at each other.

"I don't think that's a good idea." Russ bit back a smile, imagining an encounter between Maribel and Vance.

"Why not?" Vance asked.

"She's got a gun," Aimee said.

Vance shrugged. "Doesn't everybody in the UP?"

Chapter 12

*H*aunting sea smoke rolled off the great lake, and Aimee set out in the dark of an August morning for the Heikki Lunta. She missed Russ as he took advantage of the dry weather provided by Lake Superior's cool dome that deflected storm systems to the south of the Keweenaw. She had barely seen him while he pushed to finish the garage and sauna, and then the water-jet cutting tool came. But he made a point to have breakfast daily at the diner, and she appreciated that.

The sun rose and lifted the dense fog as she neared the Heikki Lunta. Not five minutes into her shift, before she even had the coffee brewed, the bell above the door chimed and Russ entered.

"Hey, Aimee," he said, "how are you doing?"

"Dog tired." She pulled the pot away from the burner and inserted a cup under the stream pouring down from the coffee maker.

"Tell me about it." Russ was looking thinner than usual.

Aimee plunked the cup in front of him. "I will. I wish I had more time with you. Time to enjoy the beautiful summer weather. But even if you didn't spend your days like a ground-hog under the cabin, I'm working all the time. I'm here until two, then I'm off to the Cornucopia at 4:30 for my evening shift."

"Sorry, babe. Could I get the usual with a farmer's omelet?"

"I think we can safely call that your new usual." Aimee scrawled the order on a pad and tore the ticket off. "Is breakfast your only meal of the day? Because you're losing weight."

Russ shrugged.

After her shift, she grabbed leftover *riisipuuroa* and walked home under deep blue skies dotted with cumulus clouds. She ate, showered, and napped before her evening shift at the Cornucopia, which wouldn't end until ten-thirty, in the last minutes of twilight.

Dawn till dusk. Six days a week. She insisted on having Sundays off to attend church.

Danny had picked her up the prior Sunday, and they talked about Russ, about Beth. Why were relationships so hard? Why was life so hard? She didn't know how much longer she could keep it up, but she had to keep going. One foot in front of the other. She had to pay down her debt.

Russ had affirmed her effort with a patronizing *attagirl*, as if her hard work mattered. It would take decades to pay off her debt, so a month less than decades mattered little. He was exasperating, but she kept the sharp edge of her tongue from cutting into him. The truth was she had to pay down her card balances so she'd have enough credit to pay for books and classes. She had received a letter from the financial aid office that said she had reached her cumulative loan limit. She didn't even know there was a limit until she got the letter, but apparently, her seven-year plan to get through her bachelor's degree added up. Aimee was worried, anxious, and honestly didn't know how she was going to pay for the last semester of school. She had talked to her Aunt Senja, who said she'd bathe it in prayer.

As she entered her final senior semester, she learned more about her future career path. Universities are in the business of selling dreams to young, impressionable kids who think they'll conquer the world. She had bought into Douglass State's four-year paralegal program, but she should have done more research because other schools had two-year programs, and some people became paralegals after simple on-the-job training. There was a market for four-year paralegals, but only in big cities with large law firms. Her debt would far exceed her annual income.

Do not worry about tomorrow, for tomorrow will worry about itself. She read the verse from her *365 Verses to Change Your Life* flip booklet that sat on the window ledge above her kitchen sink. One day at a time.

She put the pot she had used to reheat the *riisipuuroa* in the sink to soak and then headed out for an evening at the Cornucopia, the nicest restaurant in Quincy. It was the type of restaurant she wished Russ would take her to, but he said it wouldn't be fun to go on a date to a place where she worked. He stroked his beard as he said it, so she knew the truth. Too many Lord's People came into the Cornucopia. He took her to dive bars because he wanted to keep a low profile.

"Hi, Aimee," Zach said, when she slipped through the back door of the sandstone building and entered the break room.

"What's up?"

"You look tired," he said.

"Don't say that to a woman." Aimee put her purse and cell phone in her locker.

"Sorry about that." Zach was a nice kid. He'd finished his senior year of high school and planned to attend Douglass in the fall.

Aimee smiled, letting him know all was forgiven.

Her phone chirped in her locker.

"You're supposed to silence that."

Aimee flashed a look to rescind the forgiveness. When he left, she opened the locker to check her phone. She hoped it wasn't her dad. She knew it wasn't Russ—he didn't text. A twenty-five-year-old woman should have more friends.

It was a text message from Beth, Danny's ex-girlfriend. *You need a roommate?*

Aimee smiled. She and Beth had connected, had become friends after Aimee got over Danny. Aimee had been sad to see her go back to California. *You coming back?*

Aimee checked the time. She had five minutes before her shift started. She waited a minute for her phone to ding with Beth's reply. *Don't know.*

Having Beth as a roommate would cut the rent in half and stretch her dollars. It would be cramped, but even if they got a two-bedroom apartment, it'd be cheaper than what she had. Aimee typed a message. *It would be tight, but we can make it work for a while. Should I tell Danny?*

An immediate ding. *NO!*

Neither one of her friends had moved on. *He misses you.*

Beth replied, *Really? Why hasn't he contacted me?*

He said you left him. Isn't the ball in your court? Aimee's mood brightened, and she was ready to be the happy, bouncy Aimee who makes good tips. This might be the answer to her prayers.

The small commuter jet passed overhead a half hour before, so Aimee expected they'd arrive soon. Senja had told Aimee that Beth was accompanying Louisa home. After Aimee shared the news with the guys, Danny purchased material and helped Russ build a ramp as a surprise welcome-home gift for Louisa. The report was that Louisa could still walk, but she was losing strength in her legs and would need to be in a wheelchair soon. And now Danny, Mak, and Lorna were picking the women up from the airport.

Aimee rocked in a chair next to Russ in Louisa's enclosed front porch. "I won't be able to pay for classes this fall."

"It's great you're trying to pay for this semester in cash, but can't you take out a small loan?" he asked.

Aimee sighed. "I can't. I hit my loan limit."

"What's the loan limit?"

"I don't want to tell you." Aimee averted her eyes and watched a woodchuck scamper across the driveway and underneath the woodshed.

"So what will you do?"

"I guess I'll talk to the financial aid office. And it'll help my finances to have Beth living with me."

They rocked in silence as Russ rested his head against the chair, splayed his legs, and clasped his hands on his hollow stomach. Skin stretched tight over his cheekbones. His mustache had grown to cover his upper lip. His presence comforted Aimee.

"This is nice." Aimee hummed the country song *Where the Green Grass Grows*. It had been a favorite in her childhood home, before her childhood abruptly ended. "Which direction is west?" she asked.

Russ pointed to the left toward the garage and a stand of red pines that provided shade from the evening sun. Aimee scooted her chair to face that direction and Russ followed suit.

"Point our rocking chairs to the west," Aimee sang, quoting Tim McGraw. "This could be our life, Russ." For a minute Aimee forgot how deep she was into the paralegal program and where her career would likely take her. She dreamed of a simple life with Russ.

"I'd like that."

"Really?" If he was interested in her, they should move things along. "You met my mom. I should meet your family, hey."

"Yeah, you should." Russ stroked his beard.

Aimee raised an eyebrow. "Well?"

"How about Thanksgiving?"

"Russell, that's three months away."

"Hey, look. They're here." Russ stood and walked toward the door with Aimee a step behind.

Danny pulled up to the house with Louisa and Beth in his Jeep followed by Mak and Lorna in Mak's truck. Beth opened the front passenger door for her grandma, who then stood with her eyes wide and her mouth open. Even from a distance, Aimee could see tears forming in her eyes.

"Russ, did you build that?" Louisa asked.

"Danny and I built it."

Aimee crossed the lawn and hugged Louisa. "I missed you. You, too, Beth." Aimee hugged Beth.

"*Hyvää päivää*," Mak greeted the group, and Lorna hugged Aimee.

"Now, Danny, Russ," Louisa protested, "it wasn't practical building a ramp for me. I won't even be living here."

"Where will you live?" Aimee asked.

"I'll be living at High Cliff, starting at the beginning of next month." Louisa walked to the bottom of the ramp. "How much did that cost? Let me pay you."

"Don't be ridiculous, Grandma Lou," Danny said. "Even if you won't be living here, a woman's got to be able to get into her own house."

"You've lost weight, Russ," Louisa said. "I'm glad you're taking care of us old folks, but you need to take care of yourself, too."

Russ nodded.

"Now, let's go have tea." Louisa limped up the ramp, her weak arms hanging helplessly at her sides.

Once in the house, Danny and Russ went down to the basement to turn on the power and water while Beth waited at the top of the stairs.

"You don't want to let him out of your sight, hey?" Aimee teased.

Beth laughed. "I missed him, and I missed the Yooper questions, without up-speak."

"Beth, would you fill my birdfeeder?" Louisa called from the kitchen.

Beth did so and then joined the others at the kitchen table for loose-leaf tea. Louisa seemed like her old self, except she was sipping tea through a straw. Since there were only six chairs, Aimee sat on Russ's bony lap. She wondered if he should be sitting on *her* lap. Lorna had brought gluten-free cupcakes for the welcome-home party, and Aimee used a napkin to wipe a glob of frosting out of Russ's beard.

"A blue jay." Lorna nodded toward the window.

Russ and Aimee cranked their heads around to look out the window at the birdfeeder.

"*They do not sow or reap or store away in barns, and yet your heavenly Father feeds them,*" Louisa quoted Jesus.

"Beth fed them," Aimee said.

"We are God's hands," Louisa countered.

"I'm glad you're back." Aimee searched her face. "How are you doing?"

"One day at a time." Louisa smiled brightly. She had been diagnosed with ALS in February and seemed to take the death sentence in stride, or at least feigned serene acceptance, until she had a bad fall in April. "I appreciate each day, because I know the next will be harder."

"Beth, you said you might want a roommate," Aimee said. "Are you here to stay?"

Beth's and Danny's eyes were glued on each other, as if they were the only people in the room.

Russ grinned.

"Beth?" Aimee slapped the table.

Beth broke Danny's gaze. "I have two interviews at the university. Hopefully, I'll get one of the jobs, but either way, Danny and I are going to fly out to California and drive my car back."

Hope filled Aimee's heart.

"But we need to talk," Beth continued. "With Grandma moving into High Cliff, I'll be living here, at least until next spring when she puts her house on the market."

Aimee's eyes began to sting.

"What's wrong, dear?" Lorna asked.

Tears formed in Aimee's eyes. "It's nothing."

"You can tell us," Louisa said with compassion.

Aimee sighed. "I was thinking this was going to be an answer to prayer, to have Beth move in with me, to help with the rent."

"Move in with me here." Beth turned to Louisa. "That'd be okay, right?"

"Of course it would." Louisa nodded decisively.

"I'd rather not live by myself out here in the country." Beth shivered dramatically.

Aimee hesitated. "Living in town, I can manage without a car, but I'd need one up here on the hill." She was disappointed. It would have been fun to live with Beth, to have someone to talk to after work or a date with Russ. "I can't swing a car purchase. I don't even have enough credit to pay for—."

"I can't drive my car anymore," Louisa broke in, "so you may as well put it to good use. You can use it and live here in exchange for helping me sort through stuff and get the house ready for sale in the spring, as you have time between your work and studies and other pursuits." Louisa winked at Russ.

Bitter tears on Aimee's cheeks were joined by tears of joy. "I have been praying about my finances, but I never expected this."

"That's how the Lord works, dear." Louisa smiled. "He uses his people to care for each other. We take turns being his hands." She turned toward Beth. "Could you bring the bidet back from California? I didn't want to carry it on the plane, but I'd like to have that with me at High Cliff."

Beth nodded. "If Mother will let me take it. She's grown quite accustomed to it. She's telling her friends they should get one, too."

Mak let out a burst of laughter. He and Lorna had sent the bidet out to California after he had already installed one in the farmhouse. It was from extra inventory that Lorna had left over from a failed business venture. The bidet gave Louisa independence in the bathroom in spite of her weak hands and arms.

"Let her keep it," Lorna said. "I'll have Mak install another one for you at High Cliff on your very first day there."

"Yah, you betcha." Mak vigorously nodded his agreement. "I should install one for you, Russ. It'd be a good excuse for me to see your cabin. Everyone should have a bidet. You, too, Danny."

Danny laughed. "I'll pass. I'm a traditionalist."

"I'll pass, too," Russ said. "I don't exactly have running wa-

ter. Besides, I have a composting toilet called The Diverter. I've
got to separate my solids from the liquids. I don't want to have
to deal with any more liquids than necessary."

"You have a composting toilet?" Lorna's eyes twinkled as
they did every time she thought of a new business opportunity. "You think there's a market for that up here?"

Beth laughed. "I missed the UP."

As Russ drove her back to her apartment, Aimee scooted
to the center of the seat and leaned against him. "Can you believe it? I went month-to-month on my lease in May."

"God is good," Russ said.

"Yes, he is."

Russ glanced at her and then turned his eyes back to the
road. "I've been thinking about what Maribel said—about
needing to grow up. And about what you said about being a
hermit."

"Hobbit. I called you a Hobbit."

"Yes, Hobbit, and hermit and groundhog and geek."

"I'm sorry I said that, Russ. I shouldn't call you names. You
have a big heart, and I love that about you. I should say you
exhibit Hobbit-esque qualities."

Russ laughed. "Spoken like a lawyer. But you're right. To
be honest, before I got fired, I wanted the McMansion and the
good life, too. Losing my job was a wake-up call not to be materialistic, but I made self-sufficiency my goal. That's just as
wrong."

Hope rose in her heart.

"I'm thinking about our future," Russ said. "How it could
work out. What I should do."

When he pulled up to her apartment building, she moved
over to open the door of the truck.

"Aimee," Russ said her name softly and she turned back to
him. She could see longing in his eyes. She scooted back over,
tilted her head up toward his, and their lips met.

Aimee's heart sang as she walked up the stairs to her apartment. Their first kiss had been sweet. Their relationship was
moving forward. For the first time in a long time, she felt hope

for the future.

Aimee laid out her clothes for the following morning and then showered. Her phone rang while she shampooed her hair, so she let it go to voicemail. Maybe Russ was calling to say goodnight. She dried her hair and then checked her phone. A 414 phone number. She knew that area code because another waitress at the Cornucopia was a college student from Milwaukee. She listened to the voicemail.

"I'm sorry to be calling so late, but this is an urgent matter. My name is Kara Sanders. I'm a social worker at Froedtert Memorial Hospital in Milwaukee. I'm trying to reach Aimee Mallon," she mispronounced Aimee's last name with a long O. "Please call me back at 414-555-0100 extension 231."

Why would a social worker in Milwaukee be calling her? It couldn't be good.

Chapter 13

Aimee tried to shake off the sense of dread she felt as she dialed the hospital social worker.

"Kara Sanders speaking." The voice was crisp. Professional.

"This is Aimee Mallon. I'm returning your call."

"Mallon. Mallon," Ms. Sanders said in a searching voice.

"Aimee Malone," she mispronounced her surname using a long O.

"Yes. What's your father's full name?"

"Francis Dwight Mallon, spelled M-A-L-L-O-N."

"Aimee, your father was admitted to Froedtert Memorial Hospital here in Milwaukee. He has requested to see you."

Aimee felt her stomach tighten.

"Aimee? Are you there?"

"Yeah. Why's he in the hospital?"

"He has supraglottis laryngeal cancer," Ms. Sanders said in a clinical tone.

"What's that?"

"Throat cancer. He's being treated but can only speak in a whisper."

Aimee didn't know what to say. She didn't know how to

feel. It was as though she were watching her heart being im-
paled, yet felt nothing.

"I'm not sure how much time he has." Ms. Sanders' empa-
thetic tone practically demanded an emotional response.

"I'm not sure if I can come see him." Tears came to Aimee's
eyes. She wasn't sure she wanted to see him, even if she could.
She immediately felt guilty for thinking such a thing.

"I have grant money I can use if you need assistance to
come down here."

There was that, too. Aimee had meant she wasn't sure she
could deal with the emotions of reuniting with her father, but
even so, there was the cost of a trip to Milwaukee to consider.
"I'll need to think about it."

"Okay. You have my phone number. He's in room 304. It
wouldn't do much good calling him, as you wouldn't be able
to hear him, so feel free to call me, and I'll relay any messages."

Ms. Sanders gave more details, and when the call ended,
deep, gut-wrenching sobs tore through Aimee's chest.

After she calmed down, she called Russ.

"Are you okay?" he asked.

His gentle question brought on a new wave of tears. Aimee
tried to stop crying. She longed for Russ to be with her, to wrap
his arms around her and hold her.

"Are you at home?"

"Yeah." Aimee managed to say between sobs.

"I'll be right there."

By the time he arrived, she had stopped crying. She felt
silly for having him come down right away. Nonetheless, she
was glad he was there. She needed somebody with her. Russ
sat next to her on the couch and held her hand as she told him
about the phone call.

The cancer had metastasized to her father's lungs, bones,
and liver. The oncologist hoped to reduce the size of the tu-
mors that caused the most discomfort, but beyond that, he
couldn't do much. Frank's breathing was weak. He might have
six months, or maybe just weeks to live, and he wanted to see
her.

Russ squeezed her hand. "Do you want me to drive you?"

"I don't want to see him." She pulled her hand away.

He patted her shoulder. "You need to forgive him."

She glared at him. "You're one to talk, Mr. I'll-Never-Trust-a-Company-Again."

"Maybe I should let that go, but he's your dad."

Tears flowed down her cheeks. "Why should I forgive him?"

"Because you'll live with the regret if you don't."

Anger replaced sadness. "He's never asked for forgiveness. He's never made an effort to reach out."

"He is now. Maybe he wants to apologize?"

"Maybe he should've apologized years ago?" Aimee knew the sarcasm was misplaced, but it felt good to lash out. "I have mixed emotions."

"I understand anger." Russ nodded. "Not that being betrayed by a company is the same as being betrayed by a parent," he quickly added.

"Just hug me," Aimee said, and he wrapped his arms around her and rubbed her back. Her angst subsided. "I don't know what to do."

Russ held her in silence. After a few minutes, he asked, "Do you want to watch a movie?"

"Wow, you *do* feel bad for me." Aimee laughed. Her movie collection consisted of romantic comedies. Russ had once watched *The Notebook* with her, but then the next time she suggested a movie night he said it was against his religion.

Russ shrugged. "Desperate times call for desperate measures."

They snuggled on the couch and Aimee lost herself in another world. It felt good to laugh and cry about someone else's problems. It was late when the credits rolled. "Did you like it?" Aimee unwrapped Russ's arms from around her. Her adorable geek was sleeping. She kissed his cheek. "Wake up, hon. Movie's over."

Russ opened his eyes and yawned. "Maybe I should crash here on the couch tonight."

Aimee shook her head. "No way, mister." As much as she would rather not be alone, she had principles. Her mom had gotten pregnant with Rob in high school—too soon. She was not going to end up like her mom who raised two kids without first getting job skills.

He reached out and grabbed her hand, and she felt her resolve start to crumble. He was so sweet. She willed herself to stand. "People make stupid decisions when they're tired. You've got to go. I need to get up early tomorrow."

"Have you shaken the stalker yet?" Aimee asked Tammy at the Heikki Lunta.

"Ha!" Tammy burst into laughter. "I was at the Black Fly Saturday. The little Napoleon showed up. So I went to The Stope, but the creep followed me there. I had one of my guy friends have a little talk with him. He won't be bugging me anymore."

Aimee and Tammy made the rounds to the tables and then met back at the order window. "Did I tell you that my dad contacted me?" Aimee asked. Between taking orders and running plates over the next six hours, Aimee and Tammy had a dragged-out conversation about Aimee's childhood.

Aimee's family was poor, but she had many happy memories from when she was young. She had played and laughed. She had a doting mother and a fun father. Her dad built fires in their backyard, and they roasted marshmallows. Her parents took them camping at Twin Lakes where Aimee and Rob splashed in the water and played with other kids in the park. In the winter, they went sledding and drank hot chocolate out of Frank's thermos. One February, when the ice was thick enough on Lake Superior, they took a drive to the Pictured Rocks and explored the sandstone bluffs and ice caves.

Her dad was a Packers fan. Every weekend in the fall, he'd gather the family in front of their TV, at least when the power was on, or at Mak and Lorna's when it wasn't. They'd eat popcorn and drink pop. It'd be a good day if the Packers won, but a loss put Frank in a foul mood, especially if they lost due to a Favre interception. Sophia never said anything negative about Frank, so Aimee was not quite sure when the problems began.

She couldn't shake the memories seared by fear, like the time when Frank drove Aimee and Rob out on the ice in the canal. He drove down the boat landing in Douglass in late December, one year when it had been cold since November and there hadn't been much snow. Aimee panicked as he approached the water and she realized he wasn't going to stop.

"What's wrong with driving on the ice?" Tammy asked.

"Of course you wouldn't think much of it, because you're from Minnesota, but the ice doesn't get as thick here, and we usually don't see anything more than a snowmobile on the canal." Telling the story to Tammy made Aimee feel like she was still that scared little girl. Her panic had turned to terror when Frank whipped donuts in his truck. She cried. Rob yelled at him to stop, so he did, but told them to get out. They walked back, while he continued to slide around on the ice. By the time Rob and Aimee got to the boat landing, a police car was waiting for them, and Frank had taken off down the canal to get back on land via a boat landing on the Quincy side. The cop brought Rob and Aimee home and had a talk with Frank. "I never really trusted him after that. It wasn't just that he did something stupid, it was more his total disregard for how scared I was, and then kicking us out of the truck and leaving us on the ice. He could be so cruel."

Aimee wouldn't have described her dad as an alcoholic during her childhood. She didn't know what alcoholism was, and nobody talked about it. It was her normal. She remembered her dad getting depressed and despondent. She remembered the smell of alcohol on his breath that would come about the same time as his depression. She remembered him getting mean. He'd leave, and Lorna and Senja would come to comfort Sophia, who'd make excuses for Frank or blame herself. She loved him, and so did Aimee.

At times, Frank treated Aimee like a princess. She was glad for that because she expected the same from the men she dated. But her dad didn't follow through on commitments, and she cried when he would leave for days at a time.

But Rob was only happy when Frank was gone, leaving him as the man of the house. He brought in firewood and water from the hand pump. He shoveled and mowed. Rob even worked part-time jobs to help pay the bills.

When Frank was home, he was hard on Rob, never satisfied with what he did. Many evenings, Rob would push a Yooper Scooper around clearing snow from the driveway for hours, and Frank never thanked or affirmed him. He only criticized. For putting the banks in the wrong place. For scooping too early before the snow stopped. Or not scooping soon enough. Rob couldn't possibly skate well enough, shoot enough baskets, or run fast enough.

And there were fights when Rob stood between Frank and Sophia. It was no surprise to Aimee when he joined the military. He was already used to boot camp.

Life got even harder when Rob left, but who could blame him? He was eighteen years old, finished with high school, and it was time for him to spread his wings. Then Frank left for good, too, and everything spiraled down from there.

Her mom was incapable of providing for Aimee and herself. She had limited job skills and barely enough motivation to get public assistance, which was difficult because she was still married. She never did divorce Frank and wouldn't even pursue spousal abandonment.

After all that, Sophia never said anything negative about Frank.

"I thought *I* had a messed-up life," Tammy said after Aimee concluded her long, sad story. "So are you going to see him? I'm sure we can get someone to cover your shifts, at least for a couple days."

"I suppose I should. Russ thinks he might want to apologize, reconcile after all these years."

Aimee turned off the television in her mom's apartment.

Sophia woke with a start, lying on the couch in pajamas

with Mountain Dew and a bag of Doritos on the floor next to her head. She groggily sat up. "Hi, honey." She searched around her. "I was just watching..." She picked up the remote control.

"Please don't turn on the television. We need to talk."

"Of course. What's wrong?" Her mom patted the cushion next to her.

"Mom," she said tentatively, unsure of how to broach the subject. Aimee sat on the couch next to Sophia. "I got a text from Dad that said he was coming home."

"Really?" Sophia's voice brightened, and she looked around the room. "I should clean this place up." She hopped up, grabbed the chips and pop, and brought them to the kitchen. She returned with a rag and wiped off the coffee table. "You should have told me sooner." She lifted her chin with a hopeful expression. "Did he want it to be a surprise?"

"Mom, he's not going to make it here. He's in the hospital in Milwaukee."

Sophia gasped and her eyes widened. "What's happened?"

"He has throat cancer."

Sophia dropped the rag. "Oh." She sat back on the couch, shoulders slumped.

"Do you think I should go see him?"

Sophia brightened. "Of course, and I'd like to see him, too."

Aimee liked that idea. Maybe the trip wouldn't be so bad if her mom came.

Sophia wrinkled her brow. "But how would we get down there? I don't drive anymore. You don't have a car, either, do you? Could we take a bus?"

"Maybe I could use Louisa Herrala's car," Aimee said. "The social worker at the hospital said they have grant money available, but I don't know how much that will cover. Maybe you could help with the gas and motel."

"Could we wait to leave on Friday afternoon? That's when I get my paycheck."

Aimee was glad her mom was snapping back to life and acting like a mother.

"I have so much to do," Sophia continued. "I need a haircut. I need my nails done."

Aimee cringed. "Yeah mom, get your nails done when we need money for gas, the motel, food."

"I was beginning to lose hope," Sophia said, ignoring Aimee's objection.

The trip would cost the same with or without her mom, Aimee thought, but at least her mother could act as a buffer between Aimee and her dad if things didn't go well.

Chapter 14

"*L*ouisa!" Aimee scolded her from the backseat of Louisa's Subaru Outback. "You should at least get out of the car."

"I'll be fine here." With a contented smile, Louisa looked out over Big Traverse Bay where dunes lined the arc of the shoreline and wild blueberries grew like grass in the sandy soil. "You kids go and bring me back a handful of berries."

"Now, Louisa," Russ said, "you left California when you did for the express purpose of picking blueberries."

Beth had been planning to take her, but she and Danny flew back to California to get her car and most treasured possessions. Louisa had asked Aimee to stay with her for the week, and since Sophia wanted to wait for payday anyhow, Aimee postponed her trip to Milwaukee.

When Aimee learned of Louisa's great disappointment over missing blueberry season, she and Russ offered to take her blueberry picking. On the half-hour drive to the southeast corner of *Kuparisaari*, Louisa expressed concern her arms had grown so weak with ALS that she wouldn't be able to pick the berries anyhow.

"Why don't you sit at a picnic table?" Aimee suggested.

Louisa shook her head. "It's sandy. I don't want to fall."

"There's a sidewalk that leads almost all the way to the table," Russ said.

"But not all the way. I couldn't possibly walk in that soft sand."

"You can put your arms around our shoulders, and we'll help you." Aimee opened Louisa's door.

Louisa remained unmoved on her seat. "I won't be able to pick any anyhow."

"But you can pick your own sugarplums." Russ smiled as he came around the car.

Aimee and Russ assisted Louisa out of the car and walked alongside her through the parking lot. Louisa looked longingly at plump blueberries in low bushes in the sand.

Russ nodded toward the Saskatoon tree that was next to a sidewalk. He and Aimee guided Louisa to the tree.

"Why, look at this," Louisa said. "I hadn't noticed this tree before."

"Try this." Russ stretched his neck and grabbed a cluster of the small, purple fruit with his mouth.

Louisa laughed. "You look like a giraffe." She reached out with her mouth and ate sugarplums right off the tree.

As busy as Aimee was, she felt honored to help with Louisa's care for a week while Beth and Danny drove back from California. Louisa adjusted her schedule around Aimee's, rising at five in the morning so Aimee could help her change into day clothes before leaving for work.

One morning, while Louisa was in the bathroom, Aimee boiled a kettle of water and steeped Louisa's morning tea. She set a cup of tea with a straw on the table along with sweet cardamom bread.

Louisa emerged from the bathroom in tears.

"What happened?"

"Oh, it's silly. It's difficult to use the bathroom. I can't brush my teeth. If it would just stop, I could deal with it. But this disease is relentless, and I hate losing my independence."

It was difficult to watch Louisa struggle, especially when there were setbacks. "I don't think I should leave you alone today. I'll call in and say I can't make it to work."

"Nonsense. Get me my Kindle, and I'll be fine here sipping my tea and eating *nisu*."

"What if you need help in the bathroom?"

"Maybe I'll just have the *nisu*," Louisa said.

"You're going to dehydrate yourself so you don't have to use the bathroom? I'm calling Senja."

Aimee made the call. "Sorry to wake you so early, Auntie, but I don't think I should leave Louisa here alone all day. She needs help with the most basic things."

"I have one meeting first thing this morning, and then I can head up there. I can work remotely."

Louisa convinced Aimee she'd be fine for a few hours, so Aimee left. She was relieved that Senja would be there shortly to help Louisa use the toilet and to prep lunch for her.

That afternoon, Aimee stopped at Shop-Mart and picked up a spinning toothbrush. When she arrived back at the farmhouse, Louisa was lying on a massage table in the living room.

With her eyes closed, the masseuse shook Louisa's forearm. "You can let go now."

"I'm not holding on to anything," Louisa said.

"I'm not talking to you. I'm talking to your muscles."

Aimee chuckled, and the masseuse opened her eyes.

"Hi, Marcella." Aimee didn't know the woman well, but they had both attended the youth group at Pinehurst as teenagers. "How's it going?"

"I just felt a big release." Marcella held a hand above Louisa's face and flicked her fingers. "You can have some of my energy."

"Thank you, dear. That was very relaxing," Louisa said.

Marcella helped her up and into her recliner. She pulled the footrest up and set Louisa's Kindle in her lap.

Louisa leaned her head back. "I've almost lost the use of my hands, but God has replaced them with so many."

"I'm glad I can help." Marcella's eyes moistened, and

Aimee recalled that around the same time Frank left, Marcella's mom had gotten sick. They had prayed for her mom at the youth group a few times, and then Marcella quit coming. Aimee hadn't thought much about it then, being so wrapped up in her own problems. Life was hard in so many ways.

After Marcella left, Aimee made supper for Louisa and helped her get up from the recliner. They sat at the kitchen table. A window fan pulled warm mid-August air into the hot farmhouse.

For that one sticky week of the year, Louisa preferred iced tea in the evening. Her glass dripped sweat that formed a puddle on the table. "How are you doing, dear?"

"Busy. I'm working all the time. I'm anxious about my debt. Conflicted about my dad—" Aimee caught herself. "I'm sorry. I shouldn't complain." Time with Louisa put life into perspective.

"Nonsense, my child." Louisa leaned forward. "My suffering doesn't negate yours. You have concerns. I want to hear them."

"Well, I feel like the weight of the world's coming down on me."

Louisa looked concerned. "Is it too much for you to help me? I could hire help."

"No. No. It's not that. It's no trouble. Besides, I like the company." Aimee held her glass with both hands and leaned back in her chair. "I have bills I can't pay, a boyfriend who won't commit, and an estranged father who's dying in a hospital in Milwaukee and wants to see me."

"Are you going to see him? Take my car." Louisa sounded more like she was giving a directive than a suggestion.

"Thanks. I was hoping I could." Aimee smiled. "My mom wants to see him. When I told her about the text messages and the call from the hospital, she was raring to go. If you're sure it's okay for me to take your car, I guess I'll take her, but I'm not sure I want to see him."

"You should," Louisa said decisively. She sipped her tea through a straw, infecting Aimee with her calm demeanor.

"I don't know what to say to him," Aimee said.

"What would you like to ask him?"

"Why? Why did you leave us? We love you so much, why did you leave us?"

Louisa sat back in her chair and nodded.

"Russ said I need to forgive him. He said that's probably why my dad wants to see me, to ask for forgiveness."

"Well, whatever his motive, it'll bring you closure. You should see him."

Aimee nodded. Her mentor was likely right. "Next week, when Danny and Beth get back, I'll go down to Milwaukee with my mom."

Aimee helped Louisa get ready for bed before leaving for her evening shift at the Cornucopia. "I have a surprise for you." Aimee pulled a kitchen stool into the bathroom. "If you sit down in front of the sink, I think you can brush your teeth with this." Aimee showed her the spin brush. "You won't have to move it around much. Here, I'll put toothpaste on it and turn it on."

Louisa put her face down to the toothbrush as she cradled it in her shriveled hands that rested on the counter. She was able to move her face around to brush her teeth. It probably would've been more efficient for Aimee to brush Louisa's teeth, but the smile on her face when Louisa finished told Aimee that Louisa appreciated regaining some independence.

Aimee had postponed the inevitable as long as she could, but with the trip to Milwaukee planned and school starting soon after that, she scheduled a meeting with the financial advisor at Douglass State University.

"I didn't even know there was a loan limit," she pleaded.

"Just for the Stafford Loans," the counselor said. "You can apply for private loans."

"I don't know if I'd qualify if the loans aren't guaranteed. Besides, I have so much debt I'm scared." Aimee leaned forward in her chair and bowed her head. She was defeated.

"You know, we just got an anonymous grant…" The woman dug through piles of paper on her cluttered desk. "Let me ask first, you're in your senior year, right?"

"Yeah."

"And you're a local?"

Aimee nodded. "From Quincy."

The advisor opened a folder. "And you have independent student status?"

"Yes…" Aimee studied her face, a twinge of hope rising.

"A grant came in the week before last. I should've thought of you, should've reached out to you, but I've been busy. We hired somebody, but she won't start until the week after next."

"Beth Dawson?"

"Yes. She came in from California to interview. How did you know?" The woman cocked her head.

"This is the UP. But you were saying …?"

The counselor pulled a sheet of paper from the folder. "An anonymous donor offered to pay for full tuition and books for a woman who is in her final year of the paralegal program, who is local, and who has independent student status. I think you're the only one who qualifies."

Chapter 15

The porch screen door slammed and Aimee turned to Louisa. "They're here."

Beth and Danny entered with ear-to-ear smiles. Aimee stood and embraced Beth, and Danny hugged Louisa, who remained seated at the kitchen table.

"Have a seat, kids. Aimee, could you get them iced tea?" Louisa asked.

The couple sat opposite Louisa. Danny had a cheeky grin as Beth put her left elbow on the table and rested her chin in the palm of her hand with her fingers sticking up. She pressed her lips together as she fluttered her eyelids.

"What's got into you, child?" Louisa asked.

Aimee placed two glasses on the table for Danny and Beth.

Beth turned her head and stretched her fingers out, almost bending them backward. "Anything new with you?" Beth asked.

"I've been moving in slowly." Aimee sat at the table. "I got the finances figured out for my last semester." Beth didn't seem to be listening, and Aimee realized her question may have been designed to elicit a reciprocated inquiry. "Anything new with you?"

"Well," Beth held out her left hand with her wrist up and her fingers splayed out and down.

Aimee noticed the ring. "Shut up!"

"We're engaged." Beth squealed.

Aimee shrieked.

Louisa grinned. "When did that happen?"

"Danny and I've been talking about it—" Beth started.

"And since I was meeting Oliver," Danny continued, "I thought that was the perfect opportunity to—"

"Ask his blessing." Beth looked at Danny with a giddy smile.

"Have you been assimilated by the Borg?" Aimee snickered.

Danny grabbed his fiancée's hand. "This is better than science fiction."

Aimee shook her head. "Beth, I hereby appoint you the official spokesperson of the Beth-Danny collective. You tell the story."

Louisa chuckled.

Beth leaned forward eagerly. "So I knew he'd asked for my dad's blessing, but I didn't know he was prepared to propose. Then Danny wanted to take a long way home through Wyoming. He asked me at a scenic outlook on Beartooth Pass—"

"In Gallatin National Forest," Danny finished.

Aimee attempted a smile. She was happy for Beth and Danny, but it hurt because she hadn't even met Russ's family yet.

"How did Rebecca respond?" Louisa asked.

"Ha." Beth burst into laughter. "Let's just say she's growing—"

"And Oliver said he'd try to calm her down. He was thrilled," Danny said. "He told me that a man who can stand up to Rebecca with love and respect would make a good husband for his daughter."

"How's Russ?" Beth asked.

Aimee sighed and rolled her eyes.

Chapter 16

"*R*eady?" Aimee asked.

Sophia's eyes brightened. "I'm ready." Her apartment was tidy, and the TV was off. "How are we getting there?"

"Louisa Herrala's letting me use her car, and the hospital will reimburse me for gas and give me a hotel voucher."

"Perfect. I knew it would work out, so I got my nails and hair done." Sophia held out her hand with manicured fingernails.

Aimee smiled. "Then you should be all set." It was an unnecessary luxury for someone living paycheck to paycheck, but it felt good to see her mom taking an interest in life again.

Country roads carried them for nearly four hours to Green Bay, where Aimee merged onto a freeway behind a semi. All of Aimee's senses were on high alert. Driving in the city took much more concentration than in the UP.

"I haven't left the UP for twenty year—" Sophia gasped and grabbed the ceiling handle as Aimee cut across to the left lane. "Do you want me to drive?"

"I'm doing okay, Mom." After passing the truck, Aimee glanced over her shoulder and cautiously nosed back into the slow lane.

Sophia exhaled slowly and put her hand back in her lap.

"Are you nervous about my driving?"

Sophia laughed nervously. "I'm sure we'll be okay if we stay in this lane."

"We'll get into Milwaukee before rush hour, so we should be fine."

A few miles down the road, they continued their conversation about Frank, Rob, and life in general—but mostly Frank. Sophia talked fondly of him, and Aimee hadn't wanted to sour the conversation with tough questions.

"Do you remember the time we went camping on the North Shore?" Sophia asked.

"I don't remember ever being on the North Shore."

"That was in 1995." Sophia paused. "No, that had to have been '96. It was the spring after that bad winter. The water was flowing hard down Gooseberry Falls."

"I would've just turned four."

"That was so much fun," Sophia said. "Dad was such a fun guy. He was always so good about building memories for us. He didn't always have work, but he had time."

Aimee bit her lip.

"And he was so funny," Sophia continued. "Such a joker. I was nervous with him carrying you around those falls."

Her mother's comment blew the dust off an old memory. "Wait, I do remember. Did he hold me over the edge of a fall?"

"Oh, yes. He was trying to get a reaction out of me."

"I was terrified." Aimee looked over at her mom in disbelief.

Sophia glanced at her with a surprised look as if saying, "For what reason?"

"You don't find that at all disturbing? That a father would hold his daughter over the edge of a waterfall while she's crying?"

"Oh, Aimee. We were young. I was seventeen when we had Rob. We were only twenty-five years old on that trip."

"Mom, a parent shouldn't do that."

"Well, that was Frank. He loved to party, but he also loved

you. There were a lot of good years." Sophia let out a contented sigh.

"Why did Dad leave?" She willed herself to focus on the road.

"It was the alcohol. He was an addict. It's a disease, Aimee."

"But why didn't he ever call? Not even on my birthday?" Aimee bit back tears.

"You'll have to ask him, but I let bygones be bygones," Sophia said cheerily.

"Mom, aren't you sad he's dying?"

"Well," Sophia paused. "Everyone dies. I thought he might have been dead already, the way he lived. I'm glad I'll get to see him before he goes. He was my first love, you know—my only love." Sophia's face briefly drooped before she smiled again. "Did I ever tell you about the time we slept on a beach? We watched the stars and listened to the waves until I drifted off. When I woke up, Frank was sitting next to me. He had gotten a blanket from the truck and covered me. It was so romantic."

Aimee found herself smiling. She had lost two parents when her dad left, but now that he had returned, so had her mom. It was a taste of what her life might have been, if it were not for the alcohol. "I'm beginning to see the wisdom in Russ's church being against alcohol."

"Who's Russ?"

"My boyfriend, Mom."

"Oh, that's right. The quiet guy. He's a bit of a geek. Not like your father. Your father was the life of the party. Boy, did we have fun. Did I ever tell you about the time we went mud-bogging in his truck?"

Aimee drank in the rich décor of the lobby at the Radisson Hotel across from Mayfair Mall in Wauwatosa, a suburb on the west side of Milwaukee and only a few minutes from the hospital. "Wow. This is a nice place. I thought they'd put us in a budget hotel." Dark wood paneling. Marble floors. Leather furniture. "The social worker said there'd be a voucher at the front desk. I'll go check us in."

"I'll be over there." Sophia motioned to a high table set with coffee and cookies.

Aimee breathed a sigh of relief when the voucher was waiting for her as promised. She handed over her credit card for incidentals and glanced over at her mom. Sophia looked around to see if anybody was watching and then grabbed several cookies, stuffing them in her purse. She poured herself a cup of coffee.

Aimee got her credit card and walked across the room. "Ready, Mom?"

"Yep," Sophia mumbled between chews. With wide eyes, she looked like a kid in a candy store.

Aimee laughed. "Mom, the cookies are complimentary."

"I know, and so good." A few crumbs flew out of her mouth.

Up in their room, Aimee sat on the bed flipping through TV channels, occasionally looking toward the bathroom to her mother's reflection in the mirror. Sophia put on makeup and brushed her teeth. She stared at herself and smiled, hid her teeth, and then attempted another smile without showing teeth. She brushed her teeth again, as if vigorous effort could remove years of decay from acidic sugar water.

Sophia finally came out of the bathroom, took off her T-shirt, and rummaged through a paper grocery sack. She pulled out another T-shirt, but her face didn't show pleasure at that choice, either. "Do you have anything I can wear?"

"I don't think you'll fit into anything of mine."

Her mother's face saddened.

"There's a mall across the road," Aimee said. "I'll buy you something nice."

Sophia beamed. "We'll have to be quick, because visiting hours end at 4:30."

Sophia found a black top at a plus size store at Mayfair Mall. She tried it on in the dressing room and wore it to the register, where the clerk cut the tag off the shirt and rang up the sale.

Rush-hour traffic had picked up even though it was only quarter after three when they headed over to the hospital. Aimee stopped several times to read signs that directed traffic around the multiple buildings and parking ramps.

"We need to hurry." Sophia's voice was anxious. "Park anywhere. Then we'll ask someone where to go."

Aimee finally found the right building and parked in a nearby structure. They made their way to the third floor, room 304. The door was open and a janitor was mopping the floor.

"We're here to see Frank Mallon," Aimee told him.

"There's no one in here. Ask at the desk."

Sophia and Aimee headed back down the hall.

"We're here to see Frank Mallon," Aimee said to the receptionist.

"And you are?"

"Aimee Mallon."

The woman punched a few keys and studied the screen. "And who's with you?"

"This is his wife, Sophia," Aimee said.

"Just a minute," the receptionist said. She picked up her phone and dialed. Seconds later, she said into the phone, "Francis Mallon's daughter is here—and his wife." After hanging up, the woman directed Aimee and Sophia to have a seat in the waiting room.

After a few minutes, another woman appeared at a door and called for Aimee. Aimee and Sophia got up and crossed the room.

The woman held out her hand. "Hello, I'm Kara Sanders."

Aimee grasped Ms. Sanders' hand. "Can I see my dad now?"

"Yes, Aimee, but I'm so sorry, Frank was very specific. He wants to see his children, but he specifically named you," Ms. Sanders turned to Sophia and shook her hand, "Mrs. Mallon, as someone he does not want to see."

Tears filled Sophia's eyes.

"I'm not going to see him, either," Aimee said.

"I got my nails done for nothing." Sophia stopped crying

and assumed a stiffened posture like she used to do when she and Frank fought.

Aimee was so mad she could spit. She hated that feeling. She hated seeing her parents fight. She used to hide in her room, put in earbuds, and crank up her MP3 player to drown out the ruckus downstairs. Aimee turned her back to Ms. Sanders and put her arm over her mom's shoulder.

"Wait, Miss Mallon," Ms. Sanders pleaded. "It's important you see him. Whatever's going on between him and his lovely wife, he's dying."

"He's not dying well," Aimee snapped.

"Go see him," Sophia said.

"But, Mom, he's such a jerk. He won't even see you."

"Don't talk about your father like that," Sophia said sternly.

"Mom." Aimee huffed.

"He's your father. You should go see him."

"After how he treats you?"

"That's between me and him. He wants to see you. You should see him."

Aimee looked to Ms. Sanders, who nodded.

Chapter 17

*I*t was hard to tell if there was a man under the sheet below the emaciated face. Aimee walked around the bed and sat in a chair. Her father's eyes were closed under dark, sunken lids. He strained to take shallow breaths through his swollen throat. Aimee remembered seeing her great uncle in an open casket, when Frank held her up and told her he was a great man. It was too much for Aimee at the time. She must have only been five or six. That image of death never escaped her. She was looking at it again.

He had aged beyond his forty-five years. Gray stubble covered his face, and his thin, oily, black hair was combed back. Aimee had spent so much time studying that family picture taken when Frank was only thirty-five, just six years older than Russ. Now the space between his nose and his mouth had grown, his mouth widened, his ears enlarged. His skin was rough, with deep creases between his nose and cheeks, and crow's feet framing his eyes. These features would have looked distinguished on an old, healthy man, but her father should have been in the prime of his life.

Aimee sat quietly, hoping he wouldn't wake so that she would be able to say she saw him, but chose to let him sleep.

She had rehearsed her lines in the car on the way down. *We love you so much. Why did you leave us?* But now, the only thing she wanted to know was why he refused to see her mom.

Fifteen minutes passed, and visiting hours were nearing an end. A nurse walked into the room, nodded hello to Aimee, and said loudly, "Francis, do you have any special requests for dinner?"

Frank stirred and opened his eyes. He shook his head and laid it back on the pillow. Catching Aimee in his peripheral vision, he turned his head and smiled.

"Hey, kiddo," Frank mouthed. She had heard him say that—watched him say that—so many times in her life it was unmistakable, even though she couldn't quite hear him now. The term of endearment melted her bitterness. Compassion filled her heart and tears welled in her eyes. Frank twitched his head to draw Aimee near, and she leaned in. In a whisper, Frank said, "I'm dying for a smoke."

Aimee laughed and sat back. "You're dying because you smoked."

Frank laughed, coughed, and then coughed harder. He cleared phlegm from his throat and spit into a towel.

He looked so pathetic she didn't want to begin too harshly, but she had to ask. It was the reason she had come. She posed the question she'd rehearsed. "We love you so much. Why did you leave?"

Frank shrugged his shoulders and twitched his head again. Aimee leaned forward in anticipation. She'd been waiting ten years for this. The apology. If she could hear him say, "I'm sorry I missed your graduation," or "I should have sent you a birthday card," she could find it in her heart to forgive him. The man was dying.

"Long story," he said breathlessly, as if he hadn't given it enough thought to explain in a sentence or two.

"Why won't you see Mom? She's out in the lobby crying because you said you wouldn't see her." Aimee knew her tone was accusatory.

Frank look startled. "She's here?" he whispered.

"Yes, and why won't you see her?"

"She told me she didn't want to see me again until I got the money I lost at the Ojibwa Casino. That's when I left. I never got the money, kiddo."

"Dad, I've never heard Mom talk about that. I doubt she even remembers."

Frank raised his eyebrows as if wondering if it were true.

"Would you see her if she forgave you for that?"

"Oh, I'm such a mess. She wouldn't want to see me like this."

"Dad, she loves you."

Frank closed his eyes and laid his head back.

"Francis," the nurse said upon entering the room again, "do you want to get up to use the bathroom before dinner comes? And visiting hours are over, by the way."

"One more question, Dad. What's your biggest regret?" Aimee asked gently and waited.

Frank's eyes filled with tears. Maybe now he'd ask for her forgiveness.

"I wish…" Frank whispered the words and Aimee leaned in. "I wish I had made it to Lambeau Field."

"Really, Dad? That's your biggest regret? Not leaving us? Not missing my graduation?" Aimee seethed.

"I was getting sick, so I wanted to get back in time for a preseason game. I don't have money for a ticket, but I hear they give tours of the stadium." Frank shrugged. "But I was going to see you, too, kiddo."

Aimee sat back. Pitiful man. She was done with him. She stood to leave. "Mom loves you. She can't see you unless you give permission."

Chapter 18

Aimee found her mom drinking pop and eating a hotel cookie on the far end of the hospital waiting room near a silent television tuned to a cable news program. "Ready, Mom?"

Sophia grunted and shoved the rest of the cookie in her mouth. She brushed crumbs off her black shirt. Aimee led the way out of the hospital with Sophia trailing a step behind. She didn't ask about Frank or what was said in the room. Neither said a word until Aimee pulled onto the hotel ramp.

"Should I take you out to dinner?" Aimee asked. Dinner seemed like the right thing to do, even though restaurants were not in Aimee's budget. Two days before she had left, she mailed a payment for her Visa bill. She hoped the check had cleared.

"Nah, just pick up chips and pop at the Walgreens across the street."

"Mother! Snap out of it." Aimee gripped the steering wheel, pressed her lips together, and stared down Sophia who sat motionless in the passenger seat of the Outback. "Your self-worth does not depend on that man."

Sophia looked at Aimee with eyes of a child. "Well, I saw a Cheesecake Factory by the mall. I do love cheesecake."

"Okay." Aimee sighed. Baby steps. If she was going to self-medicate with food, it should at least be with a decent meal.

Even with getting to the restaurant shortly after five o'clock, there was a thirty-minute wait for a table. Aimee took a pager from the receptionist, and the women squeezed in next to other patrons on a bench. So many people. Aimee couldn't remember the last time she had waited for a table in the UP.

Sophia sat slouched, gazing at the floor.

"Just a few more classes and I graduate in December," Aimee told her mother. "I'll probably be moving then. Most paralegal jobs are in big cities."

Sophia nodded her head ever so slightly.

Aimee continued, "I want to break the cycle of poverty."

"We were never poor," Sophia said defensively.

"Our electricity was cut off. Our clothes were ratty."

"We made do with what we had. We lived better than most of the world."

Aimee shook her head. Was her mother disconnected from reality?

After they were seated, Aimee paged through the menu. Several items were out of her price range, but the sandwiches were affordable. Her mother ordered a steak.

Aimee cringed, but said nothing. In addition to providing hotel vouchers, Ms. Sanders offered to reimburse gas, but Aimee needed to fill out a form and submit receipts. In the meantime, she had to put the gas on her credit card, and she was on her own for her food and, apparently, her mother's meals.

How did the roles reverse? When did she become the responsible adult? Before even finding out that the hotel and gas would be covered, her mom had blown her money on her hair and nails. Sophia sat across from Aimee savoring a steak she couldn't possibly afford on her own with every bit of confidence her daughter would pay. Nonetheless, Sophia had seemed—if for a brief moment, if only for a few days—hopeful. Aimee longed for her mother to change, but, if she had learned anything as Frank's daughter, she knew there's only so much one can do to help other people.

Her mom ordered cheesecake after dinner, although Aimee got her to agree to split it with her. It was enough for two.

"I'm sorry, Ms. Mallon," the waiter said, returning to the table with the bill. "This card didn't go through."

Aimee took a deep breath. Her mom, oblivious to the problem, continued to eat the cheesecake. "Try this one," Aimee said, and handed another card to the waiter.

The waiter returned a short time later and shook his head.

"Do you have an ATM here?" Aimee asked.

"There's one in the mall, but we take debit cards."

"I don't have a debit card anymore after someone stole it and my bank account was drained for a week. Just give me a minute." Aimee made calls to the credit card companies, as her mom finished the lion's share of the cheesecake and sipped her third root beer refill. Aimee instructed the waiter to put a portion of the bill on one card and the rest on another.

"Ready, Mom?"

Sophia leaned back in in the booth and exhaled. Sweat formed on her brow. She took deep breaths and patted her stomach with her fist. "Heartburn."

"Are you all right, Mom?"

"Yeah, ate a bit much. I'm pretty full." Sophia dragged behind as they left the restaurant. She was out of shape. The only exercise she ever got was a short walk down to a gas station where she worked a few nights a week. She made enough cash to cover her subsidized, low-income rent, and she had a Bridge card, which paid for groceries. It's too bad the most affordable groceries are the least healthy.

Aimee sighed. "Mom, you need to get out more, do something with your life."

"I know."

"Well, are you going to?" Aimee got into the car and strapped on her seatbelt.

Sophia plopped down onto the seat, stopped for a moment to catch her breath, and then swung her legs into the car using her arms to help lift each leg in turn. She reclined her seat.

"Well?" Aimee pressed her.

"It's so hard to exercise. My feet hurt when I walk. My back hurts."

"You have to plow through it long enough until it stops hurting, until it feels good." Aimee drove across the lot and found a parking spot closer to the mall entrance. With her cards maxed out, Aimee needed gas money for the drive home the next day. "I need to find an ATM to get cash. Want to come into the mall?" The exercise would do her mom good, Aimee thought.

"I need to rest for a minute."

"You've been resting for the last ten years," Aimee said under her breath, but Sophia remained reclined in the Outback.

In the mall, Aimee asked a gray-haired man at guest services for directions to an ATM. "There's a Tyme Machine on the second floor by the food court."

Aimee laughed to herself as she rode up the escalator. That's what she needed. A time machine to go back a day and decide not to waste her time and money to see her father.

Back in the hotel, Sophia closed her eyes and leaned against the elevator wall. "Could you get me Prilosec from Walgreens? This heartburn's bad."

"I shouldn't have let you order that cheesecake."

"That was good cheesecake." Sophia chuckled. She got off on the fourth floor.

Aimee pushed the button for the lobby. "I'll be back in fifteen minutes."

She walked out of the hotel and to the intersection, where a river of cars flowed on twelve lanes in four directions. The speed and scale of the city was awe-inspiring on foot. After getting the signal to walk, she double-checked the two lanes of traffic that turned in front of her. She dashed between cars and crossed a total of nine lanes. It was a different world from the one in which she grew up. By the new year, her career would likely land her in a big city like Milwaukee. Or maybe Minneapolis or Chicago. Wherever, it was going to be different from the life she knew. She loved the UP—the nature, the people, the relaxed pace of life—but job opportunities were few.

After checking the price of Prilosec, Aimee purchased Tums. It crossed her mind to pick up pop and chips because she knew it would delight her mom, but she decided against it. Sophia had to stop her unhealthy behavior. She had to cut out the junk food. She had to exercise. Aimee wasn't sure how much influence she could have on her, but she didn't want to contribute to the problem.

Aimee made her way to the room. "I'm back." There was no answer. "Mom?" Something was wrong. Her mother should be watching TV, or at least have the TV on. It was too quiet. Aimee saw light underneath the bathroom door and breathed a sigh of relief. She lay down on the bed, and turned the TV on to HGTV. "Are you okay, Mom?" she called during a commercial break when her mom hadn't emerged.

Sophia groaned. "I'm sick."

Aimee opened the door to find her mother slumped over with her forearms on the bathroom counter. She was breathing hard and sweating profusely.

"My body aches all over." Sophia rubbed her shoulder.

"Mom, you should lie down."

Sophia nodded her head and staggered to the bed where she collapsed. "I can't catch my breath."

Aimee grabbed the phone and dialed 911.

"I need an ambulance. Something's wrong with my mom."

Mom in ER. Aimee texted Rob from the emergency waiting room.

She texted Beth. *Pray. Mom in ER.*

Beth replied immediately. *Oh no. I'll have Grandma pray too.*

Aimee stared blankly at the television. Her mentor had ALS. Her dad had cancer. Her mom had who knows what— maybe a nervous breakdown.

Aimee was tired. It had been a long day. Physically and

emotionally exhausting. She hoped her mom could get something to calm her nerves, and then they'd go back to the hotel and sleep. She was glad she'd had the presence of mind to drive to the hospital. Before the EMTs whisked Sophia away, they asked if she wanted to ride along. Aimee didn't want to be stuck at the hospital, so she verified that they were taking her to Froedtert. She knew where to go as she had passed the emergency entrance twice looking for the correct parking lot earlier in the day. Maybe in another hour, who knows—the ER didn't seem so busy—they could go back to the hotel and rest. They'd leave for the UP early the next day and get back in time for her evening shift at the Cornucopia. She was too broke to take any more time off work.

"Aimee Mallon?" A voice broke into her thoughts.

"Yes?" Aimee looked up at a nurse.

"Oh, good, you're here." The woman handed her a clipboard. "Your mom would like you to fill out the paperwork."

Aimee knew the basic information. Name. Address. Birthday. Emergency Contacts. She listed herself, her Aunt Senja, and her dad. He should know. They were still married. Insurance? She'd have to get her mom's purse from the hotel and find her insurance card.

Her phone beeped. A text from Rob. *Keep me posted.*

Anger boiled up within Aimee. Wasn't he going to come or at least call? She told herself to calm down. Rob didn't even know they had gone to Milwaukee. She breathed slowly. In. Out. In. Out. His response was not out of line. She was on edge. She texted a reply. *In Milwaukee. I'll call when I know what's going on.*

Aimee brought the clipboard up to the desk and handed it to the nurse. "I don't have an address or phone number for her husband, but he's admitted in the hospital here, too. And I'll have to check on the insurance."

"Your mother had a heart attack." The woman said the words matter-of-factly. "The doctor will be out shortly."

A heart attack? Her father was dying of cancer. Her mother had had a heart attack. *God, help. How much do you think*

I can handle? Aimee bit her lip. She walked into the restroom and locked herself in a stall. She muffled her sobs with her arm. Alone in a strange city with no support system and out of money—the emotional pain was crushing her soul. Aimee slumped against the wall, hitting her shoulder on a purse hook. Ouch. The physical pain dulled the anxiety and despair for a second. *God, help,* she prayed again.

She wished she were in the UP where she at least had her aunts. She should call her mom's sisters. And she wanted Russ. She couldn't deal with this on her own. Aimee returned to the lobby and unlocked her phone. There was no signal, and the battery was low. She walked down the hall while looking at the screen. She stopped when she had a couple bars. She called her Aunt Senja and left a message on her voicemail. She called her Aunt Lorna and left a message. She called Russ. Another message. Why was no one answering?

She again took a seat in the ER lobby. Out the windows, a deep turquoise colored the sky. The sun had set, but her day was far from over. It was going to be a long night.

Chapter 19

*R*uss leaned back in the passenger seat of Mak's crew cab truck. Mak had driven for the last few hours while Lorna and Senja relaxed in the back seat. Russ had met up with them, unexpectedly, at a gas station in Baraga, forty-five minutes south of Douglass. It was far enough off the beaten track that Russ assumed Mak was also heading down to Milwaukee. Mak offered him a ride, so he parked his truck and jumped in with Mak and the sisters. Aimee had left voice messages for each of them around nine o'clock in the evening.

No one had been able to reach Aimee. Russ tried to call, but it rolled right into voicemail. In any case, the distress in her voice prompted him to leave right away. She needed him. Once they got down the road, they didn't have cell phone reception until Green Bay. By then it was midnight, and Aimee still didn't answer.

"Call da hotel, Russ," Mak said. "Da Radisson by da mall."

"Which mall? I'm sure there's more than one."

"Da mall near da Radisson."

"There's probably a Radisson by every mall," Russ countered.

"Well, you got your little computer, you's da genius, so

why don't you figure it out." Mak snorted. "When I was your age, da only computer I had was called a pencil. Start was on one end, and escape was on da other." He glanced over to Russ as if expecting a reaction. "Da eraser,"

"Yeah, I got it." Russ groaned.

"They're staying at the Radisson by Mayfair," Senja called from the backseat. "That's a nice mall."

Russ punched away on his phone with two thumbs and found the number. "Two rooms?" he asked before dialing.

"What, you staying with Senja?" Mak asked.

"No, I could stay in a room with you. I was thinking Lorna and Senja could share a room." Russ didn't want the added expense. It crossed his mind he could stay with Aimee, but he thought he might hear another do-you-see-a-ring-on-this-finger jab. He'd be a gentleman, because even though the temptation was strong—her skin, her intoxicating fragrance—his fear of rejection was stronger.

"I'm not sharin' a room with you. I'm gonna sleep with my wife. I haven't been in a hotel with Lorna since…" Mak looked up in thought. "It was da spring of oh-nine. That was a year after da economy tanked. Lorna had one of those distributor conventions. She spent more money at da convention than she ever made in sales. But we had fun that night at da hotel."

Lorna whooped. "I remember that."

Too much information. Russ grimaced at the thought.

Mak laughed. "You kept me up all night, hon."

"Yeah. I couldn't do that now."

"You don't think so?" Mak glanced back to Lorna in the rearview mirror.

"Enough already." Russ's face was getting warm. "So three rooms?"

"Unless you want to sleep in da truck." Mak let out a belly laugh. He looked over at Russ. "Not that I want you sleeping in my truck with those filthy clothes."

Russ brushed dirt off his pants. He had crawled out of his hole and left immediately after getting the message.

He called the hotel and made the reservations for the last

three rooms, but they were available for only one night.

"You should drive," Mak said after Russ was off the phone.

"I have a hard time driving at night. Can't see."

"You tell me after driving all that way on country roads? Did you see all those deer we passed?"

"What deer?"

"I counted eight. We passed eight deer. You didn't even see them?"

"I'm sure they saw me." Mak chuckled.

"God's protective hand was over us," Senja piped in.

They stopped at a gas station south of Green Bay. Russ bought a coffee and took over driving.

Mak snorted a laugh when they got back on the freeway. "Did you hear about da time Heiki drove down to Milwaukee?" Mak slapped his knee. "Well, Selma calls him on his cell phone and says, 'Be careful, some idiot's driving da wrong way down da freeway. It's live on TV.' Heiki says—" Mak guffawed. "'It's not one driver, it's everybody.'"

Russ laughed.

Mak turned to the backseat. "Get it. It was Heiki who was driving the wrong way."

"I got it, hon, but I've heard it before—every time we get on the freeway," Lorna said.

"I heard it before, too, but it was about Toivo." Russ glanced at Mak.

"I don't tell Toivo jokes," said Toivo Maki with his most serious face. "You going again to Mexico, hey?"

"Nah."

"Why not? Don't you go every year?"

"I can't afford it this year." Russ had cleared out much of his Mexico mission fund to provide the scholarship he had secretly arranged for Aimee. The money he used to build the outhouses in Mexico came from his royalty checks. Out of principle, he didn't want to spend it on himself. His new mission, at least for the next semester, was to help his independent girlfriend graduate without being crushed under the burden of debt. It took a bit of research to find out she was the only senior paralegal student who came from the area and had independent student status. Senja had connections at the school, and Russ had sworn her to secrecy. He hoped Aimee wouldn't ask him about it.

"Slow year for construction, eh?" Mak asked.

"Well, kind of." Russ kept one hand on the wheel while he combed his beard with the other.

"That's da problem with contracting in da UP. There's no work in the winter, and too little in da summer. I used to swing a hammer more often, but now everybody's a contractor, even people who could be doing something better with their lives, Dr. Saarinen. You're cutting in on da livelihoods of us ordinary folks."

Russ shook his head. "Working for the man is not something better. And I don't think I pick up enough work to make your life any harder."

"I'm teasing," Mak said. "Da LPs would never hire me anyhow."

Russ was too busy cutting up his copper into salable specimens to worry about his lack of contracting work. The streak that ran through the copper was silver. He had learned that collectors value blended-metal specimens. He had also learned that where there's one large piece of float copper, there are typically smaller specimens that were carried along with the glacier. He used his metal detector to search across his property and found smaller pieces, most less than five pounds. He had opened an eBay store, but he hadn't yet listed anything. He was in the investment stage of his business. Mexico would have to wait until he could replenish the fund with copper proceeds.

"Have you ever thought about diversifying, getting into other businesses?" Russ asked.

"I leave that to Lorna. My specialties are making wood and moving snow. Lorna's got her business ventures. Her cupcake business is rising." Mak laughed. "Did you get that? Cake rising? I didn't even try. Lorna? Where's my journal? I need to write that down."

"You have your book business, right?" Russ asked.

"Well, that ain't so much a business as a dream."

"Don't all businesses start as dreams?" Russ countered.

"It's true," Lorna chimed in from the back.

Russ shifted in his seat. "If anybody knew how unrealistic their chances were, they'd never try."

Mak snorted. "Yep. Lorna has tried just about everything. She had her pasties, essential oils. Now she's on to cupcakes and birch bark decorations."

"And wasn't she trying to sell bidets?" Russ asked.

"I still have them for sale," Lorna pitched from the backseat. "Fifty bucks."

"She can't get rid of them. She's only sold a couple dozen since oh-nine." Mak turned back to Lorna. "Remember, hon, that's what you ordered that night at the hotel."

"Yep, that was a wild night," Lorna said.

"That's what she did all night at da hotel," Mak said to Russ. "She watched da QVC shopping channel. When those bidets came on, she got so excited she called up and ordered fifty of them at bulk rate. After that, I told her I'd had it and had to get to bed."

"You watched QVC all night?" Russ glanced at Mak.

"Yeah."

"I thought you were talking about—never mind." Russ shook his head.

They drove on, and the conversation fell silent. Mak snored deeply as the sisters slept quietly in the back.

The city was still alive in the early morning when Russ drove through the western suburbs, which reminded him of his time in a northern suburb of Detroit. Bright. Busy. Russ had spent his evenings and nights in a small apartment close to the freeway, where a constant drone of traffic penetrated his mind and a light from the parking lot shone into his window at night. He had a half-hour commute to work, worked long days, and had lonely nights in his apartment. He went out to lunch on occasion with colleagues, but the relationships were superficial. People in the city raved about the restaurants and shopping, neither of which interested him.

Aimee said he was a hermit. That wasn't true. He was more connected to people in the UP than he ever was in the city. It was a paradox—the more concentrated the inhabitants of an area, the more isolated people tend to become. She was right on one point—he wasn't independent. But at least he wasn't dependent on a corporation, on an employer, for his livelihood. He was dependent on friends and family. That was how life should be.

If he were honest with himself, he'd have to admit his concern with moving forward with Aimee was if anyone should be dependent on *him*. It was one thing for him to eke out a living as a seldom-employed contractor—to live a simple life in a cabin off the grid—but it was another thing to expect that of a wife. Or a child. He smiled at the thought of having a child, and then frowned.

There was also the issue of the Church. How could he leave it? How could he ask her to join a church he didn't even attend? Besides, she wouldn't like it.

When he moved to Detroit, there wasn't a Lord's People congregation nearby, so his mother sent him cassette recordings of the sermons. A church so set on rejecting anything of this world is slow to adopt new technology like MP3 recordings and podcasting.

He had listened to the sermons so he could honestly tell his mother that he had when she asked, but he listened to them in the background as he read or worked at home. The sermons were not particularly profound, mostly a reading of Scripture and then repeating the passages in different words in affected Jacobean English.

Aimee's church was lively and modern. The difference would shock her.

As much as he wanted her, Russ wasn't ready to commit yet. He was an engineer in every aspect of his life. He needed to have all the information before making a decision.

"We're here." Russ nudged Mak awake as he pulled to a stop at the front doors of the Radisson. His groggy passengers stretched, grabbed their bags, and went into the hotel to check in.

Russ asked the night clerk for Aimee's room number, but she wouldn't give it to him, which made sense, so he asked to leave a message for her at the front desk.

He wrote a note on a piece of hotel stationery. *Aimee, we're all here—Mak, Lorna, Senja, and me. Call my mobile number when you get up. We'll have breakfast and head over to the hospital. Love, Russ.*

Russ stared at the note. *Love.* He scribbled the word out and handed it to the front desk worker.

Chapter 20

"Someone's here to see you," a woman's voice said.

Aimee looked up in surprise as Ms. Sanders wheeled her dad next to her.

Frank twitched his head, and Aimee leaned in close. "Mom's pretty bad off, hey?" he whispered in a raspy voice.

"Yeah, Dad."

"Heart attack, hey?"

"That's what I've been told." She had been in the emergency room waiting area all night. It was a waste of the hotel voucher, and now she'd have to stay at least another night in Milwaukee with her credit cards maxed out. "Close to midnight, I asked for an update at the nurse's station. They were still stabilizing her, but I haven't heard anything since."

Frank turned to Ms. Sanders. "Can you find out what's going on with my wife?"

His interest surprised Aimee.

"I'll see what I can find out." Ms. Sanders left.

"So are you going to see her?" Aimee asked her dad.

"Of course," Frank said, as if there were no question.

Ms. Sanders returned. "We'll walk over to the next building. You can see Sophia there."

"They said the doctor would be out shortly," Aimee said.

"I'm sure the emergency night-shift doctor has gone home. They transferred your mother to Heart & Vascular Services this morning."

Aimee walked beside her dad, who sat in the wheelchair pushed by Ms. Sanders. As they passed a sign for the gift shop, Frank tapped Aimee's hand. Aimee leaned down as she walked.

"Let's get her flowers," Frank said, though barely audible.

"Do you have money?"

"No. If you buy them, I'll pay you back. Promise, kiddo."

Aimee snorted a laugh and straightened. "Promise? Since when have your promises meant anything?"

Frank shrugged his shoulders and guffawed. He coughed, coughed harder, and then spit phlegm into a towel.

"Dad, I'm broke." Aimee said the words apologetically. She stopped for a second and fell in next to Ms. Sanders. "Is there any way I could get more vouchers for the hotel?" Aimee held her breath.

"I can reimburse one two-night stay for low-income, out-of-town visitors," Ms. Sanders started, and a smile came to Aimee's face, "but it'll take me a couple days to get the voucher in your hands. If you put the room on your credit card tonight, I can reimburse one more night."

A knife twisted in Aimee's gut. Ms. Sanders took her hand off Frank's wheelchair for a half a second and patted Aimee's shoulder.

"Could I get reimbursed for my gas down here?" Aimee asked. "I have the receipt." *Please God,* Aimee prayed silently.

The social worker nodded. "I'll get you the form later today. You can turn it in, but the checks are mailed out, and I have no control over that."

Aimee nodded and bit back tears. She'd have to wait for the check. The talk of a check reminded her of her paycheck, her job. Her jobs. She had missed two shifts the night before and that morning, and now she wasn't going to be home for a few more days. Snap. She needed to call the Heikki Lunta and the Cornucopia, but her phone was dead.

And she didn't know if anybody got her message—if anybody was coming to help.

She walked with her head down through an elevated walkway that led to the next building and another lobby, where Ms. Sanders spoke to the receptionist.

Returning to Aimee and Frank, the social worker said, "It's going to be some time yet. I need to go lead a support group, but they know you're here. A nurse will call for you when you can go in. I'll come back and check on you in a couple of hours. Frank, if you'd be more comfortable waiting in your room, someone at the desk can call a CNA to help you back and forth." Ms. Sanders smiled gently at Aimee. "Hang in there."

"Thanks, Ms. Sanders," Aimee said.

"Call me Kara."

"Okay, Kara." Aimee was comforted to be on a first-name basis with the hospital social worker. She didn't feel so alone.

"Can we go out there?" Frank nodded to a door that opened to a rooftop courtyard with benches and trees in large planters.

"Ask the receptionist to give you a pager," Kara said and then walked away.

Aimee got the pager and wheeled her father to the courtyard through the door lettered with the words *Tobacco Free Campus*. Folks sat on benches eating muffins and drinking coffee.

Her stomach growled. She should've stuffed a few hotel cookies in her purse the day before. Maybe she'd buy a jar of peanut butter and a loaf of bread. The diet of her teen years after her dad left and her mom stopped cooking. Peanut butter on toast for breakfast. A peanut butter and jelly sandwich for lunch and dinner.

She pushed Frank into the courtyard next to a bench. Aimee sat and leaned her head back. The mid-August air was already hot and muggy at the early hour, a welcome relief from the over-air-conditioned hospital where Aimee had spent the night without a blanket. It took the chill out of her bones. She closed her eyes and took a deep breath. A foul cigarette smell wafted over from across the courtyard.

Frank coughed. The humidity was probably too much for him.

"Are you okay out here?" Aimee asked.

Frank twitched his head. She leaned forward. Frank looked longingly across the courtyard. "Sweetheart, can you bum a cigarette off that guy for me?"

Aimee shook her head, annoyed her dad was using the term of endearment to try to elicit a favor. "I'm not going to contribute to your health decline."

"What's a cigarette going to do to me now? Kill me?" Frank scowled. "Wheel me over there and I'll ask the guy." Frank nodded at a man in a business suit who was lighting up.

"No, Dad."

Frank's face flashed with anger. "Find a CNA to come get me and take me back to my room."

"Fine with me." She stood and moved around his wheelchair.

Frank shook his head. "Leave me alone."

She went back into the building and asked the receptionist for a nursing assistant.

Out in the courtyard, the suited man lit the tip of a cigarette in Frank's mouth.

"Francis and Aimee Mallon?" a nurse announced from the waiting room doorway.

"Yeah. I'm here." Aimee returned the pager to the receptionist and met the nurse.

The nurse asked, "And your father?"

Aimee looked back to her dad who had the cigarette dangling from his mouth. "He said he wanted to go back to his room."

"Well, maybe that's for the best. Your mother seemed pretty flustered at the thought of seeing him. She probably doesn't need any added stress."

Aimee nodded. She followed the nurse down the hallway to her mom's room.

"Hi, Mom." An IV bag hung above the bed with a tube leading down to Sophia's forearm. Wires attached to her chest led to a machine that registered every heartbeat. An oxygen monitor was clipped to her left index finger. "You gave me quite a scare."

"The cheesecake was worth every bite." Sophia chuckled. "Where's your dad? They said he was coming."

"He's tired." Aimee knew that was true, even if it wasn't the reason for his absence.

Sophia's face saddened. "Well, I don't want him to see me like this anyway."

"And you must be Sophia's daughter," a man in a white coat said after he entered the room. "I'm Dr. Adsit." He stood next to the bed and laid his hand on Sophia's shoulder. "I've been talking to your mother about treatment options. I'll explain again now that you're here." The doctor looked down at Sophia. "You have an artery that is seventy-five percent blocked. Another is fifty percent blocked. I'm recommending you have coronary artery bypass graft surgery."

Sophia shook her head. "I'm not having surgery." The heart monitor beeped a steady beat.

"Now Sophia, I'm not going to say you'll die tomorrow, but with an artery that's seventy-five percent blocked, it's only a matter of time."

"I'm not having surgery."

"You're very young, Sophia," the doctor persisted.

"You have so much to live for," Aimee pleaded. "I don't want to lose you to a heart attack like you lost your mom."

Sophia looked up at Aimee with a puzzled expression. "She didn't die of a heart attack. She died of a staph infection."

Chapter 21

Aimee sensed their presence when they entered the waiting room. She looked up to see Mak, Lorna, and Senja. Russ stood dutifully behind them. Aimee jumped out of her seat and ducked around her aunts' outstretched arms. "Russ!"

He wrapped her in a hug and twirled her around. "I brought you breakfast." Russ pulled a bagel wrapped in a napkin from his pocket. "It was free at the hotel."

"Thanks." Aimee turned and hugged her aunts. "Thank you for coming."

"Of course," Lorna said.

"I've been praying since I got the news," Senja said. "Your mom's going to be all right."

"She will if she comes to her senses and has the surgery. The doctor wants her to have bypass surgery, but she isn't listening to him. I think she's too upset about Dad. He didn't want to see her yesterday. That bummed her out, and he hasn't seen her yet today."

"We'll cheer her up." Lorna put her arm around Aimee's shoulder.

"And how're you doing?" Senja asked.

Tears came to Aimee's eyes. "Not well."

"God won't give you more than you can handle." Senja held Aimee's hands. "He's a God of comfort."

Aimee pulled her hands back. She wanted to scream. "Life is more than I can handle. And I had no idea where you guys were."

"You didn't get our messages?" Russ asked.

"My phone's dead."

"I have St. John's Wort out in the truck," Lorna said. "That helps when you're sad. Mak, could you go get my vitamin bag?"

Aimee laughed through her tears. "What I need is for my mom to get better and for my dad to apologize."

"And sleep," Mak barked. "I'm cranky when I don't sleep. You look as tired as I feel."

Aimee turned to her uncle. His crystal blue eyes didn't hold their normal sparkle. "A long drive, hey?"

"Da drive was restful, thanks to Russ driving. I'm tired because as soon as we got into da hotel, Lorna found the Home Shopping Network. She bought a half-dozen Drumi foot-powered, non-electric laundry machines." Mak turned to Russ. "She had you in mind, my filthy friend."

Russ smiled, and Aimee laughed at Mak's ribbing. There was truth in that. Russ's clothes looked as if he'd crawled out of his hole and left without having a chance to do laundry.

"Oh!" Lorna cheered. "That was a fabulous find. And I bought a Zumba trainer's set complete with DVDs and marketing material. I'm going to start a Zumba gym in Quincy."

Back in her mom's room, Aimee listened to her aunts bicker as she sat on the guest chair and ate the bagel Russ had given her. Russ and Mak had opted to stay in the waiting room, and Aimee thought that maybe she should have joined them. Senja stood on one side of Sophia's bed and Lorna on the other.

"Don't be recalcitrant," Senja said. "You're young. God has much planned for you."

"I don't know about that." Sophia shook her head.

"He does, Sophie. Everything happens for a reason. If God let this happen to you, then it's for a reason. You need to live so you can determine his purpose in your life," Senja said firmly.

Lorna rolled her eyes. "Whatever God may want of you, I want you to live. I'd miss you."

"Why would you miss *me*?" Sophia lowered her head. "You never see me."

"I see you," Lorna snapped.

"When?"

"Last Thanksgiving."

"That was almost a year ago." Sophia raised her chin. "And don't get me started on you." Sophia's heart monitor picked up pace as she turned to Senja. "I haven't seen you since Christmas two years ago."

"Oh my, has it been that long? I'm sorry."

"You're so busy with the church you don't have time to be a Christian."

Senja gasped.

Aimee's Aunt Senja *was* a rather busy Christian. She ran the women's ministry and served as the church's event coordinator. She planned weddings, coordinated dinners, and led a prayer group.

"We shouldn't fight." Sophia stiffened. "I don't even care about that. That's not why I don't want to have surgery."

"Then why not?" The two standing sisters asked the question in near unison.

"I don't want to die."

Aimee pricked up her ears, and Senja and Lorna looked at each other.

"Remember, Mom had a heart attack and she got bypass surgery," Sophia said. "She ended up dying of a staph infection."

"There's no reason to think the same thing will happen to you." Senja laid a hand on Sophia's shoulder. "God will protect you."

Sophia let out a sigh.

Aimee's mom, the youngest of the three girls, was in middle school when their mother died. Aimee wondered how that had affected her mom. The two older sisters were close in age, but then there was a twelve-year gap. The loss of their mother had been harder on Sophia than the other girls, who were already out of the house. Maybe Sophia would've made different choices in life if she hadn't lost her mom so young.

"This hospital looks very clean," Lorna said. "And I can give you colloidal silver. It's a disinfectant. You can take it orally."

Sophia shook her head. "It's not worth the risk."

Lorna leaned in. "Sophie, if you don't get the surgery you'll die."

"I could die from the surgery. I just need to lose weight."

Lorna grinned. "Sophie, I have an idea. Let's you and I start a Zumba gym in Quincy." Lorna reached a state of euphoria that often accompanied her ideas for new business ventures. "We can document your weight loss—take pictures of you every week—and put it on the Internet. It'll be a virus." She flung her arms out.

Sophia chuckled.

"It'll go viral, you mean." Aimee laughed, coming alongside Senja. She looked down at her mom. "So you do want to live?"

"Of course I want to live. Why would you think I'd want to die?"

"You seemed so sad when Dad didn't want to see you."

"I was sad. I am sad. But I like my sad life." Her mom smiled.

"I saw Dad this morning. He wants to see you today."

"Oh, I can't see him." The beeping on the heart monitor quickened. "I don't want to see him now." Sophia shook her head.

"Why not?"

"I'm such a mess. I need a shower. I need to brush my teeth." Sophia ran her tongue along the front of her teeth. "I need new teeth." She laughed.

"Mom, Dad didn't want to see you yesterday because he didn't have the money. He said that's why he didn't come back. Would you forgive him for that?"

Sophia rubbed her forehead. "What money?"

"He said he lost money at the casino."

"Well, I don't remember that, but I'll take the money if he has it. Or he can buy me a can of Mountain Dew, and I'll call it even."

"Wouldn't *that* be lovely. I can push the two of you onto the patio in the courtyard. You can die in each other's arms, you with your pop and him with a cigarette."

Aimee and her mom laughed.

"I'm not letting you go anywhere until you help me start my gym," Lorna said. "Imagine how well it'll do in Quincy with our long winters."

"Exercise will do you good, but what you need is God," Senja counteroffered. "You need to come to church with me and join my prayer group on the last Tuesday of every month."

Lorna rolled her eyes.

"Somebody always brings treats," Senja added.

"That's the last thing she needs," Lorna snapped.

A nurse entered and asked the ladies to leave so Sophia could rest. Mak drove the sisters over to Mayfair Mall while Russ stayed with Aimee.

"How long are you staying?" Aimee asked Russ as she drove to the hotel.

"As long as you need me." He reached out and squeezed her shoulder. "But I'll have to find another hotel, because the Radisson only had a room for one night."

"Do my aunts have rooms tonight?" Aimee got in the right turn lane.

"I don't think so. They checked out this morning. They called around to other hotels, but everything's booked. I think they're planning to visit your mom again this afternoon and then head home."

"Shoot." Aimee scowled.

"Shoot what?"

Aimee glanced at the clock on the dashboard. "I hope I have time to charge my phone. I need to shower, too. Check-out is at eleven o'clock. I may end up sleeping in the hospital again."

"You don't have a room tonight?"

"I had a voucher for one night, and I didn't even get to sleep in the room. I might get another voucher, but it won't do me any good if I don't have a room. I was hoping to stay with Senja and Lorna." Aimee glanced over to Russ. "Where are you going to stay?"

"Could I sleep in the Subaru? Otherwise I should head back with Mak."

"Stay. This is too hard on my own. We'll figure something out."

Aimee showered while Russ waited in the lobby. How should she tell him she was broke? She didn't want him to think she wanted him for his money, although she needed to broach the topic of borrowing money. She wanted him there to hold her, to listen to her, to comfort her. Senja had said that God was a God of comfort. That bothered her. With all that was happening, God felt distant.

Upon checking out, Aimee asked again if there were any rooms available for the night, not that she could afford one. The hotel was still booked, but the man at the desk agreed to call her if anyone canceled.

Russ took her to the food court at the mall and was gracious enough to pay for her meal. Aimee had taken her wallet out, but Russ wouldn't hear of it. She loved how he made her feel like a princess.

"Russ, do you feel God's comfort?" Aimee asked when they were seated.

"I haven't thought much about it," Russ said between bites of his burger.

"Senja said God is a God of comfort. But I don't feel it." She popped a French fry in her mouth.

"I'm here, and so are they." Russ nodded to behind Aimee. Senja and Lorna were walking shoulder to shoulder, while Mak lagged behind carrying an assortment of shopping bags.

"They're in rare form." Aimee laughed.

"Yeah, Lorna's been pressuring me to buy one of her manual washing machines."

Aimee surveyed his dirty clothes. "That might not be a bad idea."

Russ looked down at his pants.

"Are you ready to go meet my dad?"

Chapter 22

"*D*ad, I want to introduce you to my boyfriend, Russ." Aimee gestured to Russ who had entered the room behind her.

"Hi, Mr. Mallon." Russ stepped forward, as if he was going to shake hands, and then stopped.

Frank nodded his head. Aimee pulled a chair next to his bed, while Russ stood at a distance.

"Got a question for him," Frank rasped.

"He's got a question for you, Russ. Come here so you can hear him whisper."

Russ pulled up another chair and sat next to Aimee.

"Are you taking care of my daughter?" Frank whispered.

"Yes, sir."

Aimee laughed. "Thanks for looking out for me, Dad. It would've helped if you had been around for the last ten years, too."

Frank shrugged, smiling at Aimee's sardonic jab. She got her sarcasm from him. He understood it, appreciated it. That's how life was growing up—friendly jabs and jesting sarcasm. It helped her grow a thick skin. Russ had told her he too was teased growing up, but he didn't have the same appreciation for it. She had learned to be gentle around Russ.

Aimee leaned forward. "Dad, where were you for the last ten years?"

"Around."

"Around where?"

"I spent time in Vegas. San Diego. Phoenix." Frank spoke slowly as though it took effort to get each word out. "Wherever the wind blew."

"You've been living in the Southwest, and you didn't bother to tell me? You know how miserable the winters are in the UP. I would've come to see you."

Frank shrugged. "There wouldn't have been nowhere for you to stay."

"What do you mean?"

"I was homeless. I still am." Frank looked around the room. "Although, this place is nice." He laughed and coughed up phlegm.

"You were homeless? Why didn't you call? We could've helped."

Frank shrugged. He looked up at Russ and then at Aimee. "What's his last name?" he whispered.

"Saarinen," Aimee said.

Frank studied Russ and then addressed Aimee. "Aren't the Saarinens LPs?"

"Yeah, Dad."

Frank chuckled. "He's quite the Romeo. I like him."

"Mr. Mallon, can I ask you a question?" Russ leaned in.

"My dad was Mr. Mallon. Call me Frank. Shoot."

"Where did you sleep when you were homeless?"

"Here and there. Stayed in my truck for a while, until it got impounded and I didn't have money to get it out. I stayed with friends," Frank said between deep, labored breaths. "Sometimes I picked up a few bucks and rented a motel room. Sometimes I slept in a park. The city didn't like that, so they offered me a one-way bus ticket to wherever I wanted to go. I got off the bus in Milwaukee because I wasn't feeling so good, and I stayed at the Milwaukee City Mission."

"How was that?" Russ asked.

Frank looked puzzled, as if he wondered why Russ cared. "It was fine. They made me attend a chapel, which was good for me, I guess. I thought I'd get a good sleep and then head for Green Bay, but I was having trouble swallowing, so they called an ambulance. And here I am."

"Hey, Frank," Mak said as he and the sisters entered the room.

"Frank, we thought we'd pay you a visit while we're here," Lorna said.

"How are you feeling?" Senja asked.

Frank shrugged.

"He can only talk in a whisper," Aimee said.

"Cancer, hey?" Lorna asked.

Frank nodded.

"Did you know that cannabinoids have been shown to kill cancer cells?" Lorna offered. "Medical marijuana's legal in Michigan. You should come home to be treated."

Frank laughed and coughed. Tears came to his eyes and he coughed up phlegm.

"What's so funny?" Lorna asked.

Frank twitched his head, and Lorna leaned in. "I've been self-medicating for years. It hasn't helped yet."

"You don't need drugs, Frank. You need God." Senja leaned forward. "Do you believe you're a sinner?"

Frank snorted. "Ha. There ain't no question about that."

"Do you believe Christ died for you, Frank?"

"The Bible says it."

"Do you want to pray with me and receive Jesus as your Lord and Savior?"

"Senja, I prayed that prayer five times. It doesn't stick."

"God can put you back together, Frank." Senja's eyes filled with tears. "Can I pray for you?"

"Yeah, yeah. You pray for me. Maybe God will listen to you."

Aimee closed her eyes and prayed silently as Senja prayed aloud, thanking God for sending a Savior. Aimee opened her tear-filled eyes and saw her dad crying, too.

"I hope this one takes," Frank said. "Can you pray for God to heal me of this cancer while you're at it?"

"You should try medical marijuana," Lorna broke in. "They discovered the endocannabinoid system in the 1980s, and cannabis repairs the receptors. I can infuse it in coconut oil. You can take it orally so you don't need to smoke it. We'll microdose so you won't get high."

"Okay, you two." Aimee smiled at her aunts. They were quite the pair. She turned to her dad. "Are you ready to see Mom?"

Frank nodded.

A CNA got Frank out of bed and into a chair, and Aimee wheeled him down to Heart & Vascular Care. The sisters had gone before them to help Sophia freshen up.

By the time Aimee and Frank arrived, Sophia had brushed her hair and teeth. She sat up in bed with the sheets folded neatly over her. She was sick, no hiding that, but Frank didn't seem to notice.

His eyes lit up when he saw his wife. "Hi beautiful," he whispered. This tender and affectionate man was the Frank Sophia loved. He sat beside her bed and held her hand, and they talked quietly.

Aimee and the sisters left them alone. Aimee peeked in on occasion to make sure all was going well. Later in the afternoon, the sisters and Mak stepped in, said their goodbyes, and were off.

Russ and Aimee sat in Sophia's room on the guest chairs while Frank retained his place by Sophia. The doctor checked in on Sophia and reiterated the need for surgery. Frank agreed with the doctor, but Sophia didn't budge. She said she'd lose weight and she'd be fine.

"Most people don't," Dr. Adsit said. "If you've lacked the discipline thus far, you'll not likely have the discipline to stick with the program." However, he did acknowledge that with diet and exercise, reversal of her condition was possible. She'd have to take it slow and stay under the care of a physician, as the risk of another heart attack was significant. "Many women who have heart attacks die at home, alone," he warned. "Now you know how elusive the symptoms can be. If you have any discomfort, get to a hospital as soon as possible."

Sophia nodded.

"I want to keep you here for a few days to monitor you. Then we'll keep you on a blood thinner once you're discharged. You're a stubborn woman, Sophia." Dr. Adsit said.

Looking exhausted, Frank requested a CNA, who came and took him back to his room.

Aimee pulled her chair closer to the hospital bed. "Mom, Senja prayed with Dad earlier about accepting Christ as his Savior. Dad was so sincere. He cried. I believe he's a Christian now."

"Sure, he is. He became a Christian ten years ago. Remember when he took us all to church? That's when both of us made things right with God. I became a Christian, too."

Aimee frowned. She hadn't seen her dad's life change, not the way the Bible promised. "Then why did he relapse?"

"We all relapse." Sophia shrugged. "Some sins don't clean up as easy."

"Why don't you go to church, Mom?"

"I watch the 700 Club. That's my church. Hey, is Rob coming?"

"I don't know. I need to call him."

"How long are you staying?"

Aimee looked over at Russ.

"Until you're discharged," Russ said, "Then we'll take you home."

Her mom smiled, which warmed Aimee's heart, but then she was filled with dread wondering how she was going to survive two more nights in the big city with no money and no hotel room.

Chapter 23

*A*imee walked with Russ through the hospital halls until she found a waiting area with decent cell phone reception. She called Rob and updated him on their mother.

"So she's out of the woods," Rob said. "That's great. There's no need to worry."

"No, you're not understanding me." Aimee could hardly believe his indifference. "She's stabilized, but she could have another heart attack at any time."

"I'm sure she'll be fine after the surgery."

"Do we have a bad connection or are you not listening?" Aimee knew it wasn't a bad connection, because she could hear his keyboard clicking. "I was saying she's refusing to have the surgery."

"Sorry, I'm a little distracted here."

"Rob, you should come see her. The doctor's concerned she could have another heart attack at any time."

"I'll call her." So dismissive.

She'd take a direct approach. "She wants to see you. Can you please come?"

"It's hard to take time off work. I'll try to make it there for Christmas."

"You should come *now* so you can see Dad, too. He doesn't

have much time—maybe only weeks."

"I have nothing to say to the man." Rob's voice was cold.

"Did you know he was homeless?"

"Yeah. A couple years ago, he asked to stay with me when he was up in Vegas."

"He stayed with you?" Aimee asked.

"No way. I'm not going to have him in my life."

"But you heard from him, and you didn't bother to tell me?"

"You didn't ask," Rob said.

"I would have wanted to know."

"We're better off without him." Her brother sounded so bitter.

"Rob, you need to forgive him."

"Have *you*?"

Aimee fell silent. She had given Rob the directive out of instinct, because it was the right thing to do. But if she fully examined her own heart, she'd have to admit she wasn't ready to forgive him either. She hoped her dad would ask for her forgiveness, recognize the damage he had caused, but he was oblivious. It made her pain acute.

"Have you?" Rob repeated.

Aimee couldn't bring herself to forgive him because she didn't want to trivialize all the wrong he had done. Sophia accepted him unconditionally. Rob rejected him unapologetically. Aimee pitied the man, but she couldn't let go of the hurt. She wished Rob could have seen their dad's tender side and how their mom delighted in his presence. When Aimee found out he was homeless, she could see him as a human—a broken, sick, human. "He's our father."

Rob snorted. "He's *your* father. Tell Mom I love her. I'll try to be home for Christmas."

Aimee closed her phone and exhaled slowly. Russ put his arm around her, and she rested her head on his shoulder.

"I guess it's you and me," Aimee said. "Thanks for being here."

"Anything for you," Russ said.

Aimee met his gaze. "Russ, I don't want you to think I'm using you. You know I can take care of myself."

"I know that."

"But I'm in a bit of a pinch."

"How's that?"

She dropped her head. "I have to stay here for my mom, but my credit cards are maxed out. I don't have money for food or a hotel, if a room opens up."

"I can help." He squeezed her in a hug.

"I don't want you to think I'm some sort of helpless woman who needs a man."

"I don't think that. Needing help has nothing to do with your gender. Your dad's a man, and I'm sure he's had help in his life."

Aimee stiffened and turned to look at him. "Mister, I am far from being like my dad."

"That came out wrong. I'm not saying you're like your dad. I'm just saying it has nothing to do with your gender."

"I'll pay you back. Keep track of the money you spend on me."

"Aimee, I don't think any less of you because you need help. I've gotten help in my life."

Aimee put her head back down on his shoulder. "Want to take me out on a date?"

"Yeah, I'm hungry." He stood and eagerly pulled her to her feet.

PF Chang's Asian Bistro hummed with excitement. The murmur of a hundred conversations. Clanking dishes. Hostesses dressed to the nines. Aimee was glad she put on a cute shirt that morning. Russ looked out of place with shaggy hair, an overgrown beard, worn T-shirt, and dirty jeans.

A young, slender hostess in a tight black dress stood behind a lectern in the crowded entrance and ran her fingers down a list of names. "It'll be an hour wait."

"Wow. An hour." Russ frowned. "Can we sit at the bar?"

"Go right ahead." The hostess motioned for them to seat themselves as she grabbed a flashing pager from another couple.

As they made their way to open stools at the bar, Russ's eyes followed plates of food carried past them. Aimee's knight in rusty armor had lost too much weight in the past month.

"An LP sitting at a bar." Aimee elbowed Russ in the side. "I should put it on Instagram."

Aimee asked for iced tea.

"A Shirley Temple," Russ ordered.

"On the rocks?" the bartender asked with a smirk.

"And stirred, not shaken," Russ deadpanned. "And menus. We'd like to order food."

"An LP drinking. Now I've seen it all." Aimee smirked.

"It's nonalcoholic."

"That's funny. I thought you were ordering a drink." Aimee laughed. She was either looking for sunshine in her dark valley or Russ was getting funnier. Either way, he made her laugh, and she loved him for that. "Where did you learn to order a drink?"

"When I lived near Detroit, I went out to happy hour with my colleagues on occasion."

"I've never seen you drink, but I thought it might be because you were always the one driving. It's weird we've never talked about this, but do you drink at all?"

"I never have. The Lord's People don't drink."

"That's wise. Alcohol was my dad's downfall."

"So, you don't drink either?" Russ asked after they got their drinks and menus.

"Nope. That's one of my rules. I vowed I wouldn't make the same mistakes my parents made, so I'm careful about some things. My dad wasted a lot of money gambling, so I won't set foot in a casino, not even for a birthday party. I hate casinos. My mom got pregnant with Rob in high school. She married my dad—and I'm glad, because then I was born—but her life didn't turn out well. I made a couple mistakes with guys when I was younger, but that's not going to happen again. I'm not going to get pregnant before I'm ready, so I'm careful to stay out of—"

"Do you know what you want?" the bartender interrupted.

"We haven't had time to look," Aimee said.

Russ snapped open his menu. "But we're hungry, so what appetizer would you recommend that's quick?"

"They're all quick, but our lettuce wraps are popular."

"Let's do it," Russ said.

Aimee laughed. Russ had never been fussy about food. He probably didn't know what he had ordered, but if it was quick, that was good enough.

Aimee's phone rang. "Hello?"

"This is the Radisson. We have a room for you tonight."

"Just one?"

"There are two. They each have a king-size bed. Do you want one or both?"

Aimee looked at Russ. "There are two rooms at the Radisson tonight."

"Take 'em." Russ nodded.

"I'll take them," Aimee said.

"Okay. We'll need a credit card to reserve the rooms."

Aimee swallowed hard. She hated using Russ like that. She pulled the phone away from her mouth and leaned over to Russ. "They need a credit card to reserve them. My cards are maxed out."

"Okay." Russ pulled out his wallet.

Aimee handed the phone to Russ.

"How much are the rooms?" he asked. "Okay. I'll take one." He gave his name and credit card information.

He was so kind to come down, but sometimes so insensitive, Aimee thought. They had just had a conversation about values. She didn't want to share a room with him. It wasn't that she didn't trust him—she didn't trust herself. She didn't want to end up in a tempting situation, although she was irritated enough by him only reserving one room that temptation wouldn't be a problem. She didn't even want to touch him. Russ handed the phone back to Aimee.

"And here are your lettuce wraps." The bartender placed lettuce leaves and the stir-fry mixture in front of them.

Aimee considered her options for the night as Russ checked in to the hotel. She felt less irritated with him after getting food in her stomach. It was her choice not to share a room with him. She could take care of herself. She could spend the night in the emergency waiting room. It was uncomfortable, but safe, and they didn't pay much attention to her the last time she was there.

Leaving Russ at the counter, Aimee snuck across the lobby and put a few cookies into her purse. She shoved a cookie in her mouth.

"You know, those are complimentary," Russ said as he approached her.

"I know. And so good."

"Here's your key." Russ held up the room card wrapped in the holder.

"Do you see a ring on this finger, mister?" Aimee laughed uncomfortably. "I can't stay with you. I'll go back to the hospital. I'm not going to make the same mistake—"

"I mean this is your key, and the only key. It's your room. I'll sleep in the car."

Aimee hugged Russ around the neck and kissed him gently. She felt electricity pulse through her body. She looked up into his steel blue eyes. "I wish you could stay with me tonight."

Russ pulled Aimee closer and rested his chin on her head. "I could sleep on the floor."

"No way, mister." She pushed him back and shook her head.

"You just said you want me to stay with you."

"What I said I wanted and what I'm going to do are two different things." Aimee grabbed Russ's hand. "At least walk me to my room. I know it's early, but I didn't get much sleep last night."

"You slept in a hospital waiting room, hey?"

"I don't recommend it. I hardly slept a wink."

Russ pulled his lips tight and nodded his head. He looked nervous.

Chapter 24

*R*uss walked Aimee to her third-floor room, hugged her, and kissed the top of her head, breathing in the fragrance of her coconut shampoo. As he released his embrace, Russ searched for the right words to say.

Aimee peered up at him. "I love you."

"Ahh…" He could have said that, but it was too soon to commit. She hadn't even met his family. "I love being with you, Aimee."

"Okay, mister, you find a safe place and have a good rest." Aimee punched Russ lightly in the stomach. She dug in her purse for the key to the Subaru and handed it to him.

Faced with the imminent reality of homelessness, $185 for the second room didn't seem too expensive, so he checked with the front desk, but it had been taken. He called other area hotels, but none had rooms. He thought about finding a park, but he knew from his time in Detroit that they typically close at dusk. He thought about driving to a wayside rest, but doubted he'd find one close to the city. So he moved the Subaru to the top level of the Radisson parking ramp.

He slid the driver's seat back and reclined. He shifted to his right and then to his left in a futile attempt to get comfortable. He put his seatbelt on, pulled the slack from the recoil mechanism, and leaned his head against the belt.

Getting comfortable was harder than he had imagined. He had slept in vehicles before on long road trips, but only for a short nap after being exhausted from driving. After a restless few minutes, he crawled to the back of the station wagon. He folded down the rear seats and lay on his back.

His shoulder blades pressed hard against the thinly upholstered floor, and his wallet dug into his glute. He crawled to the front and put it in the glove box. He lay back down and tossed and turned. He didn't have anything to cover him, but the night was warm. His breath and body heat made it stifling hot in the Subaru. He got up, put the key in the ignition, turned it forward a click, and rolled a window down.

He stared at the ceiling a few feet above his head. He looked at the six-inch opening of the window. Somebody could reach his arm through it. He crawled back up front and closed the window to a crack. He opened another window a crack.

He began to relax. He thought about Aimee. She had been consuming much of his thoughts lately. As hard as it was to think of how she'd fit into his life, it was impossible to think of a future without her.

A car parked next to him. He rolled to the side near it, against the wheel well and passenger door, so he wouldn't be noticed. He heard the voices of a man and a woman. When the talking and laughter grew faint, Russ rolled onto his back.

He told himself he was helping Aimee with her school because he was doing mission work at home, but he hoped he was also building his own future—*their* future. He hadn't admitted to Aimee he was thinking about marriage. How was it going to work with his family, with the Church? Maybe they'd accept her if they knew she had similar values, even if for different reasons. Nah. He was dreaming.

Another car parked near his, but farther away. He was anxious for a few minutes until voices faded and he knew the guests had gone into the hotel. As Russ relaxed to the soporific sound of traffic in the distance, he thought about his float copper and how he was going to cut specimens. At some point he must have dozed off.

He found himself in his hole, cutting a small section near the silver band. Then he was in his cabin, hammering it flat. Tap, tap, tap. He hammered away. Tap, tap, tap. The noise was coming from behind him. He turned to the door. Who would visit the hermitage without notice?

Tap, tap, tap.

Russ woke.

A bright light shone through the rear window. Russ held his arm over his eyes.

"What are you doing here?" a gruff voice asked.

"Sleeping."

"You can't sleep here." A plump-faced cop—no, a security guard—scanned inside the car with his flashlight.

Russ sat up. "I'm a guest here."

"Not tonight. Get a move on. You have to sleep someplace else."

"No, sir. I really am a guest here. I'm a registered guest."

"What's your name?"

"Russ Saarinen."

The guard lifted a portable radio to his mouth. "Could you check if you have a Russ Sorry-ann staying here?"

Russ spelled his last name, and the guard relayed it.

A voice over the radio replied, "Yes, he's a guest."

"Sir, you can't sleep in your car. You have to stay in your room."

"Yes, sir."

Russ remained seated. The guard stood next to the car. Russ supposed he was not going to move until he saw Russ walk into the building, so he slipped on his shoes and got out.

The guard followed him into the hotel and to the elevator. Russ got on and pushed 3, and the doors closed with the mustached guard standing with his arms crossed on the other side. Russ quickly pressed *L*, rode to the third floor, and finally back to the lobby.

Russ went to the front desk, hoping there had been a

cancellation, but all the other guests had either checked in or guaranteed their rooms. The clerk told him other hotels in the area were full, too. He was tired and wanted to sleep, but it was just past eleven o'clock and people were still coming in and out of the hotel. Maybe he could find a quiet place to sleep later. Russ sat in the lobby and read a newspaper to pass time.

Russ turned to the business section. His blood boiled as he read of a convenience store owner who lost everything to the out-of-control government. The IRS had seized over $100,000 from his bank account for no other reason than he deposited his daily cash revenues. The government accused him of structuring, of making multiple deposits less than $10,000 to avoid reporting, and they held on to his money for years as he tried to prove his innocence. After the guy spent over $50,000 in accountant and attorney fees, the IRS agreed to settle if he forfeited half of the money. There's no protection for the ordinary person.

He flipped the page and a picture caught his eye. Sharply dressed in a tailored suit, the balding CEO of his old company was shaking the hand of another man and holding a National Safety Award. Russ felt nauseated thinking of his last days there. They're all corrupt.

He read the comics.

After it seemed an hour had passed, Russ checked the time on his phone. It had been only fifteen minutes. He put the paper down and walked around the hotel, looking for a quiet, dark corner. The bathroom off the lobby wouldn't work. People were working out in the exercise room. Maybe the business center. He peered through the glass door into the dark room.

The motion sensor lights turned on when he entered. He logged on to a computer and surfed the Internet. There was nothing on it he didn't already have access to on his phone. The business center was quiet. After another five minutes and nobody coming in, Russ lay on the floor under a desk. He relaxed, and after ten minutes, the lights turned off.

Just as he began to feel drowsy, the lights turned on. He stiffened as footsteps approached, and soft-soled, black walking shoes stopped by his head.

The beer-bellied security guard with the mustache stood over him, shaking his head. "And here's my favorite guest. You can't sleep here either."

"Okay, okay. I'll go to my room."

"I don't believe you're a guest. However you got the name of one of our guests, I don't believe for a minute you're that Russ Sorry-guy. Let's see your ID."

Russ got to his knees and reached for his wallet, the wallet he had left in the car. "I don't have my ID on me."

"Look, buddy, there's a homeless shelter downtown. If you need a place to stay, you should try there tomorrow. It's too late to go there tonight, but you can't stay here."

"I'm not homeless," Russ protested with as much indignation as he could muster.

The guard kneeled. His eyes softened. "Hey, man, I know what it's like to be down on your luck—"

"I'm not down on my luck."

The guard shook his head and his face showed pity. "When was last time you had a decent meal?"

"I ate at PF Chang's this evening."

"Have you been drinking?"

"I've never had a drink in my life."

The guard chuckled. "You're a meth head then."

"No. Look, I'm a registered guest. My girlfriend's sleeping in the room."

"Right. We'll see about that. What's your room number?"

"309."

The guard stood, and Russ got to his feet, too. The guard picked up a courtesy phone on the desk. "This is James. Can you connect me with room 309? ... Hello, ma'am, do you know a man named Russ Sorry—something? ... Can you give a description of him?" The guard looked Russ up and down. He laughed. "Yeah, that's what I thought, too. Okay, thank you. I'm bringing him up."

"I told you," Russ said.

"Well, yeah, your story checked out. I guess you're having

trouble on the home front. I know how that is." James put his hand on Russ's shoulder. "My wife kicked me out once till I came to my senses. Do you need to talk about it?"

Russ shrugged the man's hand off. "No, I don't need to talk about it."

"All right. All right. But I can't let you sleep here." James shepherded Russ to the elevator and up to room 309.

The door cracked open, and Aimee peeked through. She closed the door, Russ heard the click of the security latch, and the door opened. Aimee stood in silk pajamas, shaking her head.

"You two need to talk. Communication is vital to a healthy relationship," James said. "You have a good night." He swaggered away.

"Aimee, I can't get another room and I'm not good at being homeless. Can I stay here?"

Aimee nodded and held out her arms. As Russ hugged her, he closed his eyes and felt the warmth of her body against his. The temptation was palpable, but he'd be a gentleman. He respected her too much.

In the room, he sat next to her on the bed as he told her about his multiple encounters with the security guard.

"You're such an adorable geek." Aimee laughed groggily. "I guess we should try to get some sleep."

Russ stood. "I'll sleep on the floor. Do you mind if I use that?" Russ nodded to the bedspread folded up at the foot of the bed.

"Sure, go ahead. I put your bag in the closet. You can change into your PJs in the bathroom."

Russ smiled nervously. "I don't sleep in PJs."

"What do you sleep in?"

"I usually sleep in my boxers."

"Usually?"

"I'll sleep in my pants tonight."

Aimee made a disgusted face. "They're dirty."

"So?"

"Get the bedspread, cover yourself, and slip out of your

pants. And that T-shirt. The guard thought you were homeless. I'll wash them in the sink and hang them to dry."

Russ did as he was told. He laid the bedspread on the floor, folded it over himself like a burrito, and slipped out of his clothes and handed them to Aimee. She took his pants and shirt and went to the bathroom. He heard water sloshing and then the sound of water dripping as she wrung out his clothes.

Aimee jumped onto the bed and popped her face over the edge. "Are you comfy?"

"Compared to the last couple hours, I'm as snug as a bug in a rug."

Aimee's head disappeared and she turned off the light.

Russ stared at the popcorn ceiling illuminated by a glow that came over the top of the darkening shades. The air conditioner hummed and blew cold air above him.

"Good night, Russ."

"Good night, Aimee."

"I love you, Russ." Seconds passed. "Russ?"

"I love you, Aimee."

Chapter 25

*R*uss pulled Aimee close, feeling the curves of her body against his. "Aimee, I really do love you," he whispered the words as he held her, desire rising. Her body was soft. He squeezed her tighter. "Aimee?" He opened his eyes.

He was lying on the floor, hugging a pillow. The blanket tangled around his feet on the hard floor. He kicked to free himself. What a dream. It was unsettling how much he wanted her. How much he loved her.

Bright morning light streamed in from above the curtain. He stared at the popcorn ceiling. The air conditioner hummed. No—it wasn't the air conditioner. "Aimee?"

No answer.

Russ had to use the bathroom. What was humming? "Aimee?" he called more loudly.

No answer.

Russ sat up. She wasn't on the bed.

The humming came from the bathroom. Aha. A hairdryer.

Fully awake, Russ waited uncomfortably for Aimee to get out of the bathroom with his only pair of pants. In a hurry to leave, he had packed a relatively clean T-shirt, fresh boxers, toothbrush, and toothpaste, but no clean pants.

Attempting to distract himself from his need to pee, Russ thought of Aimee, her parents, and her upbringing. Aimee had *sisu*. She was tough and resourceful. She had worked hard and come far. She amazed him, but how did he end up saying "I love you" the night before? He had imagined he'd come to that conclusion logically, and at some point he'd tell her deliberately, perhaps even romantically, somewhere special like on the beach at Big Traverse. But then he had blurted it out.

It had been a long, exhausting day, and a few hours of homelessness bewildered him. Aimee was right. He was dependent on other people. He needed her, because she made him better. They needed each other. Their lives had intertwined. Saying "I love you" was the logical climax to such an emotional day.

Russ *really* had to use the bathroom, but Aimee was still in there.

How long had it been? Fifteen minutes? A half hour? He poked his head up to see the clock, but a pillow on the bed blocked it. His iPhone was on the desk. It was hard to believe how long she took in the bathroom. How much gasoline would the generator use to power a hairdryer for that long every morning? Russ stood and wrapped the bedspread around his body, bracing it in place by clamping his arms down against his chest. He waddled to the bathroom and knocked on the door.

"Just a minute," she called.

Russ didn't have a minute, but he was too embarrassed to tell her so. He remembered the bathroom off the hallway near the elevator on the main floor. He'd use that.

Russ walked down the hall and stepped into the elevator car, the bedspread trailing behind him. Part of the bedspread remained in the hall, and Russ gave the blanket a quick tug as the doors closed shut. He pressed his knees together, willing himself to hold it for a few more minutes. The elevator doors opened, and Russ stepped out.

James, the security guard, came around the corner, and their eyes met. James shook his head. Russ felt a tug, and he was yanked back. His feet were pulled out, and he fell to the floor as the blanket rose up the closed door and stopped. Russ lay on the floor in his boxer shorts. The elevator alarm rang.

James stood over him with his arms folded. The front desk clerk and a man in a business suit peeked down the hall.

It took some explaining, but James seemed to accept Russ's story. He was gracious enough to allow him to use the lobby bathroom, and then he escorted Russ back to his room.

"I suppose you don't have your room key on you." James looked down at Russ's boxer shorts and smirked.

Russ shook his head.

James knocked on the door.

Aimee opened the door and laughed. "Okay, mister, what have you done?"

Russ shrugged. "I need my pants."

"They're in the bathroom. I never did get them fully dry this morning."

After Russ showered and got dressed in his damp pants, which still showed evidence of days in his hole, they went down for breakfast in the hotel restaurant. Russ recounted his morning, and Aimee laughed until tears came to her eyes.

James stopped by the table. "We've had our share of bad guests, but you're the first to get the bedspread jammed in the elevator."

"Sorry about that," Russ said sheepishly.

"Don't worry. I put in a good word for you. I told them you're a kindhearted idiot, Russ, not a man bent on destruction. The hotel has another room open for tonight, but maybe you should stay with your girlfriend so she can keep an eye on you." James snorted with laughter.

Russ raised an eyebrow to Aimee. They had behaved themselves. Maybe he could sleep on the floor again.

She shook her head and raised her left hand. "Do you see a ring on this finger, mister?"

He booked the second room for the next night.

"Now, let's go shopping," Aimee said.

"I don't want to go shopping, especially not after the expense of another room."

"You can't go around the city in pants like that. I couldn't scrub those stains out, and that *fresh* T-shirt of yours has holes in it. Besides, I already made an appointment for you at a salon at the mall."

"A haircut?" Russ protested. "You didn't say anything about a haircut."

At the highfalutin salon, Russ sat next to Aimee as she thumbed through old magazines. A stylist called Russ's name, and he stood.

"Umm..." She looked at him in horror. "Let me check if Skye is done with her break." She disappeared into the back.

Embarrassing. He knew she was disgusted by his appearance. His teenage sisters gave him that same look on occasion.

A young woman with dyed, jet-black hair and bangs came up front and graciously greeted them.

Aimee held up a magazine. "Can you make him look like this?"

"Paul Walker? I'm a hairstylist, not a magician." Skye glanced at Russ. "No offense."

Aimee laughed.

"I could shave him. It'd be cheaper—only twenty dollars," Skye suggested.

Russ grimaced. "I don't want to be shaven." He should have insisted on one of those chain haircut places. Apparently, he was going to be paying more than twenty dollars for a designer cut. "I want a regular haircut."

"I can do that." Skye motioned to Russ to follow her and have a seat in one of the chairs. Aimee grabbed another magazine and followed them.

Skye stood behind him and pulled his beard to the sides to see how long it was. "I'm sorry about the commotion when you came in."

Russ shrugged.

"I volunteer at the City Mission with the Haircuts for the Homeless program," Skye said. "I keep trying to talk Amber into coming. My mom and I lived at the Mission for a few months when I was a kid. Now I have a good job and I like to give back."

"My dad stayed at the City Mission." Aimee stood near the chair and thumbed through the magazine.

"Is that why you have a heart for the homeless?" asked Skye.

Aimee shrugged. "I suppose."

"We're there the first Friday of every month. You should come." Skye wrapped Russ's neck with a thin strip of tissue paper. "We can keep up on this."

Russ studied his reflection in the mirror. So she thought he was homeless. Did he look that rough?

Skye glanced over at Aimee. "You should tell your other clients about Haircuts for the Homeless. I think about going back to school and getting a job where I can really make a difference in people's lives. How long have you been a social worker?"

"Huh?" She looked up from the magazine. "I'm not a social worker. I'm a student. I'm studying to be a paralegal."

"Well, it's so nice you're helping him out." Skye threw an apron over Russ's body and snapped it behind his neck. "That's how God works—when things affect you personally, you develop a heart."

"What are you talking about?" Aimee asked.

"Your dad. I suppose because your dad stayed at the City Mission, you want to help other homeless men." Then Skye asked Russ, "How long have you been homeless?"

"I'm not homeless." Russ huffed.

Aimee laughed. "He's been getting that lately. He's been digging a hole in the UP."

"What's the UP?" Skye asked.

"It's that part of Michigan above Wisconsin," Russ said.

"I've lived in the city my whole life. Even poor folk in the city don't look that rough unless they're really down on their luck." Skye smiled at him. "No offense." She ran her fingers through his hair.

He had showered that morning, but his hair was untamable at its current length. He supposed the clean but ratty T-shirt added to the effect.

"What would you like done?" Skye asked.

"We'd like it short, but not too short." Aimee was back to using the plural pronouns. "And could you trim his beard? Or shave it off, even?"

"I like my beard. It's warm in the winter." Russ covered his cheeks with his hands.

"It's August," Aimee countered.

Russ sighed. "Whatever she wants is fine. I don't care."

"I'd like him to look like this." Aimee flashed another magazine.

Skye studied the picture. "It'll require product."

"Okay." Aimee smiled.

It's only temporary, Russ thought. A small recompense for embarrassing her the prior night and that morning.

Skye went to work and Aimee returned to the sitting area. Hair piled up in a semicircle around the chair. After the cut, Skye shaved his beard with an electric trimmer. She shampooed his hair, lathered his face, and shaved him clean with a razor. She dried his hair and styled it with gel.

Aimee stared at Russ when he came to the front. "Get out!"

Russ looked behind him to see if she was talking to somebody else.

She smiled broadly. "Who are you and what did you do with my boyfriend?"

Russ felt his face warm.

"You're gorgeous." Aimee stood. "Can I say that about a guy? Russ, you're good-looking."

"I didn't want you to fall in love with me for my looks," Russ deadpanned.

Aimee laughed. "I'm glad you have your own room tonight. I'd be tempted."

"Because I look so good?"

"No, because you make me laugh. Now for clothes."

Aimee dragged him around the mall. She kept referring to outfits, rather than pants and shirts. She used phrases like,

"This'll look cute with that," and "That doesn't go at all." Russ loved to see her in better spirits, even at the price of his dignity.

After their adventures at the mall, they went back to visit Sophia and Frank. Sophia asked who Russ was, as if Aimee had gotten a new boyfriend. Frank seemed to be stronger, even after exerting himself visiting in Sophia's room that morning. He still looked sick, but he held his head higher and opened his eyes wider. Sophia was getting better by the hour.

That evening, Aimee and Russ explored the town and had dinner in the Third Ward. Aimee looked at Russ in a way he had seen many women look at Danny throughout the years. The hostesses and waitstaff seemed to treat them with undue respect. Russ had entered into a bizarre world far from the UP.

Later in the evening, as they walked through the hotel lobby, James, the security guard, said, "Have a good night." He smiled and gave an authoritative nod and then did a double take, looking at Russ again. "Russ? Is that you?"

Aimee put on her PJs and snuggled under the covers of the king-size bed. It would've been easy to let Russ stay with her when James had suggested it. She laughed, thinking of her adorable geek's transformation. She wouldn't be able to call him that anymore. Her guy had cleaned up well. When Russ kissed her goodnight at her door, Aimee had been tempted to let things go further, but she was proud of herself for sticking to her principles.

She had too much to lose. She wasn't going to repeat the mistake her mother made by starting a family so early and outside of marriage, although Russ was probably the safest guy to sleep with. If she got pregnant, she had no doubt he'd take care of her and the baby. His independent, cabin life was a phase. If push came to shove, he'd step it up and get a real job. She prayed a silent prayer that God would open Russ's eyes, that he would show Russ a different path—one that made more sense for a future with her.

Peace washed over her, and then she prayed for her father.

She prayed that the Spirit would move in him and he'd ask forgiveness for all he had done to hurt her and her family. Now that she'd calmed down, now that she'd seen his tender side and had come to understand where he had been for the last ten years, she was ready for a heart-to-heart with him. She was ready for closure. Tomorrow she'd say what she had come to say. She'd tell him how she felt.

Chapter 26

"*D*ad, this might be the last time I see you. I don't want to leave things like this. I forgive you, Dad. You hurt all of us, but I forgive you." Aimee rehearsed her speech as she showered.

She had woken with a sense she should initiate the conversation by offering forgiveness, and that would bring him to realize what he had done.

She dried her hair, got dressed, and packed her bags along with her mom's stuff. After dropping her room key card off at the front desk, she met Russ in front of the hotel, where he was waiting in Louisa's Subaru. They made the quick drive to the hospital. Russ dropped her off and left to gas up the car while Aimee headed to her mom's room.

Sophia sat in her bed with breakfast on her tray. "I'm being discharged today. We should go have another slice of cheesecake to celebrate."

"Mom!"

"Just kidding, honey." Sophia was a new person with bright eyes, a quick smile, and a ready laugh. Frank had spent time with her rekindling their relationship. It befuddled Aimee. After a rocky marriage and abandonment, they picked up as if nothing had happened.

Aimee knew it would be hard for her mom to leave for home that day, but they had no choice. Aimee had to work that night, Sophia had no money, and they had asked enough of Russ.

"Help me fill out the discharge papers." Sophia gestured toward a stack of papers on the bedside table.

"Oh, Mom, I never did find your insurance card in your purse."

"I don't have insurance."

Aimee grabbed the papers. "I thought everybody had to have insurance."

"I can't afford it."

"How can you not afford it with your income? You should get enough subsidies to pay for almost all of it."

"Meh." Sophia flapped her hand. "I wouldn't even know where to start."

"You never signed up?"

"And how was I supposed to do that?"

"You go online."

"Just help me with the forms."

Aimee read through the paperwork and asked her questions. Behind the last form, there was a post-cardiac care sheet. "Here, Mom. You should read through this."

Sophia looked sheepish. "Could you read it for me?"

"Mom? Can you read?"

"Sure. I can read."

Aimee wasn't so sure. She read through the instructions, which included early heart attack symptoms and steps to take if Sophia felt she might be having another heart attack. Aimee handed the clipboard back to her mother and told her to sign at the bottom.

"Okay. Now let's go see your father. Maybe we can take him out to the courtyard."

"We don't have time to take Dad outside," Aimee said firmly. It was true they had to go, but she also didn't want a repeat of the smoking incident. "I need to work tonight. Russ will be back soon."

"We can't leave your father, Aimee, not like this, not in this condition." Child-like worry came to Sophia's eyes. "We should stay a few more days. Maybe his health will improve and he could come home with us. He wants to see Lambeau Field. We could take him there on the way."

"I don't have money to stay. You don't have money. I need to get back to my job. Don't you need to work?"

"I told Senja to stop by the gas station and tell them I'm in the hospital."

"Mother, I can't take more time off work. I'm broke. We need to go home."

Sorrow darkened Sophia's eyes. It tore at Aimee's heart.

"Help me comb my hair," Sophia said. "Bring me my makeup."

"We don't have time, Mom. Your makeup is packed and in the Subaru."

"Don't you have anything in your purse?"

Aimee dug in her purse and pulled out a lipstick. "Here, you can have this."

Sophia's eyes brightened.

"While you eat your breakfast and freshen up, I'm going to go talk to Dad. I want to resolve things with him. Ask your nurse to call a CNA to take you down there."

"Dad, wake up." Aimee nudged Frank and leaned in close.

"Kiddo." Frank opened his eyes and smiled. "Did you bring me smokes?"

"No, Dad."

Disappointment washed over Frank's face. He closed his eyes.

"Mom's being discharged today. We're going home."

Frank nodded his head, but kept his eyes closed.

"Dad, I may not see you again."

Frank opened his eyes. "Then I guess this is goodbye."

"I don't want to leave things between us unresolved."

"No worries, kiddo. I forgive you. No hard feelings."

"You forgive me? Right, I'm the one who needs forgiving," Aimee said sardonically. "Why would I need to be forgiven?" She glared at him.

"For leaving me in the courtyard. For not bringing me to Lambeau Field. For not staying with me here."

Aimee felt her blood boil. She stood and breathed deeply.

"Why are you looking at me like that?" Frank looked puzzled.

Aimee retrieved a chair and put it next to the bed. She'd try a more direct approach. "Dad, you left us when I was fifteen years old. You promised you'd teach me to drive, and you missed my graduation."

"If you're gonna be mad at anyone, be mad at your mother. She told me to leave."

"You hit her."

"She hit back."

"She's a woman. You're her husband. You're supposed to protect her."

"She hit hard." Frank laughed and coughed up phlegm.

"Fantastic. You beat your wife and son, left your family, and now you're joking about it?"

"I didn't beat Rob. I disciplined him. Got him ready for the military. And look how well he turned out." Frank thrust his chin out. "Push that button for me, will you? I need to use the can."

Aimee sat back, exasperated. She pushed the call button on the hospital bed. She didn't know what else to say. The peace from the prior evening had vanished. How could she forgive him? He was unrepentant. He'd never get it—never understand how much he had hurt her when he left.

Frank closed his eyes and snored. Aimee studied his face. He was old before his time. A CNA came into the room a few minutes later, and Aimee slipped out before the aide woke him.

She found her mother sitting in a wheelchair being pushed by another CNA. Sophia's face beamed. Her lips were glossy, and it appeared she had used the lipstick to blush her cheeks.

Aimee didn't know whether to laugh or cry. "He's all yours,

Mom, as soon as he's off the can."

Sophia chuckled. "Is he getting better?"

"No, Mom. He's not going to get better."

Sophia scowled. "You don't know that."

Aimee pursed her lips together and nodded. "I'll wait for you in the lobby."

She picked up a magazine, but the words and celebrity pictures couldn't pull her mind away from the conversation she'd had with her father. She replayed it in her mind, while sadness and anger percolated. She took a deep breath and let it out slowly.

"Hey." Russ sat next to Aimee. "Are you okay?"

"Not really." Aimee leaned her head against his shoulder.

"Did you talk to your dad?"

"He's not even sorry for what he did. He had the nerve to forgive me, even though I didn't do anything." She bit her lip.

"I'm sorry," Russ said.

Aimee straightened. "Why are you sorry? You did nothing wrong."

"Sorry," Russ said again.

"Stop." Aimee focused on breathing. In. Out. In. Out.

After a few minutes passed, a CNA pushed Sophia into the lobby. Tears dripped down Sophia's cheeks, and she wiped them on her sleeve.

"It didn't go so well, hey?" Aimee asked her mother tentatively.

"It was beautiful. He told me, 'Catch you on the other side, babe.'" Sophia smiled dreamily. "After all these years, he thinks I'm a babe. He's always been so charming."

Aimee shook her head.

Chapter 27

*R*uss drove his truck north along Keweenaw Bay, where waves lapped up on rocky shores. In late August, the soft evening sun illuminated the Huron Mountains, which rose above the southeast horizon on the other side of the bay.

He had driven Aimee and Sophia in Louisa's Subaru to Baraga, where he picked up his truck. The temperature gauge in the Subaru had steadily dropped from ninety-two degrees in Milwaukee to seventy-seven degrees in Baraga. He had kept the air on for Sophia, but now that he was in his truck, he drove with the windows down to get fresh air. Real air. His nose had missed the country.

He couldn't wait to get home to his cabin where no one looked over his shoulder. No one judged his appearance. He leaned over and inspected himself in the rearview mirror. His short hair and clean face reminded him of his working days at his old company. His Banana Republic ensemble, as Aimee called it, reminded him of the preppy college kids at the University of Michigan, where he never truly fit in. As soon as he got home, he'd change into comfortable clothes. Perhaps he'd keep his old clothes cleaner now that he had committed to buying a Drumi foot-pedal washing machine from Lorna.

He should have spared the expense, considering how much money he had already spent.

The last four days had been crazy. He was glad to be in Milwaukee for Aimee, but the busyness of city life didn't appeal to him. Nor the expense. Everything was expensive. The hotel was almost $200 per night—a total of four nights between him and Aimee. Dinners were over fifty dollars. He spent hundreds of dollars on clothes. What was he thinking? How was he going to pay for it?

He had committed his royalty payments to the scholarship for Aimee—or, rather, a local female student with independent status in her last semester of the paralegal program. He didn't look for work when he was busy with the copper, so he only had one job lined up—a kitchen remodel that would provide a couple weeks of work. And now most of the other jobs had been bid out for the contracting year, which would wind down in November. He'd have to move on the copper. He'd have to cut specimens and get them listed on eBay. He was afraid that for the first time in his life he'd have a credit card balance that he wouldn't be able to pay in full. What was he thinking?

Whatever he was thinking, he was home in the UP. The UP doesn't put on airs. There's no need to compete. It's honest.

A couple nights prior, when he told Aimee he loved her, he meant it. He had repeated it since, but he didn't know how it was going to work. She loved the city. She seemed ecstatic when they went out to dinner or to the mall. Had she any idea how much he hated it? They were so different. And then there was his family. The Church. She'd have to change to be accepted by them, and if she didn't, they'd take it out on him.

As he approached Douglass, lakeside cabins became more frequent until they were built side-by-side. In the distance, he saw the big can light of a Michigan State Trooper vehicle. He checked his speedometer. He was within five. As the police truck passed, a hand waved out the window. Danny. His friend did a double take as he passed Russ. He probably recognized his truck but expected to see a shaggy-haired, bearded guy. Russ laughed. Danny was the only government official Russ trusted.

Russ drove past the university and through Douglass. As he crossed onto the island, he thought with amusement how wonderful it would be for the lift bridge to get stuck and leave 320 million people stranded on the other side.

He passed the Cornucopia, where Aimee would be working that evening. She'd barely have enough time to drop off Sophia and make it to work. Russ drove up Quincy Hill, past Louisa's, Danny's, Maribel's, and Koski's. Finally home. Tension drained from his temples.

As he pulled off the road where he parked his truck, something didn't look right. Tall grass was trampled down where a vehicle had been parked. He got out of his truck and checked his construction trailer. The lock was on the door. His four-wheeler was undisturbed behind the trailer.

He jumped on his ATV and took yet another route through the sugar maple forest to his cabin. As he approached, something else didn't look right.

The generator. Rather, the lack of a generator. It was gone. Someone had stolen his generator.

Unbelievable. For years people had been leaving equipment in plain sight, and nobody bothered it. He locked his trailer, but that was more for the safekeeping of the lock than fear of someone stealing his tools. The only time he needed the lock was when he was on a job to keep people from borrowing his tools. Panic rose in his chest. The copper? Did someone find his copper?

Russ jumped off his four-wheeler and dashed to the front of his cabin. Something was on the door. A note.

Ah, that made sense. Someone borrowed his generator and left a note.

When he got closer to the door, he could see it was more of a form. *NOTICE OF EVICTION.*

Russ read the notice. *By order of the sheriff, you are prohibited from entering these premises.*

A check marked a box next to *Failure to meet code*, and a handwritten note on the bottom of the form read, *Nonfunc-*

tioning septic system on premises with running water.

A feeling of bewilderment came over Russ. The same feeling as when he had sat across the conference table from lawyers who told him they'd sue for libel if he said anything negative about his employment at the company.

Had someone stolen his generator? Borrowed it? Did the sheriff take it?

Russ called 911.

"What's your emergency?"

"I'd like to report a stolen..." Russ hung up. The last thing he needed was more cops on his property.

Danny probably let it slip—tipped them off. Russ called his cell phone.

"Hey, buddy," Danny said.

"Are you happy?" Russ spit out the words.

"Yeah, man. Life's been good."

"Life is good now that they took my generator and kicked me out of my cabin, hey." And Russ had thought he could trust him.

"Whoa, calm down. What's going on?" Danny asked.

"My generator. It's gone. And I've been evicted—nonfunctioning septic system. You couldn't keep your big mouth shut, hey." Russ's phone beeped with a second call. "Just a second."

"This is 911. Your call was disconnected."

"I know. I hung up," Russ said.

"Young man, it's a crime to crank call 911—"

"Argh! It was not a crank call. I called a nonemergency number instead. Goodbye." Russ clicked back to his conversation with Danny. "Okay, I'm back."

"The next time you call someone upset, don't take a call waiting. It breaks your flow. Now what are you talking about?"

"You turned me in."

"I didn't say anything to anybody," Danny said.

"Then how did they find out?"

"That's the county," Danny said. "I'm a State Police officer. I don't care about county building codes. Except they made me put in those obnoxious childproof outlets. I can hardly plug anything into them."

"However they found out, I'm evicted." Russ paced in front of the cabin. "And my generator's gone."

"I'll come up. Hang on."

Sitting on his four-wheeler, Russ waited for Danny at the road. He could hear him coming, or at least someone coming at a high rate of speed. The truck with the big can light on its roof appeared in the distance, and the gap closed within seconds.

"Hey, you did get a haircut," Danny said when he got out of his truck. "I thought I saw you pass me south of Douglass. You look professional."

Russ scowled.

"And look at those clothes. You look like a college kid."

Russ rolled his eyes.

"You're good-looking." Danny laughed. "Can I say that about another guy?"

"Just hop on already."

Russ drove Danny to the cabin, where Danny inspected the property and read the note. "I'll call the sheriff." Danny dialed the number from his contacts and lifted the cell phone to his ear. "Bill? ... I'm out at Saarinen's property up on Quincy Hill. ... Yeah. ... Yeah. ... And you took the generator? ... Okay."

"Well?" Russ asked.

A shot rang out in the distance.

Danny frowned. "It's kind of early for bear season, isn't it?"

"I guess," said Russ. "What's the deal with the generator?"

"He's got it."

"Why?"

"So you can't ignore the notice and run water."

"The government. Unbelievable."

Danny's radio crackled. "Officers requested to respond to shots fired. North on Quincy Hill. Address not provided."

"I've got to go. Can you drive me back?"

Russ and Danny hopped on the ATV again. As Russ drove through the woods, Danny's radio continued to give details.

"A man is pinned down in his vehicle. He requests immediate help. A woman is firing shots at him."

"I've got this," Danny said over his radio. "It's Maribel Myers. I'm five minutes out. Tell everybody else to stand down."

After dropping Danny off at the road, Russ went back to inspect his property. The ground, which he had left saturated from the water he used to cut the copper, had mostly dried while he was in Milwaukee. Everything else appeared to be there.

In defiance of the notice, he unlocked his cabin and inspected inside. The cutting machine was down in the hole along with the copper specimens, but without the generator to run the pump, he didn't have a source of water to run the machine. He was tempted to sleep there that night but didn't want to risk arrest. Now that Danny had called him, the sheriff knew Russ was back. His truck parked at the road overnight would be a dead giveaway he was staying in the cabin.

Russ clenched his fists and screamed. "Why?" All he wanted was to be left alone. It was none of the government's business what he did on his own property.

He grabbed his laundry and headed out the door. Aimee was working at the Cornucopia and Danny was dealing with Maribel Myers, so that left his parents' as the only place to crash. Back on the road, he seethed as he passed the sheriff, who was talking to a man on the road next to Maribel's. Russ slowed. The man was Vance. He glanced down Maribel's driveway and saw Danny talking to Maribel on her stoop. He held her rifle.

It felt like a long drive out to Trap Rock Valley. As the evening waned, the temperature dropped. The setting sun cast a shadow over the valley as he drove down the hill. Aimee's words from earlier in the summer echoed in his mind. *You have the luxury of playing poor. All you have to do is hitch a ride back to Trap Rock Valley and you'll have a warm bed and food.* Russ felt gratitude for his family. They might have their issues, but they were stable. They were dependable.

He loved his parents and his family, but he dreaded stay-

ing in the dorm. Russ shuddered. So many people. No soli-
tude. When his heart was heavy, he preferred to be alone. He
had escaped the trouble he had in the city, but trouble followed
him to the UP, and now he had nowhere else to go.

Maybe Alaska, he thought. Three quarters of a million
people, if he remembered correctly from his high school ge-
ography books. Nearly a square mile for each person. He had
heard of floatplane services that dropped people off at some
desolate lake and agreed to pick them up weeks later—or
not—no questions asked. He could escape into the national
forests and build a cabin someplace no one would ever look
for him.

Russ pulled into the driveway, where his brothers Albert
and Jesse shot hoops, feebly dribbling the ball on the loose,
crushed mine rock. Jesse had finished his last year of school
and enrolled at Douglass State. Albert, a year-and-a-half older,
had been working in the North Dakota oilfields two weeks on
and one week off. Annika and Esther, sixteen and fourteen, sat
on the porch steps reading books. No one paid much attention
to Russ as he pulled up and carried paper bags into the house.
But Henri seemed glad to see him and asked if he wanted to
work on a puzzle.

Maari must have heard his voice and came down to greet
him. "Russ, look at you. You got a haircut. You shaved off that
awful beard. So glad you're resisting the temptations of this
world. What's the occasion for the visit? You're losing too
much weight. Could I get you something to eat? Why did you
come so late?" On and on she went as mothers do, not noticing
his internal angst.

"Mom, I need to crash here for a few nights."

"Sure, there's plenty of room in the boys' dorm, but why?"

Russ exploded. "I've been evicted from my cabin. It's not
the blasted government's business what I do on my land, but
they had the nerve to trespass, steal my generator, and put up
a notice that I can't enter my own house. I did anyway."

"Back up, Russ. Start from the beginning. What happened?"

"It all happened when I was in Milwaukee, and—"

"You were in Milwaukee? Why?"

"Aimee's mom had a heart attack."

"Who's Aimee?"

Russ grasped at air where his beard used to be.

"Who's Aimee?" Maari repeated in a sterner voice.

The gig was up. Russ admitted he had a girlfriend, and Maari was ecstatic. She insisted Aimee come over for dinner on Sunday. Maari failed to confirm she was Lord's People. Russ didn't offer any information.

Chapter 28

"What do you think?" Aimee twirled in a sleeveless, burgundy dress she had bought to wear to a friend's wedding a few years ago.

"You look great," said Beth, sitting on Aimee's bed in the guest room. "Where's Russ taking you to dinner? The Fitz?"

"No. I'm going to meet Russ's parents." Aimee looked over her shoulder into a full-length mirror on the inside of the closet door. "I'll need to find my backless bra."

Beth grimaced.

"What's wrong?"

"Russ's family is Lord's People, right?"

Aimee frowned. "Right."

"It's a little sexy."

Aimee sighed. "I thought this *was* conservative. It goes down to my calves. Do you have anything I could borrow?"

Beth shook her head. "Everything I have is conservative for California, but not for the Lord's People. My grandma might have something you could wear."

"Seriously?"

"She used to be LP. She switched churches after my grandpa died. She won't mind." Beth dug in the guest room closet through old clothes that Louisa no longer wore. "This," Beth exclaimed, holding up a long jean skirt. "This is perfect. You can wear it with any shirt—just pick one that covers the butterfly."

Aimee twisted her neck to see the tattoo on her shoulder. "Russ hasn't said anything about it. I know he's seen it." She shivered, remembering his gentle touch tracing the wings of the butterfly. "Is having a tattoo wrong?" she asked nervously.

"I don't think so," Beth said, "but some Christians might. There were laws in the Old Testament that Christians don't need to follow today. They were for that time."

Aimee felt anxious. "What other rules do the Lord's People have? I don't want to offend Russ's family." She slipped out of her burgundy dress.

"I don't think you'll offend them either way. But they might more readily accept you if you didn't wear makeup, or—"

"Russ has only seen me naked once," Aimee said.

Beth gasped.

"I mean without makeup. I feel naked without makeup." Aimee pulled the jean skirt up to her waist. "He's only seen me once without it."

"Oh, I thought… Anyhow, it might be good if you didn't wear makeup—or earrings. Maybe put your hair up in a bun, or at least a braid." Beth looked up as if in thought. "Oh, not a braid. There's that verse in First Timothy about that."

Aimee dug through her suitcase for a shirt. "I have a calico dress and bonnet from when I played Laura Ingalls dress-up as a kid. It's a bit small."

Beth laughed. "It's not like that. They're not old-fashioned, just excessively modest."

"How do you know so much about the Lord's People?"

"My mom was raised in the church. My grandpa was LP, and Grandma joined the church when they got married—the Quincy congregation, which is less conservative than where Russ's family attends. But they still had a lot of rules, especially back then. You should talk to my grandma."

Aimee pulled her hair back into a ponytail.

"Are you sure you want to do this? Become someone else for them?" Beth challenged.

Aimee laughed. "You should know me well enough by now. I'm not becoming someone else for anybody. But I love Russ. I want things to go smoothly. If I have to put on a jean skirt whenever we visit them, it won't be a big deal. Where do you buy these, anyway?"

"I don't know," Beth said. "Aimee, being Lord's People is a whole lifestyle. You can't go to the movies or dance or listen to music. And there's pressure to have a lot of children."

"Louisa only had two."

"Yeah, that was an issue between my grandparents. She had complicated pregnancies and put her foot down on that, but my grandpa wasn't happy about it. She kept going to the church with him and she had friends there, but when he died, she left the church and that was it. With the LPs, you're either in or out."

Aimee swallowed hard.

"Well?" Aimee asked Russ when he came to pick her up.

He stood at the front door. "Well, what?"

"You like my new look?"

Russ stepped back and looked her over. "You look like a brown-haired version of my sisters."

"Are your sisters beautiful?"

"Oh, I'm sorry. You look great." Russ enveloped Aimee in a hug.

"Thank you." Stubble on Russ's chin brushed against her neck. She reached up and ran her fingers through the nap of his hair as he held his embrace. "Okay, my adorable mountain man, you can let go."

"Mountain man? What happened to adorable geek?"

"You're too hot to call a geek. You notice anything else different about me?"

Russ pulled his eyebrows down and cocked his head. "You took your earrings out."

Aimee motioned to her face. "No makeup."

"Well, you're beautiful with or without makeup and jewelry."

Aimee smiled broadly and slapped his stomach with the back of her hand. "You've got some serious lines. It's hard to believe I'm your first girlfriend."

A look of confusion crossed Russ's face. "Ready? Let's go."

He opened the passenger door of his truck for her.

"How're you doing?" Aimee asked as Russ turned onto the highway. By that, she was asking about his eviction from the cabin—if he wanted to talk about it.

Russ glanced at Aimee and shook his head. "I haven't been able to find out anything else. Danny said he'd talk to the sheriff."

"I'm sorry."

"For what?" Russ smirked. "You didn't do anything."

She chuckled. "Well, I did pray that God would open your eyes to how your cabin may not work long term."

"You prayed for that?" He raised his voice. "Are you crazy?"

Aimee hadn't seen Russ this intense.

"You can't pray for things like that, not without people's permission."

At the Saarinen's, a short, wide woman with gray hair pulled back into a bun stood in the kitchen with other women and held out her arms. "Aimee, grace to you."

Russ stepped aside as she rushed over to the door and hugged Aimee. "This is my mom, Maari."

Other heads popped in from around the corner. Dinner was on the two stoves and in the ovens, and a large bowl with a tossed salad sat on the long center island.

His mother turned her attention to Russ. "Now why didn't you tell us about Aimee sooner?"

He shrugged.

A wave of kids entered the house, circling around the couple. Likewise, a number of men came through the door from the garage. Like a choir falling into place on a tiered stage, the family arrayed itself from shortest to tallest along both sides of the kitchen island and into the dining room beyond. Aimee tried to count but had to start over. There were dozens of people, anyhow.

"You met my mom, and that's my dad, Karl." A lean, tall man with blond hair nodded. Russ cast his eyes to the back of the crowd and, pointing, listed off names in rapid succession. "Paul, Robert, Mark, Natalie, Selma, Craig, Laura, Juhani—"

"Huh? You honey?" Aimee asked.

"Yeah, that's the Finnish version of John." Russ scanned the crowd as if trying to remember where he was. "Anna—she's Paul's wife, from Finland—Katie, Hanna, Luke. Hanna and Luke are pregnant. I mean Hanna is pregnant. Luke's her husband. That's Jill." A woman waved. "Oskar's fiancée. He's my brother. Somewhere around here, hiding behind somebody, is my brother Henri. Henri, where are you?" A boy with an upside-down smile poked his head out from behind one of the adults. Aimee smiled at him, and he ducked his head back behind the crowd. "Those two over there are my kid sisters Annika and Esther—"

"Oh, Russ." Aimee giggled.

"She's not going to remember all of these names today." Mrs. Saarinen moved to Aimee's side and ushered her into the kitchen. "Out of my kitchen. Out of my kitchen," she said to the others. "All of you, except the women."

"Thank you, Mrs. Saarinen," Aimee said to Russ's mother.

"Call me Maari, please."

"Maw'-rey," Aimee repeated back with the drawn out *A* and trilled *R*. She hadn't been sure she could pronounce it correctly after the introduction so she had erred on the side of formality. She didn't want to mess things up.

The crowd cleared from the kitchen, the kids outside and the men to the garage. As Karl passed, he put his hand on Russ's shoulder. "You'll be getting a call. I talked to Lappi. He wants a garage."

A few women stayed behind and reintroduced themselves—Russ's sisters Laura and Selma and his sisters-in-law

Anna, Natalie, and Katie. Aimee had to ask them more than once to remind her of their names.

Maari assigned tasks to her *sous chefs.* She put Aimee on fruit-rinsing duty—fresh blackberries from a patch on the Saarinen property. Aimee guessed there were a gallon and a half of blackberries. Anna whipped cream.

The women pressed Aimee for details of her relationship with Russ. How long had they been dating? Was it getting serious? How did they meet?

"He started giving me rides after my regular chauffeur flaked out on me."

"You didn't meet at church?" one of the sisters asked.

"Oh, no. He doesn't go to my church."

"That boy," Maari said. "He told me he's been going to the Quincy congregation. He hasn't been coming here."

"I think he goes there on occasion," Aimee sprang to Russ's defense. "He doesn't go to Pinehurst."

Oxygen left the room. Anna shut off the handheld mixer. Knives and utensils clicked and clanked as the women set their utensils down. Aimee felt the eyes on her as she shut off the water at the sink and turned around.

"It's a Christian church," Aimee said, as if there were a doubt.

"Well, you'll have to join us next week," Maari said. "Russ comes with us now that he's living here. House rules." As quick as that, Maari settled matters, and the women resumed their activity. "So you're enrolled at Douglass State University?"

Aimee told the women about the program and the type of work she'd end up doing. She didn't talk too much about her career ambitions.

"Is that something you can do part time when you start having kids?" Anna asked in a thick Finnish accent.

"I suppose." Aimee had a better sense now of what kind of answers the women were looking for.

The women were warm. She'd never had a family like that—a family engaged and interested in her life. She realized they were of a different culture, but she felt accepted by them.

The women laughed and told stories. This was the family she had always wanted.

The dinner table held most of the adults, with the teens overflowing to stools at the island. The kids sat at card tables in the living room. After the feast, with the blackberries and real whipped cream for dessert, the men returned to the garage with talk of stoking the sauna. The women supervised the younger adults and kids as they cleared the table, scraped dishes, and loaded two dishwashers. And then women washed by hand the dishes that didn't fit. Within forty-five minutes the kitchen was spotless.

"Women in the sauna first," Maari announced. "Will you join us, Aimee?"

"Oh, I couldn't. I didn't bring a swimsuit."

"You don't wear swimsuit to take bath," Anna said in a Finnish accent. "That would be unhygienic."

Aimee scanned the faces of the other women. Several nodded.

"We never sauna with clothes," said an adult sister, whose name she couldn't remember. "It's fine."

"Sure, okay." Aimee smiled, thrilled that they seemed to like her. When at the Saarinen's, do as the Saarinens do.

A few of the women and the two teenaged girls beat the rest to the sauna, a building about twelve by sixteen feet built next to the bank of the river. Aimee stepped into a changing room with cedar benches, hooks on the wall, and a shower on one end with a curtain drawn back. She peeked into the steam room and saw three tiers of benches built against two-and-a-half walls. The sauna stove sat against another.

"If you're not used to the heat you can sit on the bottom bench," teenaged Annika suggested. The ribbing had begun. A sure sign of acceptance in the UP.

Aimee lifted her chin. "I can take it. I'm part Finn."

"Is that so?" Anna asked.

"I'm told my dad was part Lapp."

"Yes, I see it in your eyes." Anna pointed under her brow.

Aimee smiled. She was sure that she didn't have Finnish

eyes but thought it sweet they wanted to accept her enough to believe she looked remotely Finnish.

As the other women began to disrobe, Aimee turned her back to them and took off her top.

"You have a tattoo," Annika shrieked.

"Pipe down," Selma scolded.

"Did it hurt?" Annika asked.

"Yeah, it hurt, but not for long." Aimee self-consciously continued to undress, knowing all eyes were on her.

"Sit against the wall," Selma suggested, "then mother won't see it when she joins us."

"Is she going to go to hell for that?" fourteen-year-old Esther asked.

"Never mind," Selma said sharply.

"It's pretty," Esther said, which Aimee took as an apology. "Where did you get it?"

"At the Piercing Palace in Douglass. I got it after my dad left us. It was a promise to myself that I was going to fly."

The door creaked open, and Maari entered with the other women. Aimee spun around to face her, holding her towel up as a curtain in front of her.

"Oh, good. You're all ready," Maari said. "Now clear out of here so we have room to undress."

Aimee swallowed hard and threw her towel over her tattooed shoulder. She stepped into the steam room.

Chapter 29

*I*n the sauna, Aimee sat in a corner to block anyone from sitting on her right and spying the butterfly. She wrapped her towel around her body.

"Whose underwear is this?" Maari called from the changing room.

The other women in the sauna smiled meekly at Aimee. Hers was the only underwear not white or ecru, but she wasn't about to claim her lacey, black thong. She had done such a good job looking like a conservative girl, but it hadn't occurred to her to buy drab underwear for the occasion. Banter from the dressing room continued, and Aimee surmised it was a rhetorical question, anyhow.

Russ's adult sister Selma sat on Aimee's left, and her sister-in-law Natalie sat next to Selma. Selma seemed to have taken Aimee under her wing. She had sat next to her during dinner and whispered in Aimee's ear, giving her context behind stories and reminding her of names. Russ's older sister Laura sat on the bench opposite her, along with the teenagers, Annika and Esther. The thermometer that hung from the wall read 165 degrees, and Esther filled a galvanized pail from a spigot on the wall next to her.

The stove door creaked as it was opened from the outside. Logs clunked as someone threw them into the stove, and then the door clanged shut. The stove roared as flames pounded the firebox.

The other women entered the sauna and filled the top bench, while Russ's younger and very pregnant sister Hanna sat on the cooler middle bench at Selma's feet.

Anna, lagging behind the others, seemed none too happy about being relegated to the middle bench. "Let's have steam," she told Esther.

Esther ladled water on the rocks. Steam rose to the ceiling, moved across the room, and stung Aimee's face. Aimee pulled the towel from her body, leaned forward, and covered her face. Then she remembered her tattoo. She pushed her shoulders against the wall and sat with her knees up.

Aimee looked down to Anna, who was sitting across from her, and draped her towel between her legs. Some of the women had folded their towels on the bench and sat on them. Others came empty-handed. It seemed the most natural thing for these eleven women to be naked together in a small room.

The sauna door opened once again. A straggler, the young girlfriend of one of the brothers, squeezed between Annika and Esther, giggling as she did so.

"Remind me of your name," Aimee said.

"Jenna."

"And you're whose girlfriend?"

"Albert's."

"How old are you?"

"Seventeen." She smiled and quickly added, "But I'll be eighteen in October."

"How did you meet?" Aimee felt a sense of camaraderie with the girl, as they were dating brothers.

"We met in Minnesota. We have lots of mutual friends from Church."

"We have churches across the country," Maari interjected, eager to sell Aimee on the benefits of being Lord's People. "The kids get together for fellowship and to find spouses."

Aimee smiled politely. Russ had told her how awkward he felt at those events.

"We have churches across world. I mean *the* world," Anna said. "Paul met me at services in Finland." She cocked her head around to look at Esther. "We need more steam. It's cold down here."

Esther ladled more water on the rocks.

Before the steam reached Aimee's face, Anna demanded, "More."

Aimee wasn't sure how much more she could take. The temperature gauge had already risen five degrees since she had entered the sauna.

As the other women talked amongst themselves, Aimee asked the pregnant Hanna, "Isn't the heat a bit much for you?"

Hannah smiled and shook her head.

"My mother gave birth to me in sauna," Anna said. "I would've given birth to my children in sauna, except I couldn't find midwife with enough *sisu* here."

"Hospitals are much safer," Natalie said.

"Finland has one-third infant mortality rate of United States," Anna said. "Let's have more steam."

"Enough already," Maari said. "Would someone please switch places with her?"

Aimee so badly wanted to volunteer to sit on a lower bench, but she needed to hide her tattoo.

Maari looked at the three girls sitting next to each other. "Annika and Esther, switch with her." Both girls and Jenna moved to the lower bench as Anna took their place. Now controlling the bucket, Anna ladled more water on the stove.

The women groaned.

"What?" Anna said. "You need more *sisu*."

Selma whispered in Aimee's ear, "That means toughness."

"I know. I grew up in the UP."

"And you're a quarter Finn," Laura said. "I'm so happy you're dating Russ. We didn't think he'd ever find somebody."

"You must come to church with us next Sunday," Maari said sternly.

"Yeah, maybe I will." Aimee could see the appeal of being Lord's People. She felt a sense of family she'd never experienced. Of course, she loved her own family. She loved her mother, brother, and even her father, as flawed as he was. It was her love for him that made his abandonment hurt so much. It was the alcohol, and that made the LP Church even more attractive because they didn't drink. The business with the long skirts, no makeup, and ugly underwear was a small price to be part of a large, loving family. She leaned back and closed her eyes, relaxing in the heat as she listened to the women chat.

"I can't believe Russ is dating an *un*." Maari said the words quietly, but Aimee heard her plain as day.

Aimee opened her eyes, and Maari looked away.

"Unbelievers," Selma whispered, apologizing with her eyes. "It's what we call anybody who's not from our church. Please, don't take it personally."

With all her strength, Aimee bridled her tongue as she narrowed her eyes. There was a flipside of the close-knit LP community.

The women continued to talk, and she got to know the sisters and sisters-in-law.

"Have you heard that Margaret has Alzheimer's?" a sister asked.

"I feel so bad for Ben and the kids," a sister-in-law replied.

"Alzheimer's makes me sad," Aimee attempted to contribute to the conversation. "Have you ever seen *The Notebook*?"

The room went quiet and the women stared at Aimee.

Aimee's heart sank. "The movie."

"We don't watch movies," Maari said.

She'd need to be more careful to think before she spoke. It was like she was in a time warp. Definitely a very different culture.

"I read the book," Selma whispered.

As the conversation continued around her, Aimee took to listening for fear of putting her foot in her mouth again. She stewed on the thought that Maari didn't think she was a Christian. She finally gathered her courage. "So what's your church like?"

Maari bristled. "You're a nice girl, Aimee. If only you were a Christian." She stood. "Let's have a breather."

The women filed out of the sauna, but Aimee remained seated, hiding her tattoo. Selma paused at the door. "Are you coming?"

"Maybe I'm the only true Finn here." Aimee's eyes began to sting.

Selma stepped back into the steam room and closed the door.

"Maari likes you, Aimee."

"She doesn't think I'm a Christian."

"She wants you to join the Church."

"I don't know if I can do this." Tears rolled down Aimee's face, camouflaged by her perspiration.

"I hope you do, because I can see how much Russ loves you."

While the women milled about outside wrapped in towels and the girls skinny-dipped in the river, Aimee quickly rinsed off in the shower, patted herself dry, and put on her sexy underwear over her still-damp body. The outside door creaked open, and Aimee quickly pulled her skirt up.

"You had enough, hey?" Maari asked.

"I should go. I have to work early tomorrow morning." Both statements were true, but unrelated.

Back in the house, while the other men were in the garage, Russ watched the youngest kids along with Henri and his older nieces.

"Let's go," Aimee said.

"I haven't had my sauna yet."

"Let's go—now." Aimee held back tears.

"Okay."

When they got in his truck, she let loose. "She doesn't think I'm a Christian. She has herself confused with Jesus Christ."

"Who're you talking about?"

"Your mother. Your mother doesn't think I'm a Christian."

"Well, it's complicated."

"It's complicated?" Aimee challenged Russ as he drove her back to Louisa's. "There's nothing complicated about me being a Christian. She called me an *un*."

"Aimee, that's just a term for someone who doesn't belong to the Church."

"You mean her church. I belong to *the* Church."

Russ's chest rose as he pulled his lips together and breathed deeply through his nose. He exhaled slowly.

"Well?" Aimee was itching for an argument.

"Well, what?" Russ asked timidly.

"Do you think I'm a Christian?"

"Of course I do. Our church wasn't founded until 1896. It doesn't make sense there were no Christians until then."

"Are you a Christian?" Aimee threw another jab, frustrated by arguing with a man so even tempered.

Russ cocked his head as if deep in thought.

Aimee was surprised he didn't have a reflexive answer. "Well?"

Russ glanced over as he began to recite, "I believe in God, the Father almighty, creator of heaven and earth. I believe in Jesus Christ, God's only Son, our Lord, who was conceived by the Holy Spirit, born of the Virgin Mary, suffered under Pontius Pilate, was crucified, died, and was buried; he descended into hell. On the third day he rose again—"

"That's the Apostle's Creed, right?" Aimee interjected before he could finish.

"Yeah."

"And you believe it?"

"You betcha."

"You betcha?" Aimee laughed. "With all your rules, are you telling me LPs gamble?"

"Louisa, Beth tells me you used to be Lord's People." Aimee sat with Beth and Louisa at her kitchen table.

Louisa nodded. "Yes, that's correct."

"Russ's mom doesn't think I'm a Christian." Aimee seethed.

"That's to be expected." Louisa sipped chamomile tea from a straw. Her answer calmed Aimee.

"Why?"

"It's what she's been taught."

"Jesus makes it pretty simple," Aimee said. "If all you did was read the red letters, it doesn't take long to figure out that all you need to do is believe in him."

"And follow him," Louisa added. "Faith without works is dead."

"That sounds legalistic," Beth interjected.

"I'm quoting James. Being a Christ-follower is a commitment that changes us." Louisa studied Aimee's face. "Would you question someone's faith if they were in outright rebellion against God?"

Aimee didn't answer the question immediately, but thought about how she doubted her father's faith. Finally, she nodded.

"We all do it," Louisa said. "It's how we try to make order of the world. The Lord's People do the same thing," she continued, "but their works include attending their church and following their rules."

"Why did you leave the LP church?" Aimee asked.

Louisa leaned back in her chair. "I joined the church to marry Sam. We raised our kids in the church. It wasn't the healthiest place for them, but Sam couldn't see it. I would have left long ago, but it's where all his friends were. All his family."

Aimee frowned. "He wouldn't have had his friends and family if you attended another church?"

"No, dear. That would not have worked."

"Did you lose your friends when you left the church?"

Louisa chuckled. "I didn't lose friends, but I discovered which ones were friends. Those who refused to talk to me weren't my friends after all."

Aimee sipped her tea.

"What are you going to do?" Beth asked.

Aimee massaged her temple. "What do you think I should do?"

Beth reached over and squeezed Aimee's arm. "Do you love Russ?"

"Yes. Very much."

"Does Russ love you?"

"He says he does."

"Well, maybe you should take his mom up on her offer and attend church with them on Sunday," Beth said. "You should see what you're getting into."

Aimee nodded and turned to Louisa. "What do you think?"

"Where are you thinking of going after you graduate?" Louisa seemed to change the subject.

"Wherever I can get a job."

"Well, I would suggest you consider where there are LP churches—and where there are not," Louisa added with a twinkle in her eye.

Chapter 30

"What should I do?" Aimee asked Tammy as she topped off coffee cups for diners at the counter.

"What's the big deal if you switch churches? Russ is a nice guy. It's not like we have a smorgasbord of great guys to choose from around here." Tammy picked up orange- and brown-topped coffee pots and made her rounds on the floor.

The Heikki Lunta bustled with business as parents said their last goodbyes before students started classes and tourists savored the last slice of summer in the Keweenaw.

Mikey put a wad of crumpled bills on the counter. "Tim paid me twelve dollars for the blueberries I picked. Is that enough?"

Aimee smiled. "That'll buy you whatever you want, but Tim told me it's on the house today."

"On the house?" Mikey laughed. "I don't eat on the house. I eat in here."

"That means it's free."

"No, no. I'm not taking anything for free. I have money."

"You'll have to take that up with Tim."

"Tim said I should try the *pannukakku* with the sauce, because he'd make it with the berries *I* picked. And I want bacon."

"I'll put your order in and get your milk."

"Chocolate milk."

"Do cows make any other kind?"

Mikey laughed.

Aimee went to the kitchen window and clipped the order slip to the carousel. "Bacon and *pannukakku* for Mikey," she called to Tim, who was working the grill. Tim was a hands-on owner. It was often the only way Yooper businesses survived.

"Make it two *pannukakku*," Mak bellowed.

Aimee smiled as her uncle took a seat next to Mikey.

"With extra berry sauce," Mak added.

"Extra berry sauce," Mikey echoed.

"Extra berry sauce on two *pannukakkus*," Aimee called through the kitchen window as she scribbled Mak's order on a ticket and clipped it to the carousel. She filled a glass with chocolate milk for Mikey and poured a cup of coffee for her uncle.

"Hi, Uncle Mak."

"*Hyvää päivää.*" Mak set a book on the counter—a journal with the word *Dream* and a picture of puffy white clouds and a brilliant blue sky on the cover.

"You got a new journal, hey?"

"I filled my *Inspire* journal. Been writin' since we got home. I could write a book about last week alone."

Aimee smirked. "I've got another book for you. I met the parents last night."

"Oh?" Mak opened the journal and uncapped his pen.

A bell rang and Aimee walked to the kitchen window.

"Wait, Aimee. Come back," Mak called.

Aimee delivered the *pannukakku* with extra berry sauce to the guys.

Mak set down his pen, picked up his fork, and took a bite. He sipped his coffee and readied his pen again. "How did it go?"

"It went well at first, when I showed up in Louisa's clothes with my hair up and no makeup."

"You wore Lou's clothes?"

"A jean skirt from her Lord's People days. But then I let it slip I went to Pinehurst, and Russ's mom called me an *un*."

"They usually don't say that to your face. She must've had her guard down."

"We were in the sauna. She had everything down."

"Ah." Mak scribbled furiously before he looked at her. "Why are you so sad?"

"Uncle Mak, we didn't go to church until I was fifteen. I thought all churches were basically the same." Aimee fought back tears.

"Da LPs think they have a corner on da truth. Didn't you know that?"

"I do now. His mom invited me to go with them next Sunday, but I don't know if I could be Lord's People. They believe in Jesus, but the Jesus I know from the Bible isn't that concerned with so many rules. What should I do?"

"You should go and tell me all about it next week." Mak's eyes twinkled and he showed his yellowed teeth.

"You'd like that, wouldn't you? You'll have to start eating at the Cornucopia in the evenings if you want to hear about it. I start school next week." Aimee chuckled. "Well, Russ is a nice guy and I love him. I may as well see what it's all about. I guess I'll go."

"Go where?" Russ sat next to Mak.

Aimee smiled at him. "To church with you next Sunday."

Russ groaned.

Aimee poured a cup of coffee for him and warmed Mak's cup.

"More chocolate milk, please," Mikey said.

Aimee refilled his glass, put in Russ's order of the new usual, and made her rounds to other tables.

When she returned, Mak said with his head down and pen hovering over his journal, "So Russ, how do you think it went last night?"

"Are you going to write my answer down?"

"No, no." Mak set his pen down and closed the journal. "Not now," he muttered. "By the way, you look good, if I can say that about another guy."

"Thanks, but you can't write this down." Russ sighed. "It went as expected. Did Aimee tell you I had to move back home?"

"I didn't say anything to anybody." Aimee leaned against the back service counter.

"Why did you move home?" asked Mak.

"Blasted government." Russ went on a rant of the saga, starting months prior with the helicopter circling over his cabin and ending with the eviction notice he found on his door. "So I can't move back into my cabin until I get a functioning septic system."

"They kicked you out because you have running water and no septic?"

"Yup."

"Why don't you pull your pump so you don't have running water?"

Russ slapped the counter. "Brilliant."

"Yes, and why does everybody say *you're* da genius?" Mak snorted.

Mikey followed suit.

"But how am I going to cut up that copper without running water? I only got a few pieces sliced off before we went to Milwaukee."

"Didn't you say you have a cistern above your shower?"

"That's the best idea I've had all day."

"*I* had," Mak said.

"What?" Russ looked at him, confused.

Aimee retrieved Russ's breakfast.

When she served him, Russ said, "Good news, I figured out a way…"

"*I* figured out a way," Mak corrected.

Russ glanced at him. "We figured out a way for me to get back into my cabin. I'll pull the electric pump and reinstall the hand pump. If the building inspector is cool with that and I can get in this week, we don't need to go to church on Sunday."

"Oh, I want to go to church with you. I've got to see what

this is about."

Mak slid his journal to his left, leaned forward, and blocked Russ's view as he made notes.

"He's writing," Mikey yelled.

"You can't use this," Russ said.

"Russ, I want to go to your church. If we're serious, we need to see if this is going to work. I'm not sure I can become another person. Do you want me to change who I am for you?"

"Aren't *you* trying to change *me*? Cut my hair and beard, buy me ridiculous clothes—with *my* money—have me give up my cabin, give up my church?"

"I'm not saying you have to give up your church. Maybe I'll give up my church."

"My church is very different."

"Bella Atkinson says both people need to give things up and create a common culture. I'm not sure how we're going to do that, but I'm willing to try because I love you, my adorable mountain man."

Russ smiled.

"Well?" Aimee waited for a reply.

Russ looked around. "I love you, too, buttercup," he said softly.

"What'd you say?" Mak asked. "I didn't catch that. You called her butter-what?"

"Buttercup," Mikey yelled. "He said, 'I love you, buttercup.'"

Russ groaned.

Chapter 31

"*I*'ve never seen so many fifteen-passenger vans in one parking lot," Aimee said as she and Russ approached the Lord's People's church, a plain building with a high, pitched roof and few windows. "Except maybe at a car dealership."

As Russ parked, Aimee looked in the visor mirror at her naked face. As self-conscious as she felt without makeup, she knew she'd be too conspicuous in his church with it. She tucked a few loose locks back into her bun. She adjusted her shirt and jean skirt. "How do I look?"

Russ smiled broadly. "Beautiful."

As they entered the building, a man greeted them, "Grace to you."

Other women in the narthex were dressed similarly with their hair up and no makeup, but Aimee had missed on one detail. Their long skirts were linen—not denim—and solid, drab colors. "I'm not dressed up enough," Aimee whispered to Russ.

"You're fine." Russ stroked the stubble on his face, which had grown since Thursday, when he got back into his cabin.

Aimee raised an eyebrow.

"Russell?"

"I suppose the women consider jean skirts more casual wear. Don't worry about it."

"Grace to you," a woman said with a warm smile and extended her hand to Aimee.

"Hi."

The woman looked down at Aimee's skirt. "Are you a visitor?"

"Yes," Aimee said.

The woman nodded, and then said to another, "Grace to you."

A man in his late sixties approached them with his hand outstretched.

"Grace to you, Pastor." Russ shook his hand.

"And who's this?" the man asked.

"Aimee, my girlfriend," Russ said.

"Welcome." He shook Aimee's hand. "Grace to you."

Another man approached and greeted Russ and Aimee with a "grace to you."

"Hey, Lappi," Russ said.

"It's been good to see you attending services again. When will you start the garage?" the man asked.

"Any time," said Russ. "I have your job and a kitchen remodel for Jarvi, so I can juggle both. Just good to have some business rolling again."

They walked through the narthex with a few more grace-to-you utterances and into the sanctuary, which appeared to take up most of the building.

"What's with the grace-to-you greetings?" Aimee whispered.

"It's the way several epistles begin," Russ said. "It's a greeting of fellowship." He looked around to make sure no one was in earshot. "It's like a secret handshake—you're greeted if you're part of the Church."

"So I'm part of the Church?" Aimee asked.

"They seem to think so. You're dressed the part. They probably think you're visiting from another congregation. There are Lord's People churches all over the country."

In the thousand-seat sanctuary, clusters of families stood talking to others while well-behaved children stayed close. Newborn infants cooed mildly in their mothers' arms.

Russ pointed off to the right. "That's our pew."

Sitting behind his parents, Aimee was glad to see familiar faces.

"Grace to you, my son," Maari greeted Russ. She smiled warmly at Aimee and then turned back around.

"Grace to you," Aimee blurted out.

Maari half-turned and said, "Hello."

Russ shrugged.

The organist struck a minor chord, and the congregants fell into their pews. Following Russ's lead, Aimee took a hymnal from a pew pocket. He pointed to a board that was to the right of the chancel with numbers slid into slots. She wasn't familiar with the song, so she read the words as the congregants slowly and somberly sang the first verse, "I yearn for the end of tribulation, when from misery, Christ shall set me free from all my struggles and my woes."

Aimee reflected on her dad's life and the addiction from which he couldn't break free. She too yearned for the end of tribulation. After five verses, she yearned for the end of the song. Perhaps the next song would be upbeat—a celebratory song rejoicing in salvation. The organist began another slow hymn in a minor key, and then another mournful hymn, and another.

There was no release for children's church or Sunday school. All the cherubs sat contentedly in the pews for what seemed to Aimee a dry sermon. Nonetheless, as the speaker read the passage in King James English and paraphrased it in old English, the power of God's word moved in Aimee's heart.

God forgives us our sins, even though we're undeserving. Aimee was saddened by the state in which she left her father in Milwaukee. She had been forgiven by God, so why was it so hard for her to forgive her father? Tears moistened her eyes, and Russ reached over and squeezed her hand and then quickly let go. She sniffled, and Maari glanced back at her and passed back a tissue. Aimee nodded her thanks and blew her nose.

When the service ended, Maari came around the pew, sat next to Aimee, and passed her another tissue. Maari put her hand on Aimee's arm. "Believe thy sins are forgiven thee in the Savior's holy name and blood."

Aimee snuck a sideways peek at Russ, who shrugged. "Thank you," she said to Maari.

"Grace to you, my daughter." Maari patted her shoulder and walked away.

After the service, Russ grabbed her hand as they walked through the parking lot to his truck.

"There's a nice diner in the village. Should we go have lunch?" he asked.

"Yes." Aimee beamed. Things were changing. A little affection in public, and he was willing to be seen with her in the village.

In the truck, Aimee reclined her seat back, unbuttoned the top of her jean skirt, and unzipped the zipper.

"Whoa, lady," Russ said. "What are you doing?"

"I'm getting more comfortable. Don't worry, I have shorts on under this."

Russ shook his head.

Aimee pulled the visor mirror down. She let her hair down and tossed it left and right until it landed on a shoulder. She dug in her purse, pulled out lipstick, and applied it. She puckered her lips and made a smacking sound. "Okay, I'm ready."

Russ nodded nervously. He put his truck in drive, and they drove to the diner.

"I needed to hear that message today." Aimee gave her hair a final pat and flipped the visor up.

"Did you really like the service?" Russ looked at her in disbelief.

"The message spoke to me. I need to forgive my dad. I guess God can use any church, although it was too somber for my tastes. I'm more of a joyful person." Aimee frowned. "Is the music ever more upbeat?"

"No. The Lord's People would find the music at Pinehurst worldly."

"Well, maybe we can go back and forth between the two churches."

"That wouldn't go over well. You only get the grace-to-you greeting if you keep coming, exclusively." Russ glanced over. "I guess it might seem a bit odd, but I haven't known anything different."

"I see." Aimee thought of Louisa's advice to find a job in a place where there was not an LP congregation. "Will you come with me to church next week?"

His Adam's apple jumped high in his throat. He nodded.

"And sit with me, instead of hiding out in the back?"

Russ nodded again.

At the village diner, after the waitress delivered their plates, Russ's pastor and his wife stepped into the diner.

"Grace to you," the pastor greeted Russ, and then did a double take when he noticed Aimee. "Russell, is this the young lady you brought to church today?"

"Yes, Pastor, this is Aimee."

"You should not be dating a worldly woman."

"Excuse me." Aimee couldn't stop herself. "I'm sitting right here. I can hear you."

The pastor shot Aimee a look of disdain and turned back to Russ. "Be ye holy for I am holy, sayeth the Lord. Ye must be set apart. Not of this world."

The pastor's wife lowered her head.

"I'll see you next week," the pastor continued. "You must repent."

"I'm going to Aimee's church next week," Russ said in an odd display of confidence. Aimee smiled at him.

The pastor's face flashed anger. He stiffened and walked away.

Chapter 32

"*H*ow did you stay in the LP church for as long as you did?" Aimee asked Louisa as they sat at her kitchen table while water heated in the kettle and a cool evening breeze pushed through the window screens.

Louisa's disease had noticeably progressed while Aimee had been at the house over the last couple weeks. She shuffled her feet when she walked across her maple hardwood floor. She paused and lifted each foot with great intent when she stepped onto the living room area rug. Yet she carried herself with such peace, as though life was proceeding as planned.

"There are good things about the Lord's People. They have a real sense of community." Louisa leaned to one side, using the momentum to throw her arm on the table.

The kettle whistled, and Aimee retrieved it. She packed a tea ball with loose chamomile flowers and put it in the kettle. "I don't fit into the community. I'm too worldly."

"You might be surprised at how worldly some LPs are. The ones who are most accepted in the church do a better job of hiding their worldliness."

"Isn't that hypocritical?" Aimee pulled cups from the cupboard and grabbed a straw from the drawer for Louisa.

"They put heavy loads on others' shoulders, so people have little choice but to be hypocritical. Those who don't want to go to the church do so anyhow to maintain appearances and stay a part of their community. They're not allowed to have TVs, but many watch movies on their computers."

Aimee leaned against the counter waiting for the tea to steep. "Why do they have so many rules?"

"I think they're afraid."

"Of what?"

"Of the world. Of sin." Louisa shook her head. "They put a fence around their lives, all these little rules that keep them far from sin, like perimeter security that's meant to protect them. But they've confused those rules with sin itself, and instead of the fence protecting them, it shuts the world out. And the people aren't given the freedom to question the rules. We all make judgements on what is right and wrong. The problem is when judgement crowds out love."

"I know some Lord's People from waitressing at the Heikki Lunta, and they're always so nice to me—and good tippers. I didn't think religion would be such a big issue for Russ and me. I mean, I go to church and believe in Jesus." Aimee blew air through pursed lips. "They don't even think I'm a Christian."

"It cuts both ways. Many churches think they're the only ones who have the truth," Louisa said. "I know believers who question the salvation of the Lord's People."

Aimee poured their tea. "As irritated as I was by the way the pastor treated me, I was surprised that the message touched my heart. It was on forgiveness."

"Hmmm." Louisa sipped tea through a straw.

"I was ready to forgive my dad when I went to Milwaukee, but he ended up being so unrepentant—clueless as to how much he hurt me." The all-too-familiar anger welled up in Aimee's heart. "Sometimes I hate him. That's not a very Christian thing to say, is it?"

"Maybe not, dear, but he wasn't a very Christian father. I hate what he did." Louisa spoke softly.

"Me, too, but I don't want to hate him. I want to forgive him, but he won't apologize."

Louisa nodded. "It takes both parties to reconcile, but you can choose a heart of forgiveness."

"I thought he'd soften considering he's dying."

"People tend to die like they lived. Where do people get this idea that dying people are more noble and insightful? Maybe from movies."

"I read a book—*Tuesdays with Morrie*. He had ALS. Did you ever read that?" Aimee asked.

"Yes. I read it. And I suspect Morrie Schwartz was insightful long before he knew he was dying. People who live well tend to die well, and those who live poorly often die poorly."

Cradling her cup, Aimee leaned back in her chair with her legs crossed.

"I should cut back on my liquids," Louisa said. "It's getting more inconvenient to go to the bathroom. I need to go now." Louisa scooted her chair back. She swung her other arm onto the table and leaned forward, supporting some of her weight with her forearms, and stood. She shuffled to the bathroom, with Aimee following close behind.

As Louisa crossed over the bathroom threshold, her legs crumpled underneath her. Aimee tried to catch her, but Louisa slipped between her hands and landed on the bathroom floor, legs folded awkwardly underneath, her torso pitched forward, resting on her right shoulder.

"Louisa," Aimee screamed.

"I'm okay," Louisa said. "Can you help me up?"

Aimee grabbed her under the arms and pulled her to a seated position. She lifted her to her feet. She was surprised by her own strength, to have lifted a woman of about equal size. "What happened?"

Louisa glanced at a thin wooden transition strip that separated the maple hardwood and the bathroom linoleum floors. "I tripped." She had toppled on the most benign obstacle.

Louisa seemed more embarrassed than upset. Aimee didn't press the matter, just helped her pull down her pants

and sit on the toilet. When Louisa was done, Aimee turned the
knob on the bidet sprayer. She helped her stand and pulled up
her pants. She walked backward in front of Louisa on her way
out of the bathroom, holding her arms. "Would you like more
tea?" Aimee asked as they entered the kitchen.

"No, I better not. Help me to the living room, and I'll sit in
my recliner until Beth gets home."

Aimee guided her through the kitchen and into the living room, but Louisa paused before the rug. Her face showed
anxiety.

"Let me get that for you." Aimee rolled up the rug and set
it aside. "Do you think it's time for a wheelchair?"

Louisa's chest rose and fell. "I'm afraid so. I move into
High Cliff on Thursday, and they have chairs there. I just need
to stay upright until then." Louisa smiled.

Those who live well, die well, Aimee thought as she wiped
a tear from her eye.

Louisa shuffled along until she got to the recliner. Aimee
helped her turn, and Louisa plopped down. Aimee put a pillow on her lap, a Kindle on her pillow, and her arms in position to tap the screen to turn pages. The e-reader was a gift
from Louisa's son, who kept it stocked with the great classics
Louisa loved.

Later that night, Aimee readied herself for bed early and
crawled under a sheet. As exhausted as she was, she couldn't
sleep with the evening sun brightening the room and acrid
feelings of rejection darkening her soul.

She cried, releasing tension and stress. Tears came harder,
and she curled up, buried her face in her pillow, and sobbed
until she got drowsy. She drifted off to sleep. She dreamed
in short clips of her childhood with her mom and dad. Her
dad watched her from the bleachers as she received her di-
ploma, and then he disappeared. She searched the crowd, but
he wasn't there. She called for him, and again he was in front
of her. He lifted her and held her over a waterfall, and she
screamed. She yelled at her dad, telling him how despicable
he was. He smirked at her with contempt. Then a tear rolled

down his cheek. He mouthed, "I love you." She felt pity for him and she forgave him.

When she woke, twilight was fading into night, and she heard voices downstairs. Danny and Beth were talking to Louisa. Aimee wasn't sure if the dream had been a nightmare or a gift. It was unpleasant, but it felt good to scream at her father. And she had felt relief when she forgave him.

Aimee knew what she had to do. She got out of bed and sat at her desk with a pen and legal pad.

"Dear Dad," Aimee started the letter to her father. "I love you and I forgive you." She put her pen down and wiped her eyes. She had reflexively written the beginning line. She wanted it to be true, but it was so hard to say.

Why couldn't she be more like Rob? Why did she have to care? They say the son carries the burdens of his father, but it's the daughter who's left to clean up the mess. What a mess her father had made.

She thought back to her childhood, and the rest of the letter came to her. The letter had been waiting to be written. She allowed her hand to cooperate and spell out the words.

She folded the letter. She'd mail it in the morning.

Chapter 33

Looking at his side mirrors, Russ backed his truck until he neared his construction trailer. A camera he had mounted above his license plate showed the narrowing gap between the trailer hitch and receiver in a video monitor on the rearview mirror. He put the truck in park, and as he got out, his phone rang.

"Russ Saarinen," he answered.

"Hey, Russ, Clyde here." Clyde Jarvi was the man with a kitchen remodel.

"Grace to you," Russ said.

"Well, yes, um." Jarvi hemmed and hawed and then blurted, "We're going to have to pass on that kitchen remodel."

"That's no problem," Russ said. "You let me know if you decide to move forward with it." He'd have work on Lappi's garage for the next month, anyhow.

Russ cranked the tongue jack, and the trailer lowered onto the ball. He pulled the trailer out of the ditch and onto the road. He drove past Koski's, wondering if he'd ever come down on the price of the property. He passed Maribel's and shook his head at the thought of Vance being pinned down in his car.

Danny had told him that Maribel had gone through a competency hearing in July. The judge found no reason to confiscate her guns, but after the incident, Danny confiscated them anyhow. A new competency hearing was scheduled. Maribel insisted that Vance was stealing from her and was indignant that law enforcement didn't take her complaints seriously.

When Danny told him that, Russ didn't mention the pocket watch that fell out of Vance's briefcase at the diner. Danny was a good friend, but he worked for the government. Russ wasn't sure they'd treat Vance fairly. His story seemed credible enough.

As Russ pulled onto US Highway 41, his phone rang. "Russ Saarinen," he answered.

"Yeah, Russ." It was Lappi.

"Hey, I'll be there in fifteen minutes. I just hitched my trailer."

"Yeah, about that…" Lappi fell silent.

Finally, Russ asked. "Are you there?"

"Yeah, I'm here. Russ, I can't have you working on the garage."

"What?" Fury boiled Russ's blood. "You got to be kidding me." It was no coincidence that two LPs called within fifteen minutes of each other to cancel work. "Why are you canceling?"

"I heard you've been doing the devil's work. I've gotta go."

Russ turned around and headed back to the cabin. As he neared his parking ditch, his phone rang again. "Arg." Who was it now? He checked his phone. His dad.

"Russell, what's going on?"

"You tell me." Russ parked his truck.

"I got a call from the pastor telling me I need to get my family in order."

"He's apparently already had words with Lappi and Jarvi. They called this morning to cancel my jobs." Russ slammed his hand on the steering wheel.

"Look, Russell, whatever's going on between you and that woman, you need to get to church this Sunday."

"Do you think I'm going back to that church after how

they treated me?"

Karl didn't respond, but Russ could hear breathing on the other end.

"I'll see you Sunday," his dad finally said and then hung up.

Russ spent the next few days working in his hole with renewed determination to develop the copper specimens, his only source of income. He lost valuable time rigging up a hose to the cistern, and he missed seeing Aimee. She was back in school and was buried in homework when she wasn't in class or working.

On Thursday, when she didn't have classes, Russ met Aimee in a corner booth at The Stope, a newer mine-themed restaurant and bar with a bowling alley and arcade. They ordered pizza.

"I think you'll like Pinehurst," Aimee said after Russ reported on his work saga.

"I'll try it again, but I'm not sure how to round up business outside of the Lord's People. I can't survive without work."

Aimee's phone rang. Her eyes got big when she saw the incoming number. "It's a 414 number." She answered it, said yes a few times, and then her mouth gaped open and tears began to flow. She sobbed through the rest of the call before hanging up.

"What's wrong?" Russ suspected the worst.

"My dad died."

"Oh, Aimee." Russ got up and scooted in next to her. He put his arm around her and she leaned against him and sobbed into his chest. He caressed her shoulder at a loss for what to say. There was nothing to say.

The pizza came, but they left it untouched.

After some time, Aimee regained her composure and told Russ the details. Her dad had passed away that morning. Kara said Frank's body would be cremated according to his wishes and the ashes would be available the following week.

"I don't know if he got my letter." Aimee's tears spilled over again. "I wrote him a letter that said I forgive him and I mailed it on Monday. I doubt it got there in time."

"There's a chance it did." Russ squeezed her tighter. "I've gotten letters a day after they were postmarked." Even as he said the words, he knew chances were slim it had gotten to the big city that quickly.

Aimee took a deep breath and wiped her tears on a napkin. "Thanks, but what if he didn't get it?"

Chapter 34

"Mom, where are you?" Aimee asked over her cell phone as she stood outside Sophia's apartment door.

"What was that?" Sophia asked between heavy breaths.

Aimee's heart sank. "Mom, tell me where you are. I'll call an ambulance." She couldn't bear the thought of losing both of her parents in the same week.

Sophia panted over the phone. "I need to catch my breath. I'm okay." Her panting slowed to deep breathing. "Okay, caught it."

"Mom, what's going on? Are you having another heart attack?"

"I'm at Lorna's doing the Zumba videos. Exercising." Sophia laughed. "Did you ever think you'd see the day?"

Aimee had last seen her mom at Senja's prayer group where she was still upbeat after having reunited with Frank. "I was hoping you'd get on a program, but I don't want you to push yourself too hard."

"Lorna's videos came in the mail Monday. We're going through the program before we go to the instructor training in Minneapolis. Then we'll open our own Zumba studio. We just need to find a place to rent."

"Wow, Mom. I don't know what to say, but we need to talk."

"What's wrong?"

Aimee's throat tightened. She couldn't tell her over the phone. "When will you be home?"

"Not till later. Lorna's waiting for me to restart the video, and then I need to go get something to eat. I've been so busy, I haven't eaten since breakfast."

"Am I talking to Sophia Mallon? You sound like my mother, but who are you?"

Sophia laughed.

"Mom, I need to see you now. I'll meet you at Lorna's. I'll pick up dinner."

"I guess that'll be fine. Get me a salad—no croutons."

Aimee could hardly believe her ears. Her mother was turning over a new leaf, but would the news of Frank's death send her back over the edge?

She picked up deli salads at the co-op and then drove to Lorna's house, an old mining house outside Quincy. It was similar to the house Aimee grew up in, but well maintained.

When she arrived, Sophia and Lorna were still exercising. Lorna, dressed in spandex pants and a sports bra, made exaggerated movements mimicking the Zumba video. Sophia followed a half beat behind with a quarter of the range of motion. Her sweatpants were pulled high on her waist. Her T-shirt, soaked in perspiration, was tucked into her pants. She wore a sweatband around her head.

"Hey, ladies," Aimee yelled over the music.

Lorna paused the video, and Sophia stretched her arms out.

"How about we hug after you shower? Is it safe that you're exercising this hard?"

"I'm keeping my heart rate below 150," Sophia said between heavy pants. "Did you get the food?"

"Yup, right here." Aimee motioned to a bag she had set on the table. "I got a salad for you, too, Aunt Lorna. You should hear this, too."

Lorna sighed. "Well, okay. I suppose we can get back to this after we have a bite to eat, and then we'll take that picture." She pointed to a white sheet draped over a bookshelf. "That's our photo studio."

"Mom, we need to talk." Aimee's eyes began to sting.

"Oh, honey, what's wrong?" Sophia placed a hand on her arm.

Aimee had planned on being the strong one, but she couldn't stop the tears from flowing. "Dad died," she said flatly.

"Oh, my child." Sophia embraced her.

Aimee was comforted but aware she was absorbing her mom's sweat. "Mom, you're wet."

Sophia laughed as she released her.

"Aren't you upset?" Aimee asked.

"Of course. He was my husband."

"I thought you'd be devastated." Aimee studied her mom's face.

"I cried for ten years. I didn't lose him just now. I got him back." Sophia's eyes were moist. "Now let's eat."

Lorna plated the salads, and Aimee relayed the details of Frank's passing and his cremation.

As they ate, Lorna explained Sophia's new program—exercise, supplements, essential oils. "And she's on a Paleo diet."

"What's that?"

"Sophia only eats what the cavemen ate—meat, vegetables, fruit, and nuts. No grains."

"Do you think you can stick with it?" Aimee asked her mother incredulously.

"Sure. Lorna's keeping me accountable." Sophia lifted her chin. "And Senja's praying for me."

Lorna patted Sophia on the shoulder. "Your mom's been doing a great job."

Sophia beamed. "Frank's gonna be surprised when he sees me."

Aimee quickly looked up from her salad. "Mom, Dad's not with us anymore."

"Oh, you know what I mean."

"You mean in heaven?"

"No, next week, when we pick up his ashes. We should take him to Lambeau."

"He'd like that. Aimee felt laughter rising. It felt good to laugh in the midst of sorrow.

"By the way, tell your boyfriend he can pick up his Drumi." Lorna motioned to a stack of cardboard boxes stacked in the corner of the kitchen. "My shipment came in."

"I can grab it for him."

"I don't take credit. Especially from him," Lorna said. "He doesn't have steady enough work."

Aimee laughed. "Especially now that he's fallen from the good graces of his church."

"How's that?" Lorna asked. "Mak said you visited the Lord's People church last weekend. Didn't it go well?"

"The service wasn't so bad, but the pastor's a piece of work." Aimee told them about her experience. "Russ is coming to church with me this Sunday. I hope he likes it."

Chapter 35

"Where're all the cars?" Russ asked as he and Aimee approached Pinehurst Church, a log building with a low, red roof and a number of windows across the front. Balsam firs stood like sentries on either side of the building.

"We're a little early," Aimee said.

"The service starts in five minutes." Russ pulled into the parking lot.

Aimee pulled down the visor mirror. She pulled lipstick out of her shorts pocket, applied another coat, and smacked her lips. She tossed her hair until it landed on her shoulder and pushed aside a few locks that had fallen on her face. "I'm ready."

As Aimee and Russ approached the building, a man held the door. "Good morning."

A few of the men in the lobby wore suits, but most were in jeans or even shorts. Russ certainly wasn't underdressed in the preppy ensemble Aimee had picked out for him.

"Good morning." A woman with a warm smile and a name tag that read *Nancy* extended her hand to Russ.

"Grace to you." Russ shook her hand.

"Are you a visitor?"

"Yes," said Russ.

"I'm so glad you're here. We have two services. Since you're here for the first, I hope you'll join our adult discussion in the basement during the second hour."

Russ hadn't seen this type of enthusiasm since the sales people sold him clothes at Mayfair Mall.

A middle-aged man approached them with his hand stretched out to Russ. "And who's this?" He directed the question to Aimee.

"This is my boyfriend, Russ."

"It's a pleasure to meet you, Russ. I'm Chip Atkinson. I'm the pastor here."

Russ recognized him from the last time he visited the church, when he quietly slipped in the back and left early without talking to anybody.

Music began to play from the sanctuary.

"That's my cue." Pastor Chip smiled and left.

Russ and Aimee jostled through the lobby. People greeted Russ with eager smiles and firm handshakes. A young woman hugged Aimee and asked about her first week back in school. Aimee told her the news of her father, and they hugged again.

In the sanctuary, a rock band with a piano, acoustic and bass guitars, drums, and several singers played an upbeat song. The congregants were standing and singing, some with their hands raised and eyes closed.

"I usually sit with the college students, but let's sit by Beth, Danny, Senja, and Louisa." Aimee led the way along the right side.

Russ saw Louisa in her wheelchair next to the first row of seats. He groaned inwardly, and as he feared, Aimee proceeded to the first pew and stood next to Danny, leaving an open space between her and the pastor. How conspicuous.

Decidedly uncomfortable, Russ wished he could sit. He would have, if he hadn't been standing right next to the pastor. The words for the song were displayed on a projector screen. As he didn't know the tune, he studied the lyrics. *On that day I was set free, from sin which had a hold on me. And I will never be the same again. You changed my life and made me yours. Put a new song in my heart. I want to dance and worship you, my Lord.*

He wasn't sure if that was orthodoxy, with the dancing and all, but the lyrics of the closing verse were okay. Some thoughts on heaven. *No more crying, no more fear, no more pain, no more tears.*

After three songs with rhythmic beats, wispy verses, and overly repetitive choruses, the congregation was allowed to sit. A sixty-something man introduced himself as Mike Rogers and announced upcoming events. The ushers took an offering while the worship team, as Mike called them, performed. Then Pastor Chip led a prayer time. He asked the congregation for their prayer requests or praises. Aimee stood and shared the sad news of her dad's death, and various others offered intimate details of their lives—a troubled pregnancy, a brother on drugs, a mother with cancer. The worship leader asked the congregation to stand again, and they sang more pop songs. The congregants sat while children scurried to children's church, and then Pastor Chip patted Russ on the back and walked to the lectern.

Russ had seen most of the service once before, but he took particular note of how it contrasted with the Lord's People. Pinehurst did church differently.

Pastor Chip's sermon was on First Peter 1, about being born again to a living hope, not conforming to the world, and being holy. "We Christians need to be set apart, distinguished from the world."

Russ laughed inwardly, because that's what his pastor had told them in the restaurant. The LP church was probably too set apart, but in his view, Pinehurst had a long way to go to look different from the world.

"So what did you think?" Aimee asked after the sermon.

"It was good," Russ said.

Aimee beamed. "That's great. Well, then let's attend the adult table groups."

Russ sighed. She had misinterpreted his polite response as

an open door to suggest they stay. He felt exhausted, but she seemed happy, and she needed that after the week she'd had.

The adult table discussions were in a wing of the building that served as a dual-purpose gymnasium and fellowship hall. Tables were set up, and a dividing curtain separated men and women.

Russ sat at an empty table, thinking that if no one joined him, he'd wait for Aimee out in the truck. He wasn't able to sit in peace for more than a minute when a few men at another table confused his aloneness for loneliness and moved to his table.

They introduced themselves. One of the men passed out sheets of paper with questions. The first question was easy to answer. "Describe a time when you had difficulty fitting into a new group?"

"Right now," Russ said.

The men laughed, and they each in turn shared humbling stories. About fifteen minutes into the discussion, Mike Rogers joined them, sitting next to Russ.

The next question was more of a command. "Describe the hope you felt after being born again."

The man to Russ's right started with his testimony of how God turned his life around. One day, he hit rock bottom and pulled off the road. He told Jesus he was a sinner and he asked him into his heart. From that moment on, he was a new man. When he finished his inspiring tale, all the men stared at Russ.

Russ finally said, "Can you go around the other way?"

The other men responded to the command, each telling in turn of the hope they felt after saying a similar prayer.

After Mike Rogers shared his transformation story, he asked Russ, "What hope did you feel after you were born again?"

"I don't know. I've been a believer as long as I can remember."

"You've never repented and accepted Christ?" Mike asked.

"I repent all the time," Russ said, somewhat baffled by the question.

"If you don't know when you committed your life to the Lord, how could you possibly know you were born again?" another man asked.

Russ felt his defenses rise at the challenge in the man's question. "I don't remember my first birth, yet I'm here."

The man looked at him solemnly. "True converts know their story of before and after Christ."

"My faith is in Christ—not in a prayer." The nerve of these guys to judge his salvation. Russ left the building and waited in his truck until Aimee got out.

"Oh, there you are." Aimee climbed in the truck. "Did you like it? What did you think?" Her face was more expectant than inquisitive.

Russ knew what she wanted to hear, but he couldn't help himself. "They don't even think I'm a Christian." He realized his tone was harsh when Aimee's smiled flipped upside down. Russ tried to speak more calmly as he shared his impressions of the church. Irreverent music. Casual clothing. "And we're not saved through our works, but they think saying one prayer makes it all good. Then they don't even live like Christians."

"Are you saying I'm not a Christian?" Aimee turned the tables so quickly she threw him off guard.

"No, that's not what I'm saying. But what's wrong with having a little modesty, at least when we go to church?"

"Russell Saarinen, you did *not* go there."

Russ was tired of being pushed around. He stood firm. "You asked me what I thought."

"You're the one who was streaking through the hotel in your boxer shorts," Aimee said in one of the most sarcastic tones he had ever heard. "And when I let you back in the room, you weren't too quick to get dressed. I know what was on your mind."

Russ snorted. He knew what Aimee meant, but she was wrong. "That was the last thing on my mind."

"What? You're in a hotel room with your girlfriend and you don't even find me attractive enough to be tempted?" Aimee looked out the passenger window. "There's Danny and

Beth. I'll get a ride from them." She jumped out and slammed the door behind her before Russ could protest. He wasn't even sure he wanted to.

Chapter 36

"What was I thinking?" Aimee glanced at Sophia, who sat in the passenger's seat on their overnight trip to Milwaukee to pick up Frank's ashes.

Summer had ended in the Keweenaw. Yellows, reds, and oranges appeared on the tips of tree branches. As they drove south into Wisconsin, trees were still green on the edges of golden fields. Aimee was anxious to find out if her dad had received the letter, but at least she didn't have to worry about maxing out her credit cards. She was on more stable footing financially, living at the farmhouse rent free. Her future was looking brighter, except for her relationship with Russ.

"He's not going anywhere with his life," she continued. "He's too afraid to take risks. He doesn't love me enough to leave that crazy church."

"I thought he was nice. He's kind of a geek, not as charming as your dad, but a nice guy."

"He's not the only nice guy out there." Keeping one eye on the road, Aimee looked across rolling hills to wind turbines in the distance. There was so much of the world yet to see. "I think I was with him out of convenience."

"Uh-huh," Sophia said quietly.

Aimee wasn't sure if she was concurring with her or just letting her know she was listening. "Mom, what do you think I should do?"

"You have to decide that for yourself. My folks didn't like Frank at all, but I was in love. I'm glad I didn't listen to them, because he was my soulmate."

"It's hard to get advice. Louisa is evasive. Senja said she wasn't qualified."

Sophia laughed out loud.

"What's so funny?"

"Oh, Senja was so in love once. Her and a guy named Sherman dated for a while."

"What happened?"

"I don't know. I was just a kid. You've just got to make sure you're on the same page. Frank and I were always on the same page, but not everybody has it as good as us."

Aimee shook her head. Her mom was delusional, but there was no harm now in Sophia thinking the man was a saint. A ghost couldn't hit her. Dead men can never leave.

"Russ and I aren't on the same page. Louisa said he'd grow up, but I don't think it's a matter of his maturity. He's too different of a person."

"Here are Frank's belongings." Kara set a ragged backpack on the desk.

Sophia eagerly hugged it to herself before unzipping it. A foul smell of dried beer and cigarette ashes came from the bag. She began taking items out. A single pair of pants, shorts, two T-shirts, a hoodie sweatshirt, boots, socks, and underwear. Sophia opened the front pocket and found Frank's wallet and a coin purse.

Aimee's heart sank. No letter. "So that's all he had?" she asked Kara.

"And this." Kara held out the envelope with Aimee's handwriting addressed to Frank Mallon c/o Kara Sanders.

Hope rose in Aimee's heart. Maybe Kara had read it to Frank.

"Go ahead. Take it."

Aimee willed her arm to reach for the letter. She turned it over. The seal had not been broken. Her eyes filled with tears, and she buried her face in her hands and sobbed. She felt her mother's arm over her shoulder and Kara standing on her other side.

"You take as much time as you need," Kara said.

"Cry it out." Sophia clasped Aimee's hands.

Aimee cried until her eyes could produce no more tears. She regained her composure and put the letter in her purse.

"Here's a card for the funeral home. You can stop by there during business hours to pick up the ashes. Are you going to plan a funeral?"

Sophia shrugged.

"I think we'll have a private ceremony," Aimee said.

Sophia smiled at that.

"Will you spread his ashes?" Kara asked.

"Oh, I haven't thought of that," Sophia said with excitement.

"Well, I want to advise you not to spread them all, if you do, because you might regret not holding on to them or having spread them in the wrong place."

"There's a lot to think about being a widow." Sophia lifted her chin, as if her new responsibilities gave her life meaning.

Kara smiled. "Frank seemed to adore you."

"I adore him."

"Come on, Mom. Let's go get Dad's ashes so we can get on the road and be home at a decent time." Aimee stuffed Frank's belongings into the backpack.

"Yes, let's go get him."

In the car, Aimee explained the letter of forgiveness. "I wish I had sent it sooner."

"It doesn't matter. He loves you." Sophia held Frank's bag.

Aimee pulled the letter from her purse and handed it to her mother. "You can read it." She put the car in reverse and backed out.

"Oh, no. I want to hear it in your voice. You read it to me."

"I'm driving." Aimee glanced at her mother as she pulled out on the street.

"Read it to me later." Sophia looked out the passenger window.

As they drove to the funeral home, Aimee grieved her loss—not just Frank's death, but the loss of him as a father years ago. The betrayal, even though ten years prior, seemed raw and in some ways more difficult to handle than his death. She was baffled by her mother's positive attitude. Sophia seemed like a different, yet familiar, person—the mother who raised Aimee, but had gone missing for a decade. "Why did Dad leave?"

"He was a free spirit. That's why he liked over-the-road hauling so much."

"He drove truck?"

"Yeah, when you were young. But he lost his CDL when his blood sugar was out of control. He kind of spiraled downhill from there."

Aimee checked the address on the business card. Driving slowly, she searched the fronts of buildings for the corresponding numbers. "But what kind of dad would leave his family?" Having been deprived of a real argument with her dad, Aimee wanted answers. Why was her mother such a stalwart defender of the narcissistic man?

"Oh, Aimee. You told me you forgave him. Why do you seem so angry?"

"Humph. I forgave him so I could start healing, but it still hurts. And it hurts so much because he was so unrepentant." Aimee pulled into the parking lot of the funeral home.

"Your dad has trouble saying he's sorry. He said sorry by coming home."

"He was on his way to Lambeau." She couldn't keep the disgust from her voice.

"He's the number one Packer backer." Sophia squeezed Frank's bag.

Aimee rolled her eyes.

In the funeral home, Aimee stood from her chair, put her hands on the mortician's desk. "We didn't agree on a price beforehand."

"Please sit, Ms. Mallon. I understand this is a hardship case. That's why I'm only charging $2,000. Our services are normally $4,000."

Aimee sat. "Look, my mom works at a gas station. It'll take her forever to pay a $2,000 bill. And she's under no obligation to."

The mortician dug in a file cabinet and removed a folder. "I have the paperwork here." He handed Aimee a form. *Authorization to Cremate.*

"What's this?" She looked at her mother.

"Umm," Sophia said sheepishly. "That looks like the papers I signed last week and mailed back."

"Without consulting me?" Aimee grabbed a stack of papers and thumbed through it. Sophia had signed that she was responsible for all applicable charges, but the form didn't specify a price.

"I'm the widow." Sophia lifted her chin high. "I saw it had something to do with Frank, and I figured it was just more forms."

"Did you even understand what you were signing?"

Sophia averted her eyes.

Aimee turned to the mortician. "Let us have the ashes in a cheap vase. I don't care. And we're not asking for any other service. Can you give her a break?"

"Hey, I don't want a cheap vase." Sophia grabbed Aimee's arm. "Frank deserves the best."

"I'm sure that's true, Mrs. Mallon." The mortician nodded affirmatively. "We have quite comfortable payment plans available."

"That's fine." Sophia smiled.

"Mother," Aimee scolded.

"Aimee, you're making a scene."

Leaning back in her chair, Aimee threw her head back in

defeat.

"Ms. Mallon, the cremation service costs us $1,500. I can give you an urn, a sample of a model we no longer sell, but anything less than that and I'm losing money."

"I'll take it," Sophia said.

Sophia signed up for the payment plan, and the mortician retrieved the urn and gave it to her.

"Sorry it took so long, Frank," Sophia whispered.

In the Subaru, Sophia cradled the urn in both arms. "Now I think Aimee has something to read to you." She held the vase toward Aimee. "It's his letter. Read it to him."

Aimee pulled the letter from her purse. She got a finger under the edge of the envelope and carefully tore the top, pulled the letter from the envelope, and unfolded it. She held the letter against the steering wheel.

"I love you, and I forgive you. I forgive you for all the ways you hurt me." She read slowly and distinctly so that each word would penetrate the ceramic urn and find the specks of dust that used to be her father's ears. "You may not have even realized you hurt me. It doesn't even matter anymore. You did teach me valuable lessons in life. For that I'm grateful. I'm sorry I held such bitterness for so long. I ask that you forgive me if you've ever felt anything less than love from me." Aimee swallowed hard and continued reading as she fought back tears. "Mom loves you so much. I'm so glad you had time with her. She seems excited about life now."

At that line, Sophia sobbed and Aimee's tears flowed over. A tear dropped on the paper and smeared the ink of the word bitterness.

Minutes passed until there were no more tears left.

Aimee neatly folded the letter and put it back in her purse. "You okay, Mom?"

Sophia smiled and hugged the urn. "Now, let's go see Lambeau."

Chapter 37

*A*imee pulled into the Lambeau Field parking lot.

"Look, Frank, there it is." Sophia held the urn up to the window. Her mom was set on fulfilling Frank's wishes to see the field, so Aimee had agreed to stop for a tour of the Packers' stadium on their way back to the UP.

Holding the urn, she strutted a step ahead of Aimee across the parking lot to the box office. Although Sophia was still grossly overweight, she seemed healthier, perhaps because she held herself more upright with confidence. She certainly had changed her habits. The prior night, she ate a salad with grilled chicken for dinner and then dragged Aimee down to the fitness center to exercise.

As they passed through glass doors into the stadium, a security guard called out, "You can't bring that in here."

Sophia looked over her shoulder as if he was talking to somebody behind her.

"Yeah, you." The man pointed at her.

Sophia held the urn tight and walked with increased determination.

The guard blocked her path. "There's always someone trying to dump ashes on the field. We don't allow that. You have to take that back to your vehicle."

Sophia turned to Aimee, pleading with her eyes as if expecting her to be as assertive as she had been at the funeral home.

Aimee shrugged her shoulders. "Here are the keys. Bring it back to the car, and I'll get in line for tickets."

Sophia took the keys without saying a word.

Aimee purchased the tickets and gathered with the tour group of about twenty people. The tour guide made small talk and told them they'd get started in a minute. Aimee waited anxiously for her mother. She should have returned already. Could she not find the car? There weren't that many in the parking lot.

Finally, Sophia came through the glass doors. Aimee waved to her as the tour began.

In the atrium, the guide told them about the renovation—the cost, the architecture, and the symbolism. He took them to the south end zone where he talked about the technology of the massive scoreboard. Aimee had only seen games on television full of fans clad in green and yellow, so she hadn't realized the stadium had backless, metal bleachers like at a high school football field. It gave the field a certain authentic charm that reflected the small-town roots of the legendary team.

Toward the end of the tour, the guide led them to the hallowed ground of the field. A buzz grew within the group. "We're going to walk along the edge of the field," the guide announced loudly. "We ask that you stay off the field."

As they walked behind the Packers' home benches, Aimee turned to see her mom's reaction to being so close to where the players sit, but she wasn't by her side. Aimee looked back.

Sophia was walking at a fast waddle, making a break for the 50-yard line.

"Hey, stop," yelled the tour guide, dashing after her.

Sophia picked up speed, and reaching the field, dug her hands into her pockets and turned them inside out.

Ashes scattered into the wind.

The guide slowed to a walk and spoke into his radio.

Sophia lifted her arms in victory while the rest of the tour group clapped and hooted.

A guard came and escorted Aimee and Sophia out of the stadium.

Chapter 38

Russ sat on the top bench of the sauna with Danny on a late September evening. The thermometer, mounted on the wall at shoulder height, read 170 degrees.

"Haven't seen you for a while," Danny said. The Saturday sauna at Danny's parents' home had become somewhat of a tradition for the friends, but this was the first since June.

"I've been busy." Gray beads formed on Russ's skin as sweat pushed dirt out of his pores.

"With Aimee?"

"I wish. I've been working my copper. Aimee's not returning my calls." Russ swatted at a fly that buzzed around his face. "I don't get it. We didn't even have that big of a fight. She was a little miffed I didn't like her church, but she didn't like mine."

"When marriages end, they end in a bang, but when dating relationships end, they fizzle out." Danny picked up the end of the hose and sprayed the stove. Rocks sizzled, and steam rose quickly to the ceiling and cooked the fly. It dropped to the floor.

Russ wiped sweat from his eyes with a washcloth. "You think it's ended, hey?"

"I have no idea. I've hardly seen you guys. I took that as a good sign."

"Did I tell you I love her?" Russ asked.

"You don't need to tell me. Tell her."

"Yeah, that's what I mean. I told her I loved her."

"Did she say 'thank you'?" Danny laughed.

"She said she loves me, too. I mean she also said she loves me. She said it first, and I said I love her, too."

"So what's the problem?"

"That's what I don't know. I don't know what the problem is." Russ pondered the question for a while. "Put more water on, hey."

Danny soaked the stove, climbed down from the bench, and stepped outside.

Russ waited a minute to prove his *sisu*. "Wimp," he said when they were both standing outside naked, having a breather. Crisp, cold evening air filled Russ's lungs. The northern night sky showed streaks of green, barely noticeable at first, jutting from the horizon. After his eyes adjusted to the dark, he could clearly see the Aurora Borealis dancing in the evening sky.

Danny laughed. "Remember when you first met Beth?" She had come to the Johnsons' to pick up maple syrup one evening in January and caught them taking a breather.

Russ chuckled.

"The wedding date's been set for December 24. Christmas Eve. Would you stand up for me?" Danny asked.

"Of course. I'd be honored."

"My brother Jack's going to be my best man. You'll be the other groomsman."

Russ nodded.

"Beth's going to have her friend Julie, from California, as her matron of honor. Aimee will be a bridesmaid."

"Well, at least I'll get to see her again."

Having cooled off, they returned to the sauna.

"Another steam?" Danny asked.

"You betcha."

Danny sprayed the stove again, and the steam warmed

Russ's skin.

Russ wiped his face with a washcloth. "What should I do?"

"Rinse off in the shower. You're disgustingly dirty." Danny laughed.

Russ chuckled. His beard had grown out. His hair was getting shaggy. He was dirty from working in his hole for the last month trying to keep his mind off Aimee. That had worked for a while, until he got an idea to make a special gift for her. As he fashioned the gift, he wondered if he'd ever have a chance to give it to her, and he replayed their last conversation in his mind over and over again. Why was she shutting him out? "I mean, what should I do about Aimee?"

"Let her go. That's what I did with Beth, and she came back. It's like the butterfly—"

Russ groaned. "Yeah, yeah. If it comes back, it's yours. With lines like that, you should write romances like Mak does."

"Watch it, man. I've got the hose."

Most days, Russ worked in his hole. He continued to rent the water-jet cutting machine from his dad's distant kin, who, even though Lord's People, must not have heard about the drama in the local congregation and hadn't blacklisted him. Russ sold a few specimens for a good price to collectors interested in the mixed metal. The other chunks of copper had somewhat of a market as bookends or doorstops but didn't command a price much beyond scrap value.

He visited his parents on Sunday evenings, but he refused to go to the Trap Rock Valley Sunday morning services. His disdain for organized religion grew. He was done with the church. As much as he needed the work, he was too offended to put up with the judgmental attitude of the LPs. Pinehurst was no better. They were judgmental in a different way.

His life had little purpose without Aimee. He thought back to the days before her and how much satisfaction he got out of fixing up the cabin—hooking up the LED lights, building the shower, installing the composting toilet. That's what he needed to do. He needed to refocus on his cabin.

He purchased bats of insulation and spent days on his back under the cabin stapling the paper backing onto the floor trusses. He insulated the bottom of his trap door and put a rubber seal around the edges, preparing for a long, cold winter.

One morning he had breakfast at the Heikki Lunta. Aimee wasn't around as she only worked there in the summers. He sat at the counter and Tammy served him coffee.

"Have you heard from Aimee?" He tried to keep his tone casual.

"Are you going to stalk her?"

"No," Russ said indignantly.

"You better not. I've got friends who could take care of you."

Russ swallowed hard. "You know, I could always have my breakfast at the Lapland."

"I'm teasing you, Russ. What d'ya want?"

"The usual."

"I'm not a psychic or your lover. You're gonna have to use words to describe what you want to eat."

"A farmer's omelet with hash browns, extra crispy, bacon, and pancakes."

"Extra crispy hash browns or bacon?"

"Hash browns. No, both."

"Living life on the edge. You got it." Tammy took the order to the kitchen.

Koski sat on the stool next to Russ. "Hey, neighbor."

"Hey, Bobby."

"Are you interested in buying that land yet?"

"I don't have the money, and I don't need the land."

Tammy set a cup in front of Koski and filled it with coffee. She set dishes of creamers and sugar on the counter. "The usual?" Tammy asked.

"Yeah." Koski smiled.

Tammy smirked at Russ.

"Well, neighbor," Koski took a swig, "I see that construction trailer of yours parked next to the road more times than not. Maybe we can work something out on the price."

Russ did everything he could to hold back a smile.

"Can I speak to Russell…" The man on the other end of the line paused momentarily and then finished, "Sorry-inen?"

"Speaking." Russ didn't recognize the 262 area code on the caller ID.

"I see you're the patent holder on a slow-release hinge mechanism."

"Yes?" It was the patent that paid him the modest royalties that funded his Mexico mission and, for the next few months, Aimee's final semester at Douglass State.

"My name is Kenneth Rasmussen. I'm the vice president of engineering at FHPS, Inc. in Kenosha, Wisconsin."

"I'm not interested."

As Russ pulled the phone from his ear, he heard the man blurt, "How would you know?"

Russ was intrigued by the question, and even chuckled, because the man was correct. He put the phone back to his ear.

"How would you know you're not interested without even knowing why I called?" Mr. Rasmussen repeated his question.

"Why are you calling?"

"I'd like to know if you'd be interested in exploring career opportunities at FHPS."

"I don't even know what FHPS is."

"Fractional Horse Power Solutions. We're an original equipment manufacturer for several popular power tool brands. We design and manufacture a variety of products utilizing fractional horsepower motors. Based on your patent, I like how you think. I'd like to talk to you."

"I'm still not interested. The last company I worked for crushed my soul." Russ hung up.

Chapter 39

Aimee collected a tip, wiped the table, and headed back to the kitchen. Her evenings at the Cornucopia were almost unbearable with the end in sight. Two law firms from Chicago and one from Detroit would be at the Douglass State job fair that week. She had polished her résumé and attended mock interviews. She was prepared and confident.

She picked up her order and kicked the swinging door with her foot. Across the dining room, Russ sat in her section. She avoided eye contact as she dropped off the order at a table next to him.

He can't take a hint, she thought. Russ had called her again, before her shift, but she let it go to voicemail. She listened to the message and then put her phone in a locker. It tore at her heart to hear his innocent voice asking how she was and when they could get together. After the fight, they didn't have a break-up conversation, but she thought it best just to cut ties. He wasn't going anywhere with his life. She was.

She acted busy—busier than she was with as few tables as she had—and headed back to the kitchen. "Zach, could you take table 14?"

"In your section? Why?"

"Because he's a big tipper, and I'm feeling charitable to-night," Aimee said.

"Sure, I guess." Zach looked more afraid than pleased.

It was mid-October, and she hadn't seen Russ for a month. You'd think he'd get the hint. The guy dragged his feet for months and months. He had finally said he loved her after she took him into the hotel room that night he was homeless. She wasn't even sure he meant it. He hadn't said it much after that night.

Out on the floor, she snuck a few glances at him. It appeared he was getting back to his old life with his ratty clothes and overgrown beard. He'd never change.

"Aimee," Russ said when she passed by his table.

"I'm working, Russ. This isn't a good time."

"When is a good time?"

Aimee rolled her eyes and kept walking.

"You're going to leave with no explanation, like your dad did?" Russ lobbed a parting shot, and it almost stopped her in her tracks, but she kept walking to the kitchen.

Aimee kicked the door. It slammed against the wall and bounced back. She put her shoulder into it and checked it back into the wall. The clatter in the kitchen stopped, and all eyes were on her.

"What?" She glared at her co-workers.

A quiet second passed, and then clinking and banging resumed. She folded her arms and leaned against the wall. She needed to get her customers' drinks but she couldn't remember what they had ordered.

The door opened and Zach appeared. "Hey, where did he go? Table 14."

Aimee exhaled in relief.

"But you're right. He's a big tipper. He left me five dollars for a glass of water."

The women gathered in Louisa's kitchen to plan Beth's wedding. Senja was the wedding coordinator for Pinehurst

Church, and Beth had asked Lorna to cater the reception. As Beth's roommate and bridesmaid, Aimee was there to help.

Marcella and Louisa arrived on the High Cliff shuttle bus, and Louisa wheeled up the ramp and into the house in a power wheelchair.

Aimee bent and hugged Louisa. "I'm sorry I haven't been to see you."

Louisa had moved to High Cliff at the beginning of September. Aimee had meant to stop by, but work, classes, and homework had consumed all of her time.

"It's no problem, dear." Louisa leaned her head against Aimee's shoulder. "God has provided many hands to help with my care, and hearts have been opened to me. I'm sorry to hear of your father's passing. I would have sent my condolences, but I can't write any longer."

"That's okay." Aimee pulled a chair aside to make room for Louisa at the kitchen table. It saddened her to see the toll the disease had taken.

"It's good to be home." Using a joystick to control her movements, Louisa pulled up to the table. "Marcella, my chair is so much easier to control after that massage. Thank you."

Beth hugged Louisa and Marcella. "Marcella is going to help with my hair for the wedding," she told the group.

They sat at the table along with Sophia, who had become Lorna's sidekick. She was positively thinner, mostly in her face and neck.

"Louisa," Aimee said with empathy, "it breaks my heart to see you confined to a wheelchair."

"I am *not* confined to a wheelchair. I'm liberated by it." Louisa backed up and spun circles in her chair. A smile emerged on her face when she stopped.

"Beth, I could make birch bark hearts for the ends of the pews," Lorna offered.

"I do bows. I always do bows. They're ready and no fuss." Senja did not seem to appreciate her sister's input.

"I'll make birch bark pockets and put balsam fir sprays and red berries in them."

"That sounds lovely," Beth said. "And maybe white roses."

"Humph." Senja bristled. "Balsam firs don't have berries."

"I love your ideas, too, Senja." Beth attempted to repair her broken ego. "I love the trellis idea."

"Mak can make it from birch bows." Lorna beamed at the thought.

Senja groaned, and Sophia refereed. "Okay girls. This is about Beth."

Louisa chuckled.

"We have plenty of time to think about the decorations," Aimee said. It was late October, a full two months until the wedding, and it was already beginning to look like Christmas. Copper Island had awoken to a dusting of snow.

"Aimee's right." Beth took control of the planning party. "Today our task is to get these invitations out." Beth stood and grabbed a box of envelopes off the hutch. She passed out a small stack to each of the women. "I printed off a few copies of the invitation list. Let's each take ten names to start with. We'll have these addressed in short order."

Each of the women readied a pen, except for Sophia. Aimee noticed a flash of fear in her mom's eyes.

"Senja, you take Aho through Gary Dawson." Beth addressed each woman by name and assigned her task.

Sophia excused herself and went to the bathroom.

"I'll take her names." Aimee grabbed her mom's stack of envelopes.

Louisa pulled up to the table, leaned forward, and sipped tea through a straw. "How's school going, Aimee?"

"Well. This has been my best semester yet thanks to you and the scholarship."

"Scholarship?"

"Yeah, I got a scholarship for my last semester. And with living here and saving on rent, I'm plowing my wages and tips into paying down my debt. And I have money to spare."

"Do you know where you're going when you graduate?"

"Not yet. I had on-campus interviews last week. This guy from a law firm in Chicago said I had moxie, which I guess is an Illinois version of *sisu*. I had other interviews, too. I should know something within a few weeks."

"Have you checked if there's a Lord's People assembly in Chicago?" Louisa smiled.

"Oh, I didn't tell you yet. Russ and I broke up."

"Oh, dear, I'm so sorry."

"Don't be sorry. I was sad, but it's for the best. He's not going anywhere with his life. As much as I love him—loved him—I'm sure I'll find somebody else wherever I end up." She managed a smile. Maybe if she kept telling herself that, she'd get over him.

Sophia came out of the bathroom. "Louisa has a bidet, too, Lorna. You sold a lot of them, haven't you?"

"Ha," Senja exclaimed.

"Are you ready to address envelopes?" Beth asked.

Aimee cleared her throat and gently shook her head no.

"I'm tired. I'm gonna go sit in the living room," Sophia said.

"What's going on?" Beth whispered to Aimee after Sophia left.

"I don't think my mom can read, at least not well," Aimee whispered. Perhaps her mom could get help from Beth. Before coming to Michigan, Beth had run a tutoring program in California, where she taught kids to read.

Beth nodded her head and stood, determination in her eyes. She discreetly left the table and joined Sophia in the living room.

"How big of a wedding does Beth plan to have?" Senja asked after completing her stack of envelopes and checking the names off the master list.

"The nice thing about having a UP wedding in the winter," Louisa said, "is that you can invite everybody down to your second cousin once removed and not worry about too many showing up."

Chapter 40

Russ stood rigidly as Aimee inspected him.

"You clean up well." She reached up and adjusted the knot on his tie.

He had trimmed his beard and cut his hair for Danny and Beth's special day. The men, gathered in a small room off the sanctuary, wore black suits with charcoal gray ties to match the bridesmaids' gray dresses.

"I miss you," Russ said.

Aimee kept her hands on his tie, well past the point of perfecting the knot. "I miss you, too. But it's for the best." She didn't look him in the eye.

"No, it's not."

Aimee pulled her hands away. "I don't want to get into it here."

"Let's get the awkwardness out of the way before we stand in front of a couple hundred people."

"We're too different. I'm leaving." Aimee stepped away and inspected Jack and Danny.

Russ unbuttoned his jacket and sat on a chair.

"Don't sit down. I just got you looking perfect," she corrected him as she adjusted Jack's tie.

"You'll just have to spruce me up again." Russ stood and attempted to straighten his coat.

When Aimee finished with the other guys, she adjusted his tie for the second time.

"Where are you going?" He was keenly aware of her closeness, of her touch.

"Chicago. I got a job with a law firm downtown."

"You'll live in the city?" Russ loved her, but that would be a challenge for him.

"No. I found an apartment in a northern suburb. I'll take the Metra into the Loop. I won't even need a car, because there's a grocery store within walking distance of my apartment."

Russ nodded. Maybe he could—

"You hurt me when you said I was immodest." She glared at him.

"When did I say that?" He scratched his forehead. She must have misinterpreted something he said because he certainly had never thought it.

"When we got into that big fight after church."

Russ groaned. "I'm sorry, Aimee. Sometimes I say stupid things. I wasn't even thinking of you. I was just so offended that they don't think I'm a Christian."

"What do you care what they think? Why don't you care what I think?" Aimee walked around him, tugged down on his coat tails, and smoothed the wrinkles out. "And you hurt me when you said I was like my dad."

"I shouldn't have said that." Russ turned and faced her.

"Do you think it's true? Do you really think I'm like my dad?" She raised an eyebrow.

He stroked his beard. "I just said it because you're leaving and he left."

"Watch it, mister. If I have smeared mascara on Beth's wedding day, I'll have Danny shoot you."

He moved toward her. "I don't want you to leave me, Aimee. I love you."

Her face softened momentarily. "I love you, too—I mean I loved you, but I'm young and I'm moving on with my life. But we can be friends." She patted his arm.

"I've never hated the word *friends* so much in my life."

Senja poked her head in. "Five minutes. Wedding party to the narthex, come with me."

Aimee gave him a quick hug. "Well, I'm moving on with my life. It's up to you if you want to do something with yours." She stepped back.

They followed Senja to the narthex.

Russ faced the closed sanctuary door with his left elbow jutted out, and Aimee held his arm. Ushers opened the door, and Senja nudged him to move. They walked through a birch bark trellis and down the aisle adorned with hearts. As it was Christmas Eve day, a fifteen-foot balsam fir stood in the front right corner of the nave, ornamented with white, glittery, cut-outs of angels and the Star of Bethlehem at the top.

As the processional played, Russ and Aimee walked slowly down the aisle. He delivered her to the base of the steps and took his position below Danny, opposite her. Jack filled the space next to Danny, and Julie stood across from him.

After Beth's six-year-old niece walked the aisle and spread flower petals, a pianist began to play Pachelbel's Canon in D. The congregation stood, except for Louisa, who remained seated in her power wheelchair.

Beth walked the aisle with her father to where Danny stood, his expression radiant. Russ wanted that joy for himself. Aimee caught his eye, and he quickly looked down. Although it was Beth and Danny's day, all Russ could think about was Aimee. He loved her and prayed it wasn't too late.

Was Danny right? Should he let her go and wait for her to come back? That's what Danny did with Beth, but he had always been the kind of guy that women wanted. Should Russ really expect Aimee to pursue him? And what was there to pursue? A scrawny, unkempt man who lived in a cabin off the grid and spent his time cutting up copper in a hole.

After a prayer and a hymn, Pastor Chip led the couple through the ceremony that would make them one. "To have and to hold, from this day forward, for better, for worse, for richer, for poorer, in sickness and in health, to love you as Christ loved the church, for as long as we both shall live. This is my solemn vow," Danny and Beth said to each other.

The words reverberated in Russ's mind. He wanted that for himself and he wanted it with Aimee.

Danny and Beth exchanged rings and then lit a deer-tallow unity candle that Lorna had made from a deer Russ processed.

Pastor Chip pronounced the couple husband and wife, and Danny kissed his bride. The couple made their way down the aisle followed by Jack and Julie. Russ met Aimee at the base of the steps. He grabbed her hand with determination. He wasn't going to let her slip away without a fight.

Outside the church, Danny held the door of his Jeep open for Beth. The single women, including Aimee, clustered on the sidewalk behind Beth, who peeked over her shoulder and then tossed her bouquet into the air. Senja reached for the bouquet as it came down, but it bounced off her fingertips toward Aimee, who grabbed it and held it close to her chest. Russ smiled. Her eyes scanned the crowd and their eyes met.

Chapter 41

W hen she told Russ they could be friends, Aimee didn't expect him to act like one. They spent time together on Christmas Day, and he even gave her a gift. A candle in a Mason jar half-filled with sand.

"Sand from Big Traverse, so you'll have our beach no matter where you go." Russ gave her cheeky smile. "I had to dig through snow this morning to get that."

"Russ, that is so sweet, and so much like you to make the gift."

"Except the candle. I had to buy that, even though Lorna made it from the deer I processed. I was hoping to give you another gift, but now is not the right time."

"We're just friends, Russ." He was such a nice guy, but Aimee didn't know if it was wise to even spend time with him. She didn't want to break his heart.

"A friend is a friend until something more or something less." Russ seemed more confident, and she found that attractive.

Aimee's new job would start after the new year, and Russ had volunteered to help her move. They loaded the bed of his pickup and her newly purchased car with her modest possessions.

Louisa had offered to sell her the Subaru. Aimee first declined, saying she didn't need a car.

"Everybody needs a car—$500, I insist."

"The car's worth at least $5,000," Aimee said.

"Perfect, $500, and that's my final offer," Louisa said. "If you find you don't need it, you can sell it. What good does the car do me when I get to drive a $32,000 wheelchair?"

So Aimee followed Russ down to Illinois. They took a break in Milwaukee for dinner at PF Chang's, arriving at the restaurant between the lunch and dinner rushes.

"We can seat you right away," the hostess told them.

"Can we sit at the bar?" Russ asked.

Russ ordered a Shirley Temple. "Iced tea?" he asked Aimee.

She nodded. "You're a good friend, Russ. I saw you at my graduation ceremony."

"I wouldn't have missed it for the world." Russ ordered lettuce wraps and the same dinner he'd had back in August. It was as though he was trying to re-create the past.

"I haven't talked to you much in the last few months." She took a sip of her tea. "We have a lot of catching up to do. How was Mexico?"

"I didn't go."

"Why not? Isn't that your passion? Building outhouses in Mexico?"

He wiped condensation from his glass. "I didn't have the money to go this year."

"It seems like we've switched places. You're broke, and I'm finally crawling out. This was the easiest semester I've had. Did you know I got a scholarship?"

"Yeah, I heard about that." He mumbled the words.

"And now with this job, I feel like I've made it. But I'm sad we're not going to be able to hang out anymore."

"I've been keeping a secret from you, Aimee." Russ picked up his Shirley Temple and sipped through the straw.

"You can't keep secrets. You're the worst liar I've ever met." She grinned.

"It helped that we drove down in separate vehicles."

"What's your secret?" Aimee asked.

The bartender dropped off the plate of lettuce wraps. Russ grabbed a leaf and scooped the mixture of chicken and water chestnuts into it.

"Well?" Aimee pressed.

"Do you ever have things happen and you're left wondering if it's coincidence or God?" He put the lettuce wrap on an appetizer plate, pushed it toward her, and started assembling a second one.

"What's your secret, mister?" She took a bite.

"I got a call awhile back from a company in Kenosha, Wisconsin. I wasn't too interested until I found out you were moving to the northern suburbs of Chicago. Did you know that Kenosha is the southeast-most county in Wisconsin? Right above Illinois?"

"And?" Her heart fluttered and hope rose.

"I called the guy back, and we had a phone interview. He asked me a bunch of questions, it seemed to go pretty well… then he asked why I left my prior company."

She let out the breath she had been holding. "Oh, no."

"Oh, yes. I told him everything. The design flaw. The lost fingers. Getting fired after recommending a recall. The guy said he'd never had anybody be that honest in an interview, and I was the kind of man he was looking for. Their company motto is *Do It Right the First Time.* I have an in-person interview tomorrow."

"That's great." She couldn't keep the smile from her face. Maybe, just maybe, Russ was right and their friendship would have another chance to grow into something more. "We're right next to Mayfair Mall. We should buy a suit for you."

Russ laughed. "Okay." He took a big bite of his lettuce wrap and set it down. He swallowed. "Remember that gift I said I had for you? I want to give it to you now." He reached into his jacket pocket and pulled out a small box wrapped in silver paper. He gave it to Aimee. "Open it."

Aimee tore the paper, pulled the cover off the box, and saw

a velvet-covered ring box. "Shut up," she said.

Russ smiled.

Aimee opened the hinged lid. Inside it was most unusual ring she'd ever seen—a band of copper and silver with three small diamonds set on top.

"I made it myself, except for the setting," Russ said.

"You made me a ring?" Tears formed in her eyes as his words from Christmas Day echoed in her head. *A friend is a friend until something more or something less.* She pulled the ring out of the box and examined it more closely.

"It's supposed to look like an engagement ring," he said sheepishly.

"It does, kind of." Aimee saw hope and love in his eyes. "Russ, are you asking me?"

"Yes, Aimee. Will you marry me?"

Aimee shrieked and clapped her hand over her mouth. She looked down at the table before returning his gaze. "You do realize there are no Lord's People churches down here."

"Exactly. Nor is there Pinehurst. We'll choose a church together. And I am looking forward to having running water again." Russ slid off his stool and down to one knee. "So, will you?"

"Yes, my adorable mountain man. Wait, I can't call you that if you're moving to the city." She squeezed his shoulder. "My love."

Russ slid the band on her finger.

Acknowledgments

Many thanks to my editors—Alexandra, Andrea, Cyndi, Dan, Jana, Steve, Susan, Todd, and Mom. Your eyes caught many typos and plot holes. I'm blessed to have an amazing team.

To the people who helped during the brainstorming and writing process, thank you for sharing your perspectives and letting me mine your experiences for creative inspiration.

To my family who lives with these characters as part of our everyday conversations—yes, I know they are not real—thank you.

Explore Copper Island and
find discussion questions at

KristinNeva.com

Read Beth and Danny's story, the first
in the Copper Island Novel series.

KRISTIN NEVA

SNOW COUNTRY

A Copper Island Novel
One

Made in the USA
Lexington, KY
13 September 2017